KATWALK

KAREN KIJEWSKI

AVON BOOKS ◆ NEW YORK

AVON BOOKS
A division of
The Hearst Corporation
105 Madison Avenue
New York, New York 10016

"A Thomas Dunne book"
Copyright © 1989 by Karen Kijewski
Published by arrangement with St. Martin's Press, Inc.
Library of Congress Catalog Card Number: 89-30134
ISBN: 0-380-71187-7

First Avon Books Printing: September 1990

AVON TRADEMARK REG. U.S. PAT. OFF. AND IN OTHER COUNTRIES, MARCA REGISTRADA, HECHO EN U.S.A.

Printed in the U.S.A.

RA 10 9 8 7 6 5 4 3 2 1

KAT IN TROUBLE

"OK," I told him. "Give me the stuff."

"Not here. Inside, where no one can see."

What the hell, I thought. Humor the paranoid. He opened the door and I stepped in—and knew right away. I heard nothing and saw nothing, but I smelled the cigarette smoke, fresh and close.

I ducked and twisted, tried to scramble out the door. I didn't make it. A thick arm wound around me, pinning my arms to my side. Another arm closed around my neck. I was conscious of a rough sleeve and the acrid smell of tobacco smoke. Hands slipped around my neck, cutting off life and air. This is my last breath, I thought—and it's cigarette smoke.

What a bummer!

For their help and support the author wishes to thank Bridget McKenna, Tom Ghormley, and Joe Hamelin.

Dear Charity,

What is a real friend? I say it's someone who will lend you a thousand bucks, no questions asked. My buddy says it's somebody who will stand by you in a tight spot. Answer, okay? We got ten bucks on this.

T&B

Dear T&B,

A friend is someone who takes you in in the middle of the night.

Charity

The banging started about one in the morning. The cat stretched, yawned, then moseyed off toward her food bowl. I put my book down and headed for the door.

"Kat, let me in!" More bangs, some thumps. I opened the door and stood back so Charity wouldn't fall on me. She pitched in, caught herself on the wall and hung there panting slightly. Her usual serene expression was absent, her hair and eyes wild.

"Why all the fuss, Charity? You've got a key."

"I didn't want to startle you by coming in unannounced."

"Aren't you thoughtful," I said, but it was over her head—a waste of sarcasm.

"Kat, I've got to talk to you."

"We talked at lunch today."

"That's just friends. Now I need your professional help."

I swore under my breath; she headed for the kitchen.

"Have you got any food? I'm starving."

Charity made herself at home while I watched morosely. I don't like working for friends—the complications are endless—and I avoid it whenever possible. I wanted to get out of this, and knew I couldn't. Charity had a problem, I'm an investigator; it was easy to figure how it was all going to add up.

"You're out of mayonnaise, the cheese is moldy, and all you have is stone ground, overkill, whole wheat bread. Stone ground, phooey. As if they sit around with a bunch of mortars and pestles and go for it."

I stared at her.

"The pasta salad looks okay though." She grabbed a fork and dove in. "How about a glass of wine?"

I nodded and watched glumly as she popped the cork on a bottle of cabernet I'd been saving.

"It's after one, Charity." I took a slug of wine, her locust approach to food and drink rubbing off on me.

"It is? I had no idea it was so late. I just finished talking with my accountant and then with Sam. More wine?" I nodded. "The accountant says there's two-hundred-thousand-dollars missing." Her voice rose in a shriek. "Two-hundred-thousand! That bastard! I could kill him."

"The accountant?"

"No, of course not. Sam. Pay attention, Kat, this is important."

I nodded and chugged my wine, then caught myself and slowed down.

"I know Sam's siphoned it off before the divorce so it won't be part of the community property settlement. Kat, you've got to help me."

I sighed. I knew I did, and I dreaded the whole messy thing.

"Did you confront Sam on it?"

"Of course."

"What did he say?"

"That he lost the money gambling in Las Vegas. I don't believe it."

I didn't, either. She splashed wine into our glasses.

"Kat, what am I going to do? I could lose the house, my horses, everything—"

"Slow down. If he's got it, I'll find it. That's my job."

"Yes, thank goodness. You know, I hate these little bottles, they run out so fast. Isn't there anything else to drink? Ah!" She scanned the open refrigerator, pounced on a bottle of white wine and uncorked it.

"How much of Sam's business stuff is still at the house?"

"Lots."

"Go through it." She started to get up. "Not tonight, you've had too much to drink and you're staying here. Tomorrow. Look for any kind of business dealings in Nevada. Also copies of your phone bills for the last few months if you have them. I need the section with long-distance calls itemized. And a copy of last year's income tax records. Okay? Now I'm going to sleep. The spare bed's made up, have a bath if you want to."

"Thanks." She hugged me.

"Make yourself at home," I added unnecessarily as she poured more wine and hauled out a carton of ice cream.

"Kat, you're a peach. What would I do without a friend like you?"

To my credit I bit back the obvious answer about advice columnists calmly sitting down and making use of the sage counsel they dish out to the rest of us.

"Don't you have any fudge?" It came out somewhat muffled, her mouth was full of ice cream.

"Charity, that's rainbow sherbert, it doesn't need fudge."

"Yes, it does. In a crisis fudge is very comforting. It doesn't matter what you put it on, even toast will do—not that stone ground crap, of course."

I shook off the idea of toast and hot fudge. "Don't wake me at dawn when you get up, all right? I'll meet you at the Cornerstone for breakfast at eight-thirty. Do you think you can have everything together then?"

"I'll try. I know! Hot chocolate, that's what I'll have."

From cabernet to hot chocolate. I shuddered and went to bed.

The alarm went off at seven and I lay there for a while thinking about friendship and how hard it is to get out of a warm bed. It is on record that I am not a morning person. I started to doze off, startled myself awake and got up.

My morning routine was shot and I hate it when that happens. Then I hate it when I hate it, because it makes me feel old and set in my ways. At thirty-three that's not a good feeling.

Usually I drink tea and read the paper, the *Sacramento Bee*. I was an investigative reporter for them for five years and old habits die hard. This morning I skimmed the headlines and then had my first cup of tea in the bathtub. I almost fell asleep there, not a good sign, and that made me late and grumpy again, all of which is why I don't like to get up early.

It takes me about half an hour to get into town from where I live in an unincorporated area of Sacramento County. At eight o'clock the news on the radio was depressing and the traffic heavy. I took I-80 to the J Street exit and then parked on 24th at J. There aren't any meters on 24th.

Charity had beaten me to the café and looked as though she had had about thirteen cups of coffee in the last two hours. Her elbows were on the table, her head was in her hands, and she was twitching. My good morning left her gasping in surprise and gulping in air. I patted her on the back.

"Didn't you sleep well?" Stupid question. Divorce with pasta salad, wine, ice cream, and hot chocolate. Who would?

"Kat, I'm a wreck." I thought that was an overly generous description but I let it go.

"It'll be okay, you're tough."

She made a liar out of me and started to cry. I was glad her readers couldn't see her, and fed up enough to wish I were someplace else.

Ruby slapped our plates down. We eat at the Cornerstone so often we rarely bother to order anymore. Ruby takes care of us with the built-in, honed judgment of a twenty-year veteran on coffee-shop tiles. And the dictatorial outlook of a marine drill sergeant. She shook Charity slightly and said in a firm voice, "Shut up and drink your juice. I brought you chocolate milk too, no more coffee for you, and fresh cinnamon rolls. Eat all your eggs."

"Atta way, Ruby." I grinned. Charity frowned. "It's okay," I added quickly, and before she could start crying again. "I have a ticket on tomorrow's nine o'clock plane to Vegas. I'm going to get it straightened out."

"Good." She snuffled up some tears and then some scrambled eggs. "Two hundred thousand is a lot of money. I know he's got it, that bastard. That bastard!" She started crying again. Damn.

"If he has, I'll find it." I patted her arm. "You've hired the best."

I finished half my breakfast, which is the absolute most I can do that early in the morning, tossed money on the table and picked up the overstuffed manila envelope Charity had brought. We hugged and I hollered at Ruby back in the kitchen. She came out, winked at me and waved her apron. It reminds me of my adopted grandmother, the way she stands there with her hands twisted in her apron. It always makes my heart twist a little.

I thought about it as I drove home. It's things that make your heart twist that are worth doing, I guess. Like friendship—which was why I was doing something my business sense was dead set against.

Dear Charity,
  Is anything worth fighting for?
                    Doubtful

Dear Doubtful,
  Yes, many things: children, friendship, the future. Sour cream fudge rum cake with pecans. Fight with your mind, your heart, your words. Violence is always a last resort.

                    Charity

I have a two-bedroom house and I've turned one bedroom into an office. I share an office downtown for appearance's sake, but it's at home that I do most of my work. I made a cup of tea and sat down to the pile Charity had given me, starting with the phone bills. Charity and Sam's separation was recent and bitter, something that Charity, an advice columnist, couldn't get over.

I didn't find it surprising, but then I have a more down-to-earth, even cynical, view of life than she does.

It's hard to tell what's really going on in divorce cases. Sam's story was that he'd lost two hundred grand at the casinos in Vegas. Charity's was that he was ripping her off. I was neutral for now, but past history tends to substantiate her version. I worked my way through the phone bill, making a note of half a dozen Nevada numbers, most of them in Las Vegas. Then I looked through the Las Vegas reverse directory and put names to the numbers.

There was a construction company, a Realtor, and an investment corporation. I got on the phone and made appointments with them to build, buy, and invest. The others were private individuals and I decided to wait until Vegas to check them out. I spent the rest of the afternoon clearing off my desk and getting ready to leave town for a few days. Then I left a note for the neighbor kid who picks up the mail and paper and looks after my living things, plant and animal, while I'm gone.

The next morning I had to get up early to catch the plane, which meant I again started the day off in a bad mood. Not good, not at all, and not like me.

I got to the airport in plenty of time to wait in a long, slow-moving line. Naturally. Even banks aren't this bad anymore, just post offices. The lady in front of me had black hair out of a bottle, tight knit pants and two toy poodles on leashes. Their names were LaLa and DaDa. She told me, I didn't ask. She told me a lot more that I didn't ask about and, in general, reminded me why I never choose to go to the city of neon and glitter.

By the time I got into my seat I was feeling drained and must have looked like I needed a Bloody Mary, because the flight attendant was surprised when I declined a drink. I had coffee instead, and unfolded the paper. Two cups and half the paper later, I was in a more mellow mood. I blew that by reading Charity's "Consult Charity" column. It didn't surprise me, but it didn't pick up my spirits any, either. Her personal life was affecting her professional approach.

Dear Charity,

My friends save whales, stamp out wildfires and work for world peace. All I want to do is eat ice cream (coconut chocolate chip is my favorite flavor), read science fiction and marry a rock star. Have I missed the boat?

Wondering

Dear Wondering,

Yes. The boat, the train, the plane and the turnip truck. If you're a teenager, that's some excuse and would make you eligible for deportation to an experimental colony on Pluto in the year 2002. Otherwise you're a lower life form.

Charity

I groaned and had glum thoughts. Then, a glutton for punishment, I read my horoscope.

Be discreet in matters of business; old friends and new figure prominently; avoid travel and beware of promises given too readily.

That didn't pick up my spirits either; I decided to have a nap and start the day over later. I woke up when the plane bumped down at McCarran Airport in a way that makes you hope, but not believe, that the pilot has gotten past the training-wheel stage. I stuck the newspaper in the seat pocket in front of me, grabbed my carry-on bag, and started out the airplane to the Muzak Hurry Up and Wait Shuffle.

Head-on collision is the only way to describe my first encounter in Las Vegas. Once I might have called it an unthinkable coincidence, but I'd stopped believing in coincidences, along with horoscopes, a long time ago. When my head cleared and my eyes refocused I looked around for the tank, or steamroller, or whatever it was that had hit me. I could hear it apologizing long before I could see it.

It was a businessman disguised as a thug, or a thug trying to pass as a businessman; even money on that call, though I leaned toward the latter. Either way, it was not love at first sight—not on my part. The tank was built like a linebacker going fuzzy around the edges. The balance had clearly shifted away from sit-ups and toward beer and Cheetos.

"Well, I'll be damned, it's Katy. Katy, it's you, isn't it? Hey, remember me? It's Deck, Deck Hamilton."

I looked into the lined fried-chicken face—the hard dark eyes, the flaring nostrils with halos of little burst blood vessels around them—and tried to find Deck. I couldn't.

"Katy, it's Deck."

It was the Katy that forced me to believe, and only because that goes back years and nobody uses it now. They're all gone, or dead.

"Deck, have you ever changed." A lot of things had run through my mind but that was the only one I could say out loud.

"Not you." His eyes raked me quickly, "or only for the better. Same curly, bouncy brown hair, green eyes, and knock 'em dead smile. You look great, Katy."

"It's Kate now, Deck, or Kat."

"Oh, yeah, sure, that makes sense. Me, I'm still the same old Deck."

"The Deck stuck." I smiled.

"Yeah," he agreed, and we both lapsed into a momentary memory break. "Watch it, bud," Deck broke the silence and snarled at a kid in motorcycle leathers who started to snarl back but wisely thought better of it. "We don't need his kind," he said to me.

"That's what they used to say about you."

"Yeah? Well, maybe they were right." The memories really started coming back then, memories of a tall, skinny kid, all elbows and knees, with big fists that were mostly knobby knuckles. He moved into our neighborhood, a tough neighborhood where no one cut you any slack and you were dead if you asked for it. You stood on your own, or had an older kid in the family who fought for you, or you crawled and ate dirt.

The first day the kids taunted him he yelled back, "Mess with me and I'll deck you," which he did, and then we got to calling him Deck. A long time ago Deck had been a friend; he had stuck up and fought for me more than once.

"You coming or going, Kat?"

"Hmmm? Oh, coming, I'm here on business. How about you?"

"I live here. C'mon, I'll give you a ride into town. Where you going?"

"Thanks, Deck, I've got to rent a car."

"Okay, hey, how about dinner tonight for old times' sake?" I thought it over. Why not? "Meet me in the main bar at the Glitterdome at six for a drink?" I nodded. I'm always curious about the way things happen, like how the little boy I'd known had become the man standing in front of me.

Later, in that futile exercise known as What If? or If Only I Had Known, I wished I'd said no and walked off. But I couldn't have done that. Old friends have a claim on you, and Deck used to fight for me. To be honest, I guess I couldn't have walked off anyway. I've never been able to walk away from something that caught my interest.

"Curiosity kills the cat," Ma used to tell me in one of those rare lucid spells when she took an interest in me. And it does at that.

Dear Charity,

Somehow I got into something way over my head. If I do anything about it, which I should, I betray a friend's trust. If I don't, horrible things could happen. Either way, it's big trouble. Help me, please!

Scared Silly

Dear Scared,

It's for people like you that we have the proverbial, "Look before you leap," not to mention, "You made your bed, now lie in it." Good luck, and stay out of dark alleys for a while.

Charity

We said good-bye, Deck and I, and I let a wave of people surf me over to the rental-car counter. I took a few deep breaths and hoped that for once the car people had gotten it right. They hadn't. I wasted a nostalgic moment longing for Deck and brute force; then the clerk and I had a spirited discussion about how I wanted what I had ordered, and yes, it really did have to be an economy model and a radio would be nice. In the end we compromised—I took what she gave me.

The clerk dropped the paperwork into my waiting hand and snarled briefly. I thanked her and smiled, just to prove to myself that I still had the strength of character to be polite.

When I walked outside the midsummer heat dropped on me like a translucent tarp. I staggered underneath it, sagging slightly and fighting for breath as I groped my way through air the consistency of heated caramel. The car was not the pick of the litter, but it ran; although it is true that I had been hoping for something a little more subtle than canary yellow. In the investigative field we lean toward beige, gray, and other emblems of nondescript middle-range America. Hope is another thing Ma used to warn me about. After three tries the engine caught and spluttered in a moribund way.

At night Las Vegas is a beautiful city of neon, bright lights, and promise. Hope plays then in the flickering lights, the laughter, the roll of the dice and the soft clink of ice under aged bourbon. In the daytime it is another story and the harsh sunlight is pitiless and uncaring. The promise is as squalid and tawdry then as a twelve-dollar whore. It is spelled out in casinos, motels, marriage chapels, and bars. Going to Vegas always makes me want to go home again.

I checked into a modestly priced motel called the Pink Flamingo. I was on an expense account, Charity's, and I didn't want to run it up. Some mindless interior decorator had run amok there, untouched by good taste or subtlety. Hot pink had been the beginning and end of the designer's color imagination. Flamingos stood one-legged over the bed, danced across the walls, fished in the shower and winked from the toilet seat. It was too awful to be true. I gave up all thought of a nap and decided to start tracking down the financial status of Charity's soon-to-be ex-husband, Sam. Work now, play later.

I'd brought maps with me, and it didn't take long to orient

myself and figure out where the courthouse was. Getting there was something else.

Somebody had declared driver-training week and the yo-yos and clowns were on the road in full force, showing off what they couldn't do, especially on Fremont. I made two wrong turns before I got there and parked in the sun. No choice. The heat was already starting to make waves and ripples in the air. Maybe in my brain, too.

The courthouse was blissfully cool. I paused to look around. A three-piece-suit type whomped me and brought me rudely back to attention. He didn't apologize. A hungry crowd of sleek and smarmy lawyers engulfed me. I wormed my way through them to the information desk. There I learned that the assessor's office was down the street from the courthouse, on Third. I walked. It wasn't far, but the heat made it ugly.

The assessor's office was the first stop on the hunch I was playing. People tend to run true to form. It takes a lot to jolt us out of our ruts, especially the unconscious and automatic ones, and investigators rely heavily on that. It's easier to change your name and identity than the way you walk or nervously clear your throat. Or change your MO in business. In the past Sam had bought a lot of property on spec and either built on it or sold it, usually at a profit. My hunch was that if he'd sunk money into Vegas it was in real estate, not in blackjack or craps.

A young woman sat on a tall stool behind the high counter of the county assessor's office. Her coloring owed more to Maybelline than to Mother Nature and her hair was peroxide blond. She had a huge pimple on her chin that bobbed around as she chewed and popped her gum. The weight and majesty of the legal system had not percolated downward to her.

I told her what I wanted and gave her names, Sam's and those of the people he had called. Then I wrote it down and handed it to her. She stared at me blankly for a long time and finally levered herself off the stool. It was my turn to stare. She was a size seven on top and a thirty-eight below, a teacup riding on a tanker.

Off she waddled into the back regions, and then nothing

happened for quite a while. I did not regard it as an auspicious beginning. Still, I could hear her popping and snapping her gum, so I didn't give up hope. Finally she reemerged with my information. Bingo. Sam had bought property. So had one of the others. The parcel numbers indicated that they were in the same general area. We got out a parcel map and I asked her to track down ownership of the surrounding properties. More names, more addresses, more gum. She sighed loudly, spit out the old tired wad and stuffed a new batch in.

In the end I left the assessor's office with information involving quite a lot of property and a number of names. A picture was forming in my mind.

I made my way back to the courthouse and to the recorder's office. There I looked up marriage statistics. The names were linking up. Some of the property was owned outright by a corporation, New Capital Ventures. Most of it was in the names of private individuals, one of whom was Sam. A number of the other owners turned out to be involved with New Capital Ventures, or married to someone who was. The latter were generally listed in their maiden names. Interesting.

It added up to this: New Capital Ventures controlled a major chunk of real estate and did not want that fact known. They had buried it in the names of small investors. It wasn't a fancy or slick dodge—it wouldn't fool anyone for long—but a cursory glance wouldn't catch it. It had taken me four hours, forms, and fees. Packs of gum figured in there somewhere, too.

All in all it had been a profitable afternoon. Sam was not as clever as he thought, or I was cleverer. Either way it put me in a good mood. At the five o'clock shutdown I bounced happily out the door, slowed down fast as the heat smashed into me, and headed at a crawl for the canary car. Then back to the Pink Flamingo motel.

There I made myself do sit-ups, stretches, and yoga exercises. Then I went out to the pool, swam laps for twenty minutes, and lay in the sun. That left me ten minutes to shower and get dressed. I had one almost-cocktail dress with me, so decision making was not a difficult process. It was hot pink; I looked great with the flamingos.

I needn't have wondered about finding the Glitterdome; Las Vegas is a city of the obvious. I parked the car, avoiding the scornful stares of pimply parking attendants, and headed for the bar. It was dark there and eyes slid around: the hard appraising eyes of men looking for available women and wondering if you are one of them; the unfocused eyes of gamblers who don't care about people, only numbers, 21, 7 come 11; the shrewd eyes of opportunists who don't care about anything and notice everything.

I sat at the bar, looked into blank bartender eyes and ordered a draft beer. I was just getting my money out when Deck moved in next to me and propped his elbows up with the bar.

"I'll get that," he said, waving my money away. Damn, I thought, I should have had an import. "And a shot of Crown, Joe."

"Okay, Deck. Water back?"

"Nah, no time. Chug it, Kat. We're going to an event, a slice of Las Vegas. Dinner will have to wait."

Okay, I was flexible. I left most of my beer in the still chilly mug and took Deck's offered arm. People parted for us in waves as we walked out. It was in deference to Deck, not me. Muscle talks.

"You're looking great, Kat." His hard eyes softened. I could see the little boy in them for a moment, then he was gone. I was glad that I'd seen it though. "Yeah, this is a treat. It sure is good to see you."

We stepped out of the Glitterdome and into this year's Lincoln Mark VII. It was white with glove leather upholstery, and neither bird nor bug had dared besmirch it. There was no question but that I showed up to greater advantage in it than in the lemon. We pulled up to another elegant hotel, and there I was handed out with a deference unknown to the possessors of canary yellow compacts. We made our way inside to a vast meeting room.

Someone had named it Eden, though I'd always thought of

Eden as a smallish, cozy place and this wasn't. Skylights arched high over us and fountains and ponds trickled, splashed, and sang. Palm trees, ferns, and a dazzling array of tropical plants grew in nose-thumbing defiance of the surrounding desert. There was a tree with huge red apples on it, Vegas style and artificial. I did not see Adam or Eve but I did see a lot of snakes. It did not take a reporter's eye or an investigator's smarts to figure that one out.

"Welcome to the preview of The Auction."

"An auction preview?" I found that odd. "It doesn't sound like you."

"No? Things are not always what they seem, Kat, especially in a town like Vegas." Good point and one I neglect too often. I made a mental note to sharpen up—I do that frequently.

"What's being auctioned?"

"Antiques and art. It's the social occasion of the year. Everybody who's anybody is here. I have to make an appearance and then we can go to dinner." He paused to say hello to a couple of guys who looked like cretins in business suits. It made me wonder.

"Are they anybody?" He shrugged and his eyes slid away from mine as he grabbed my elbow. Vaguely he said that they were associates of his. I looked around at people and saw plenty of business and society types, all dressed to the teeth in the glitter and dazzle that Vegas does so well.

"Hey, look at this painting. What do you think?"

I thought it looked like a nightmare in yellow vomit but, as that seemed an inappropriate comment, I said nothing. Instead my attention was caught by a short fat bald man in a lime-green golf outfit, with an amazon redhead in a leopard-print dress that had been poured on her. She was a foot taller than he, but they were laughing and looking in each other's eyes. She leaned over and started blowing in his ear.

"Las Vegas," I muttered, half in disbelief.

Two scantily dressed and overly made-up women came into

view and started cooing and pawing at Deck. They were about as subtle as jackhammers in heat and Deck seemed embarrassed. Next to them I must have looked like an Iowa farm girl on my first date, as wholesome as fresh corn and whole wheat bread. Deck made no attempt to introduce us. Feeling left out, I refocused on the lime-green and leopard couple. Except for the *l*'s they seemed to have nothing in common. Could alliteration alone make a relationship work? I doubted it.

I got bored and moved on to look at another picture, one that looked like rockets on a time warp. It was in blues with vicious-looking stars in orange and yellow. I wondered what kind of person saw the world like that. I wondered if I'd want to meet the artist. I wondered if I'd been in Vegas too long.

"Like it?"

I turned. A tall, good looking man of about forty-five stood next to me. He looked like he had everything money could buy and wasn't bored with it yet. And he had drop-dead dimples.

"No. Do you?"

He shook his head and smiled. The dimples got deeper. I'm kind of a pushover for dimples.

"It's fashionable, though."

"Ah."

He threw back his head and laughed. "I guess that doesn't cut much ice with you."

"No."

"What does?"

"A lot of things. Most of them don't come up in social chitchat."

He laughed again. "Let me get you another drink. Then will you sit down with me for a moment? Let's talk about the things that don't come up in social chitchat." We didn't actually do that, but we passed an agreeable ten minutes.

"Kat." Deck said, appearing out of the crowd and putting his hand on my shoulder. "Sorry to keep you waiting. Hello, Don," he added, and started to steer me off.

"Introduce me, won't you Deck? Your friend and I haven't formally met yet."

"Don Blackford, Kat Colorado." Deck said it with reluctance and bad grace.

"Delighted, Miss Colorado, and I hope to have the pleasure of continuing our conversation at another time."

I smiled and murmured the usual nothing much. He was a mixed-message package; fun and trouble were both in there. And, true to form, I was attracted. Deck piloted me away.

The scantily dressed women walked by again, smiling at Deck and leaving us awash in their wake of sexual suggestions and expensive perfume. I asked about them but Deck ignored my questions. I'm never really sure about reality in places like Las Vegas. We made our way through the crowd, previewing the other displayed items.

"Tell me about him, Deck."

"Don Blackford?" I nodded. "He's a big mover in Vegas. Got a hand in just about everything—casinos, real estate, you name it."

"What's he like?" I asked, and Deck surprised me by glowering.

"Forget him, Kat, okay?"

"Why?"

"Just do it."

I shrugged. Deck had always been stubborn; I could see I wasn't going to get any more out of him than that.

"What kind of an auction is this, anyway?"

He relaxed. "This year it's to raise money for a new cultural center. Last year it was for a hospital wing, and the year before it was school scholarships. We've expanded it over the years."

"Who sponsors it?"

"The whole community, our association too."

"What association?"

"Businessmen," he said vaguely. I didn't remember Deck being vague as a kid.

"What kind of businessmen?"

"You sound like a reporter, Kat. You don't have to nail down every detail, ask questions about everything." He smiled at me. It wasn't a nice smile. It wouldn't have won any prizes; at an auction, nobody would have bid on it.

"I *was* a reporter."

He shrugged, still wearing the same grimace. "Too many questions can make trouble. You know that."

I stared back at him, not smiling. I wasn't born yesterday and I didn't need to lick my finger to figure out which way the wind was blowing. He hadn't answered a lot of my questions or introduced me to his friends and associates. Briefly I debated about the wisdom of saying what I was thinking. It didn't help. In the "fools rush in where angels fear to tread" breakdown, I'm a fool every time.

"You've changed a lot, Deck. I'm not sure I like it."

"Hey, old buddy." A guy in a shiny green, wide-lapelled suit clapped Deck too hard on the shoulder, the way men do when they're one upping each other. "Nice," he said, looking at me in a not-nice way, "but not your style, Deck."

I looked at the man's gangster suit. "What would you know about style?" I asked in a hard, cold voice that made him mad and then he tried not to show it. Deck laughed and took my arm.

"Go pick on someone your size, Frank, big girls are always too much for you." The guy stared at us as we walked away. He looked like he might not forget me in a hurry and I wished he would. Already I regretted my smartass comment. The comment and the regret are both typical of me.

Deck cut in front of a waiter with a half-empty tray of champagne glasses, grabbed two, handed me one, downed his in a gulp and grabbed another. I followed suit. When in Rome . . . Then we walked around looking at the auction items and talking like regular old friends playing catch-up with the past.

He told me about himself, but never in words that tied him to anything, though I tried to pin him down.

"Aw, Kat, you remember how it was when we were kids, poor and beat up on. I didn't care for it and decided to go for money and power. I work for a company called New Capital Ventures and—"

I lost the rest of the sentence. New Capital Ventures had come up a lot that day. Suddenly I felt like I had to get away and think things out. For starters I excused myself to go to the bathroom.

Dear Charity,

My friend once went calling on a neighbor lady and found her dead as a doornail. She called the doctor and the police and then just sat there. I say it's sick and morbid to stay with dead people and that flowers at the funeral would have been enough. She says it's a question of respect and what's right. We fight about this all the time and agreed to let you settle it.

Sick of It

Dear Sick,

Your friend is right. It is only in times of war and great catastrophe that the conventions on which our society has been built can be ignored. Flowers have nothing to do with it.

Charity

A rose may be a rose may be a rose, but a bathroom is not a bathroom. Bathrooms range from stinking cubicles that no one in her right mind would set foot in to glorious, luxurious suites. Las Vegas has some great bathrooms—bathrooms that took their inspiration from Versailles or San Simeon. The one I entered was close to great. Mirrors, crystal chandeliers and flowers were abundant in the lounge and there was pink marble, white tile, and scented soap in the bathroom.

There was one flaw, one out-of-place detail—the body on the floor. The blood did not go well with the pink marble. And there was a lot of it, splashes, puddles, unreadable Rorschach blots everywhere.

Force of circumstance made me a good citizen. I'd like to say I always am, but it's not true. This time, however, I had no choice—discreet departure was out of the question. A middle-aged, overweight woman wearing a glove for playing the slot machines had come in behind me and was screaming her head off. Her shrieks echoed off the pink marble and bounced around in my mind slowing me down a little. Telling her to shut up had absolutely no effect. I tried several times and then I left. In the hall outside I looked for a house dick or a hotel employee. It didn't take long to find one; it never does in casinos and screaming brings them out of the woodwork fast.

"There's a body in the bathroom. I'll call the cops."

I started to move off but, surprisingly, he was too quick for me. He grabbed me by the elbow and the two of us went into the bathroom, his five-foot-eight-inch, 215-pound idea, not mine. He took one look around and whipped out his radio. A foot the size of a shoe box slammed up against the door and blocked it.

"Shut the fat broad up so I can get through."

I walked her over to a couch in the lounge, plopped her down and stuck a cushion in her face. She grabbed on and held it, sobbing into its pinky velvet and adding blush, snot and mascara to its cultured tones. I walked back and looked at the body on the red and white tile of the bathroom floor.

She was young, middle twenties, somewhat plain, and she looked like the kind of girl who stands wistfully on the sidelines of life but never jumps in. Her clothing was simple, conservative and inexpensive. Her throat was cut.

Next to the body was a raincoat stained with blood. It looked like a man's size and style. I wondered who the girl was, and why her number had come up. I didn't remember her from the Eden room, but she could have been there, or in the gambling rooms, or in a restaurant or bar. The bathroom was centrally located.

"Get outta there." The house dick stood next to me gesturing angrily with one hand, his sputtering radio in the other. "Sit over there with the fat broad." He was less than diplomatic and it set her off again, sobbing and rolling her eyes around and up until the whites were showing. I went over and shook her firmly by the shoulders.

"Stop it. Calm yourself."

She looked at me, wide-eyed and blubbering. "My name is Myrtle," she babbled. "I'm from Minnesota and this is the worst thing that's ever happened to me, worse than the tornado, or Harry's heart attack, or the car accident or . . ."

I patted her arm in an attempt to be reassuring and hoped the cops would get here fast. She rambled on. I ignored it.

"Tell her to shaddup, would ya." He'd been watching too many old gangster movies, I could tell. I ignored him, too. What I couldn't ignore was the dead girl—hopes, dreams, and possibilities spilled in blood around her.

The Las Vegas Metropolitan Police Department got there not long afterward. The first thing they did was cut the house dick down to size. I watched with satisfaction that I didn't try real hard to hide. Then they started on me.

"You discovered the body?"

"With this lady, yes."

"What were you doing here?" I looked at him and wondered if cops ever get tired of asking the obvious. I do, even though it's not all so obvious and every once in a while there's more to obvious than meets the eye. Not here though, not with me.

"I needed to go to the bathroom, which reminds me—" He cut

me off callously. Of course he hadn't been drinking champagne steadily for the last hour.

"Name. Address." It was an order, not a question. I gave the answers. "What were you doing in the building?"

"I came with a friend to see the auction preview."

"What are you doing in Las Vegas?" I was hoping we wouldn't get to that.

"Partly pleasure, partly business. I'm looking into a possible real-estate investment for a client."

"You're in real estate?"

"Not exactly." I was hoping we wouldn't get to that, either.

"What exactly, Miss?" There was just a hint of sarcasm there.

"I'm an investigator." I could tell that didn't make a big hit or earn me any points. I reached for my purse and handed him a photostat of my licence. He looked at me sharply, scrutinized it and handed it back. Then he asked me a bunch of questions about the girl and the murder that I couldn't answer. He took my local address, told me not to leave town in the next few days without telling him, handed me his card and said I could go.

I was out of there like a bat out of hell. Deck was waiting.

"Kat, for God's sake, what's going on?"

"Find me a bathroom, Deck, fast!" I said it through clenched teeth and sounded as desperate as I felt.

"Okay, but—"

"Bathroom!"

"Down there and to your left." I sped off, leaving Deck to follow at a reasonable and measured pace. I nearly took the door off its hinges and had my panty hose down in record time. There is very little dignity in a situation like that. Afterward I spent a long time washing my hands even though I hadn't come close to the blood and you can't wash memories away with soap. I felt like Lady Macbeth, only innocent and sane. I took a bunch of deep breaths and walked out.

"Kat—"

"I need a drink, Deck." One look at my face convinced him.

"This way." He put an arm around my shoulders and patted

me as we started walking. In Las Vegas liquor is never very far away. I headed straight for the bar and climbed up on a stool, the fastest way to get a drink.

"Two shots of Rémy and a Pacifico," Deck said. The bartender placed a shot of cognac in front of me. "Drink it, Kat." Deck's voice was gentle. It's not like me but I did, shuddering as it went down. Then I asked for a glass of white wine. Deck waited patiently.

"I found a body." His eyebrows moved infinitesimally. "A young woman with her throat cut. I had to wait for the cops and make a statement."

"Had you ever seen her before?"

"No. At least I tried to think if she'd been at the auction. She could have been, I don't know, I don't think so," I added distractedly, noting how unprofessional I sounded. I polished off the last of my wine, noting how unprofessional I looked.

I am an investigator, yes, but murder is out of my league. Mostly I do leg work for lobbyists or lawyers, run down corporate histories for potentially merging partners or companies, investigate insurance fraud. Occasionally I find a missing person, but not a dead one. I hadn't found a dead person since I'd come home from my high-school graduation to find my mother at the foot of our inside stairs, dead drunk and with her neck broken from the fall.

I was shook then. I was shook now.

Deck signaled the bartender for another round.

"Did my name come up?"

"Huh?"

"When you were talking to the police?"

"No." The question didn't strike me as strange, not until later.

"Good. I like to keep a low profile." We sat in silence for a while and I chugged wine.

"Let's get some dinner in you, Kat."

"I couldn't, Deck." I felt my stomach rise.

"It would be better to eat."

"Yes, but I can't."

"Slow down on the wine then, girl." I did, and we talked about nothing much for a while. Then I said I wanted to go back to my room and sleep. I knew I could sleep the wine off. I wasn't sure about the rest. I wouldn't let Deck drive me back to my car, so he peeled off a twenty and insisted on giving me cab fare. I thanked him, too tired to argue.

He gave me his card and a bear hug that flirted with the possibility of cracking a rib or two. "This has been great, Kat. Well, most of it," he amended. "I'm counting on dinner real soon, maybe even a lot of dinners. Let's pick up where we left off and be good friends again."

"I don't know, Deck." He looked surprised, like a little kid whose hand had been slapped for no reason he can figure out. For a moment I could swear that his lower lip started to tremble, but that was stupid, a slip into the past that never really was.

"We can't go back. We knew each other growing up—that's a long time ago. It's been great seeing you, but I think we're too different to be close friends now. We don't fit. We're pieces from different puzzles."

"Hey, Kat, why so? I'm a businessman and you're—" he looked at me with his question hanging.

"An investigator, slow time in Sacramento. It's a new business and I'm barely making it. Sometimes I think I never should have quit bartending."

"You're a bartender?"

"Was, past tense."

"I always thought that'd be a great job. What's in a stinger, Kat?"

"Brandy, white crème de menthe float." We started to walk out. He was whistling under his breath and the refrain from "The Twilight Zone" started playing through my mind. If I'd been smart I would have seen it as a clue—make that one more clue—and gotten the hell out of there for good. Make tracks. Run like a bunny. See you later, alligator. I didn't, of course.

"How about a top-shelf margarita, Kat? Bet you don't know that one, huh?"

"Gold, Grand Marnier, sweet and sour, and lime—with a salt rim and lime wheel."

"A rusty nail?"

"What are we playing, Stump the Bartender? Knock it off, Deck." It had been a hard day and I was a little peckish. He looked at me sheepishly.

"Sorry, it's a game I used to play with a buddy of mine. I haven't even thought about it since he died. I don't have many friends like that."

"Just associates?" I asked. He glanced at me and his face hardened. "Yeah, it's not the same. That's why I value friendship and the old times."

The old times. I had a sudden flash. "Deck, the kitten, that was you, wasn't it?"

"What are you talking about?" He looked at me as though I'd lost it, and maybe I had.

"Years ago when we were about ten . . . that little black kitten on Mary Beth's porch . . . strangled . . . it was you, wasn't it?"

There was a long, ugly silence. His voice hardened like his face. Then he got all red and white and the dark five o'clock shadow of his beard stood out. He didn't look like a businessman. "It was a long time ago and I'm not proud of it."

After that I wanted to leave and I did. We said goodnight and vaguely I agreed to have dinner soon. God knows why . . . but no, I know why. I can still see my mother's twisted face as she spat out, "Curiosity kills the cat." I always hated to admit that my mother was right.

Dead cats. I shivered. I had a feeling there were stakes here I knew nothing about. High stakes. And I had a feeling I'd learn soon. I wasn't sure I wanted to.

Dear Charity,

Nobody approves of my career choice. Not my mom, my dad, my best friend, or my fiancé. Why shouldn't a woman be a sanitary engineer? The money's good. They threaten never to have anything to do with me if I don't drop it and become a kindergarten teacher. What should I do? Just sign me

Heartsick and in a Quandry

Dear Heartsick,

Who has to live with you twenty-four hours a day? Your mom, your dad, your friends, your fiancé? No. You. Do what you want with your life.

Charity

P.S.

You might try pointing out that it could have been a lot worse. For instance, you could have been a private investigator.

I slept late the next morning, partly because I was still a little sideways from the wine, and partly because every time I woke up sleep seemed a lot more appealing than reality. It worries me when that happens. I finally got up and swam in the Flamingo pool for half an hour. Then I bought a paper, ate breakfast—pain relievers, four Tums and a ginger ale were the best I could do—and skimmed the paper looking for a report on the dead girl. Nothing.

I took a cab over to pick up my car at the Glitterdome—I'd had just enough sense the night before not to try to drive—then headed for the downtown real-estate office that Sam had dealt with. I had a 10:30 appointment that I'd made back in Sacramento.

They were polite and friendly until I indicated exactly why I was there. Exactly according to the story I'd cooked up, anyway. I sat in a deeply cushioned chair across from an expensive desk with real leather accoutrements and looked at a fat, sleek young man with a Rolex watch. He was too young for any of it: the fat, the sleek, or the Rolex. Then I launched into the bullshit.

"I represent a group of investors in Sacramento. We've done business with Sam Collins on several occasions, and we're considering it now. I understand he's involved in a deal down here with a lot of potential, New Capital Ventures. We're interested. What can you tell me about it?"

"Nothing. I mean I've never heard of Sam, uh, Mr. Collins."

"Perhaps somebody else in the office has been handling the deal and I should direct my inquiries to him or her." I said it pointedly.

"No, no. No one's heard of him."

I raised my eyebrows. "So sure without even inquiring?" He flushed slightly. "We don't do deals like that," he added firmly.

"Like what? I haven't defined specifics, or deals, or made any offers."

He sputtered a bit. I rolled on. "How about New Capital Ventures? What do you know about the company?"

"Nothing."

"Nothing?" I said it politely enough, but raised my eyebrows in a "just what do you know?" manner.

That made him angry. It must feel awful to wear a Rolex and act so stupid. "I'm sorry I can't help you." He stood up. "You'll have to excuse me, I'm due in a meeting."

I laughed at him. He bit back a comment but I could feel the four letter words hanging in the air. That's the trouble with wearing a Rolex before you're ready. I showed myself out; it was 10:40 and I had no new information.

At 11:30 I had an appointment with a construction company not far from the real-estate office. My stomach was feeling braver so I stopped for a large glass of milk and some more Tums. I considered a doughnut, but wisely refrained. Doughnuts are food substitutes that always look better than they really are. I've been through it hundreds of times and I know. What I don't know is why I've had to do it hundreds of times, why I didn't learn right away.

At 11:29 I walked into the main office of Trainor Construction and was received promptly. A gentleman who introduced himself as Mike Bolt offered me coffee and a doughnut. I accepted the coffee and struggled, again, over the doughnut. There must be a deep-seated doughnut subliminal message planted inside me somewhere.

I ran basically the same spiel across to Mike. He was too slick to bite, even to bat an eye. "Sam Collins? I'm afraid I don't recognize the name but let me run a quick check through our records." He walked over to a filing cabinet and whipped busily through a batch of folders, stopping and going hmmm, ha, huh, every now and then. I didn't buy it for a minute but it was a better performance by far than the previous one. He shut the file drawer.

"Sorry." He wagged his head regretfully. "I was right. We've never done business with a Sam Collins. Actually we rarely rely on outside money for our projects. What financing we do is local and with people we've worked with for years."

"What do you know about New Capital Ventures?"

He thought about it for a moment. "I've heard the name, but that's about it. We've never done business with them. Sorry, I wish I could help you." He looked quickly at his watch. "Anything else?"

I took the hint and declined. No point in stonewalling it. "Thanks, you've been most kind." We shook hands cordially and I saw myself out. It was becoming a habit. Bolt was on the phone before I was through the door. Interesting.

It was 11:47. I had no new information but I was hungry.

The car was like a yellow cubicle in hell and the air conditioner took a while to slide into the barely functional mode that was apparently the best it could do. I was looking for a down-home place, not fast food or glitz, and I was hot by the time I found it. My blouse stuck damply to my back and I had to shake my skirt away from my legs and brush my hair back from my face. It wasn't that much hotter than what I was used to, but anything over 110 degrees is hot, whether you're used to it or not.

The air conditioning rolled over me in a wave as I walked in the restaurant, making my skin prickle and my body shiver. It was an old-fashioned mom-and-pop café. I found a seat at the counter and Sis came to take my order. She was pert and sassy and didn't, you could tell, believe in any of the same things her parents did. The waistband of her white uniform skirt was rolled over several times to make it short and show off long, tan legs. I told her what I wanted; she flashed brown legs and white teeth and put the biggest glass of ice tea I'd ever seen in front of me. I drank a third of it before slowing down enough to squeeze the lemon.

I had time to think before my sandwich and potato salad came shooting expertly across the counter at me. Charity was right. Sam had money and he hadn't lost it playing the tables as he'd said. He'd invested at least some of it in real estate. Did Sam know what he was doing? I wondered.

New Capital Ventures showed up loud and clear, though they

were reticent about revealing the extent of their involvement. Real-estate purchases in the same area were made in the company name, in the names of individual partners, even in the partners' wives' maiden names. A coincidence? I didn't think so. What was Sam's connection with New Capital Ventures? What was going on, and why did it have to be so hush hush? Would the Democrats make it this year? How many angels can dance on the head of a pin? To hell with it.

I had an afternoon appointment with an investment company, but I didn't think I'd bother to go. To hell with that, too; Sam's name was getting me nowhere fast. If I could read between the lines there was a story there, I was sure of it, but I hadn't gotten that far yet.

Still, I had gotten the answers I'd come for. There were a lot more questions, but the ones Charity had asked were answered. The rest was clear and simple enough. Time to report home. I mopped up a bit of potato salad with a crust of my sandwich and made a loud and satisfactory sound slurping up the last of my ice tea.

I tipped the pert and sassy waitress well. I'd had a few pert and sassy days myself. I was just getting up when a hunch dropped me back on the counter stool. I couldn't read between the lines but I could play my hunches.

Pert scooped up my tip and grinned. "Thanks. Women don't usually tip much."

"Been there," I said. "I was a bartender for a long time."

She nodded. "That explains it."

"Where do you go for a good time in this town?"

"What kind of fun?" She looked at me appraisingly.

"Hmmm," I said, "A nice place, one where everybody goes—" I shrugged the rest of the sentence into that desert of unspoken words where phrases droop, conjunctions drift aimlessly and question marks prowl.

She laughed and looked at me for a long time. It's a big help, the network: bartenders, waitresses, people who work for tips—

you can walk into any town, drop that information and get answers.

She told me.

I decided to take the afternoon off and gamble. Maybe I'd be hotter on the tables. But I wasn't.

Dear Charity,

Is it proper for me to call a boy? My mom says girls never call boys, and ladies never call gentlemen.

Wondering

Dear Wondering,

Girls do what their mothers tell them. Ladies do what society tells them. Women make up their own minds.

Charity

P.S.

The same thing applies to boys, gentlemen and men.

There's an art to behaving well in a bar and it's not as easy as falling off a log—or a bar stool in this case. Most people, women especially, are clueless about it. After my time as a bartender (seven years, two months and three days, but who's counting?), I ought to give a class in it. Adult Education 101, "Drinking With Style."

So there I sat, drinking with style. The restaurant was everything my lunch waitress had implied, and the people were too, I guess. I have to admit they weren't really my choice. I prefer folks who look like they pump their own gas, mean it when they smile and occasionally pet kittens.

The place was starting to fill up. It was an elegant steak house, the restaurant off to one side, the bar area on the other. A heavy old wooden bar with a brass rail ran almost the full length of the cocktail lounge. Behind the bar the mirrors reflected dully, pretty much like most of the people. There were plants and trees scattered around desperately trying to photosynthesize in fake light; a tough assignment, and they had my sympathy.

I swung slightly on my bar stool scanning the room and idly wondering what the man I was meeting looked like.

I'd called Tom Marovic at the *Sacramento Bee* that afternoon. With Tom and me it wasn't a case of calling in favors. We'd worked together for a long time, covered for each other, bailed each other out and kicked each other in the pants. Tom is a twenty-five-year veteran in the business and knows people all over the country, a walking gold mine.

"Yeah, Kat, sure, I know a couple of guys down there," Tom had said when I'd called. "What are you looking for?"

"I want someone who knows local business names, legitimate and otherwise, knows the casino scene and something about local politics and real estate. Skimming, too."

Tom started laughing at me. "You haven't changed a bit, Kat. Still biting off more than you can chew, I bet."

"Well, it's a mouthful. Look, Tom—"

"Skimming?" he whistled. "I'd be real careful playing around with those boys. That's not only dangerous ground, it's their ground." His voice ran down thoughtfully. "Kat, you there? Cat got your tongue?" I shivered at the idea and the cats.

"I'm here, Tom, and I'll be careful." I hoped those weren't famous last words.

"Yeah, okay. Call Joe Rider at the *Review-Journal*. Use my name. He's an ornery old bastard but good, and what he doesn't know about that town isn't worth knowing."

"Thanks, Tom."

"You be careful."

"I promise."

Talk is cheap and promises are easy to make. I make them to myself all the time. Just last week I promised to start leading a settled, regular life. Sometimes I wonder why I didn't stick with being a reporter. The pay is lousy, but there are benefits and vacations. I sighed.

"Ms. Colorado?" I looked up into the tanned, leathery face of a middle-aged, stocky guy with hard eyes. I nodded and the eyes softened.

"Joe Rider." We shook hands.

"It's good to meet you. Thanks for making time for me."

He nodded. "A pleasure. Any friend of Tommy's is a friend of mine."

I love clichés. They make you feel so homey somehow. It's amazing how often writers use them, too, and they should know better.

"I'm so hungry I could eat a horse, saddle and all. How about you, Ms. Colorado?"

I laughed. I was going to like this guy. "It's Kat, Mr. Rider." He shook his head. "Joe, then. And maybe not a whole horse, certainly not the saddle."

The bartender came over and Joe ordered a drink and asked him to get us a table. "Tell me about Tom. I haven't seen him in a dog's age." We talked like that until we were seated and the waiter had taken our orders. A bar is generally not a good place to talk. Too many people can hear, starting with the bartender.

"What can you tell me about skimming, Joe?" I said as I forked in a bite of salad. "Mmm," I added, and he raised his eyebrows. "Big lump of blue cheese," I explained.

"Skimming? You get right to it, don't you? It's the process of taking money off the top, like cream off milk. Pure profit. It never gets reported." I nodded. "You set it up so you bring in enough to make it look reasonable, deduct your operating costs and expenses, then pay taxes on the rest of it, which is usually not much as you've skimmed it all off. The incentives for skimming are, naturally, considerable. So are the penalties; the government takes a dim view of tax evasion.

"There are a number of ways of doing it. One of the simplest is a pyramid hierarchy with one man at the top. He gives the orders, controls everything, and never lets anyone else in on the the whole picture. He's the only one with all the information on the intake and cash flow, and he can adjust it accordingly."

I listened carefully. "Does it happen often, Joe?"

"It happens. Pure profit is a helluva nice thing in anyone's eyes." The waiter brought our food. I tried to be ladylike and not dive into my broiled salmon and baked potato.

"Okay, once you've skimmed it then it has to be laundered, right?"

"Right, especially when we're talking big money. Of course these guys buy, cash on the barrel head, enough luxury houses, fancy cars, and diamonds to choke a stable full of horses."

"I know there are a number of ways to accomplish that, to clean up the money. I'm guessing that buying real estate would be one, and not a bad one at that."

"Yeah. The best way is not to do it directly but to set up a dummy corporation to handle it."

"Like New Capital Ventures, maybe?"

He whistled. "Been here a day and a half and spotted that, have you? Well, I think you're right, but I couldn't prove it and I sure as hell wouldn't advise you to try either. Those are not the kind of toes you want to step on, Kat." He said it firmly and from what I'd already learned, I could only agree with him. I piled sour cream on the last bite of my potato skin and popped it into my mouth.

"Let me run some names past you, Joe," I said after a long chewing pause.

"Dessert?" the waiter inquired. I shook my head.

"Just coffee."

"Make it two."

"Don Blackford?"

"Owns casinos, real estate and God knows what else. He's big in this town, respected but not liked."

"Jim Browning and Al Torrents?"

"Both in the casinos and high up. It's hard to tell—they're not big talkers—whether they're managers, owner/managers, acting partners, or what. You can count on it that they are heavily committed." I nodded and blew on my coffee to cool it. Then I started in.

"New Capital Ventures has recently invested a lot of money in real estate. So has a group of individuals including Browning and Torrents, their wives using their maiden names, and several others I haven't been able to track down yet. The investments are all in undeveloped land in an area just outside of town."

I took a map out of my purse and started unfolding it. "It looks to me like there's a single business interest behind this, even though a number of different names keep popping up. Here." We pushed cups and silverware out of the way and I spread out the map. "I only had parcel numbers so it's a rough approximation. This area, east central and out of town a bit that I've cross-hatched, does it mean anything to you?"

Joe whistled again, long and low. "All this land has been bought up?"

I nodded. "Is it worth anything?"

"Not now. Last year there was a helluva fight about roughly this same area. We've got two ways of thinking around here. The old way is to build it big, build it rich, build an oasis of golf-course green in the desert and to hell with anything else. The new way is starting to count the costs, not just money but water in desert country. The issue is whether to provide luxury housing for a few rich or to spread it around. You get the picture?"

I got the picture. The same issues were coming up all over the west. And they were bitter. The Fly Now, Pay Later contingent doesn't have anything in common with the Plan Ahead folks; they don't even speak the same language.

"A group of investors and developers wanted to put in luxury-living estates with golf courses, swimming pools, tennis courts, the works. These are people who live in the desert and don't want to compromise their concept of the good life with water-saving design and planning. I don't think they really reckoned on the strength of the—for lack of a better word—ecologically minded plan-ahead group either.

"It got very ugly. What? No, no more coffee." He waved the waiter away. "It ended in a stalemate but I'd say the dust hasn't settled yet, too many accusations. There was talk of bribery, corruption, and zoning changes to order on the part of the planning board and the city council. There were rumors of votes bought and sold under the table and unreported contributions. None of it was ever proven and it left a nasty taste in everybody's mouth with no way to rinse it out."

The check came and Joe refused to let me pick it up. "No way, Kat. Not a friend of Tommy's, not this time." I thanked him and mused on friendship. Joe got up and we headed back to the bar. "Nightcap?" he asked, and I nodded. We sat silently at a table and waited for our drinks.

"You've given me a few things to think about, Joe," I said finally.

"What's your angle in all this?" I told him about Charity and Sam. "Sam Collins. Does the name mean anything to you?" Joe shook his head. "He's a developer, works a lot in the Sacramento area. He bought land, too."

"Is that so," Joe commented softly. "Something's going on here, Kat. If these boys are buying land they sure as hell know something we don't. I'd like to jump in on this."

"Good. I was hoping you'd say that. You have access to information that I wouldn't have a shot at."

"You interested in using this as a story?"

"No, it's all yours and my pleasure. I just want to nail Sam and help Charity untangle her life." The drinks came; Joe reached for his wallet.

"Absolutely not."

Joe shook his head. "This is expense account now, Kat, a story like this." He paid and fished out a tattered business card. "Where are you staying?" I told him and he nodded. "Clean and decent. You have any trouble or don't feel safe, you call me or the wife and come out to stay with us."

"Trouble? Joe, c'mon."

"I'm not kidding, and you shouldn't be either. You've been in this business long enough to see the possibilities here. Watch your step, kid, I'm starting to like you." He slugged his bourbon down, winked and squeezed my shoulder. "We'll be in touch the next day or so. Walk you out?"

I shook my head. "I'm going to finish my Irish coffee and think about tomorrow." I watched him walk out. I was starting to like him, too.

The whipped cream on my Irish coffee was real and it was like eating dessert. I licked the cream mustache off my lips. Now for tomorrow. I started ticking off a mental list. Find out about Sam's current projects, take a drive out to the property in question, talk to a real-estate agent—. The scrape of a chair rudely interrupted my thoughts.

"Hi." Tall, suave, and debonair flashed a $2000 orthodontic smile under a toupee and sat down. "Hope you don't mind if I join you. You're a lot prettier than the guys," he waved at a couple of guys who waved back on their way out. One of them looked familiar but I couldn't place him in the dim light.

"Actually, I do."

"Do what?"

"Mind."

He shrugged it off. "I ordered drinks for us." The bartender approached my table. "Would you care for a drink, miss, the gentleman would like to buy you one?"

"No, thank you." I smiled at him and was grateful. "I'm going to finish this and head home. I just want to be alone with my thoughts," I added, addressing myself to suave, and we waited for him to leave. He did so, although not with grace, and left the bar right after that. I finished my drink and my mental list.

It was a beautiful evening when I walked out, clear, not too warm. I could even see a few stars. I was still looking at the stars when I heard a noise behind me. I moved fast, put a car between me and the noise. I turned then and saw suave with an ugly leer on his face.

"I like girls who play hard to get. It really turns me on," he said softly. That soft voice gave me the creeps and then I remembered where I'd seen his friend. It was the guy in the gangster suit at the auction preview, the one I'd put down.

"Beat it or I start screaming." The restaurant was not far away, the parking lot was well lit. Best to make a dash for the restaurant, I thought, even though I was not wearing good running shoes, not by any stretch of the imagination.

"Hey, you!" I addressed a point just over the creep's left shoulder. "Help!" I hollered.

It worked. He looked. I ran.

Dear Charity,

    My mom and I always fight over table manners, opening the door for old people, saying please and thank you. She says it's important. I say it's stupid, sissy stuff. What do you say?

                                 Bobby in Bakersfield

Dear Bobby,

    Manners are never stupid. People without manners are.

                                          Charity

I would have made it, too, would have gotten clear away except for a bump in the pavement. In high heels it threw me off balance and slowed me down just long enough for him to catch up. He grabbed me by the arm and slammed me into the side of a car. I dropped my purse to leave my hands free.

    "Wow, are you persistent." I was a little out of breath; he hadn't needed to slam me that hard. Macho is generally a pretty ugly thing in a man's personality. "So I'll have a drink with you. Let's go inside and discuss it."

"We'll go someplace else and discuss it."

I shrugged. "Okay. Can I at least pick up my purse?" I pointed at the ground.

"Allow me," he said more graciously and bent over. On his way up I slammed my knee under his chin. Hard. His head jerked up and his body started to reel back from the impact. Then I kicked him in the groin. Real hard. Just like Ma told me to. I timed it perfectly and watched with considerable satisfaction as he doubled up moaning and writhing on the ground.

A group of people came out of the restaurant. Out of the corner of my eye I thought I saw another movement, maybe make it plural. I reached down, picked up my purse and started accelerating. My toe hurt and I wasn't as fast as usual. A small knot of people appeared. Where had they been when I'd needed them?

"What happened?"

"What's wrong with him?"

I shrugged and started to walk away.

"Hey, you!"

"I don't even know him," I said over my shoulder and kept on moving, picking up my pace a little.

"Hold it. Police." I sighed and stopped. Bummer. It may have been police but it wasn't uniformed police. He started talking to the other people and I started edging away. "Hold it," he snapped again, so I did. He found out pretty quickly that they didn't know anything and told them nicely to get lost. That left me and whosits on the ground, still incapable, I was happy to see, of rational speech or just about anything else.

"Well?" he asked.

"Well, what?" I asked back.

"Look, miss, I'm a cop. What's going on here?"

"Yeah, and I'm Tinkerbell." He looked at me. "Okay, you're a cop. Let's see some ID." He showed it to me; it looked real, all right.

"Well," I said, as we watched whosits writhe on the ground. "I think he's got stomach cramps and I've got to be going. My mother's waiting up for me." I started to walk off, but he caught me by the arm just above the elbow. He didn't hold me hard or squeeze, but I felt the possibilities there.

"Try again." He wasn't smiling. Me either.

"I'm in town on business. He spoke to me in the bar and then, without encouragement, decided to pursue the acquaintance. He followed me out here and used more than words to persuade me. I used my knee to end the conversation. Now, can I go? I've got to feed my cat." Damn, cats again.

"Do you want to press charges?" He still had hold of my arm.

I shook my head. "We're even." He let go of my arm.

"You, buddy, you want an ambulance?" The guy was still writhing and moaning but he managed to shake his head. "C'mon, then, stand up." The cop hauled him to his feet and propped him on a Trans Am, spoke to him hard and turned back to me. We started walking.

"Let's go inside for a drink."

I sighed. Boy, was it ever my night. Maybe the moon was full. I looked, but couldn't find it. "I've got to go, I told you. Tonight's the night I always grout my tile and wash my hair." He took my arm again and marched me along.

"Look, bozo, just because you're a cop and show up at the wrong time doesn't mean I have to have a drink with you. That's not in the rule book and you can damn well quit throwing your weight around."

"No, ma'am," he sighed, "it's not in the rule book. I can tell you a little bit about that clown though. He's bad news and travels in a pack. His buddies are around somewhere. I could walk you to your car and you might get back to your place or you might not. You might sleep through the night or you might not. And, if they stopped by, it wouldn't be to offer you a drink." I shivered. I couldn't help it.

"A drink would be nice," I said trying to sound confident and casual, although I didn't feel like it much at all. I stuck out my hand. "Kat Colorado, pleased to meet you."

"Hank Parker." He almost smiled and we shook hands.

"Kat, that's an unusual name."

"It's Kate actually, Kat's a nickname."

"Kate, not Katherine?"

"Kate. My mother had a literal and limited imagination. And an even more limited maternal instinct, since she named me after Kate in *The Taming of the Shrew*."

"Are you a shrew?"

"No, but I'm not tame either."

This time he laughed.

"And the Colorado?" I felt myself go stiff and it made me mad; I'd thought I was over that. It was dark but he noticed. Cops are paid to notice.

"Sorry. Hey, forget it," he said.

"It doesn't matter. I mentioned my mother's limited and literal imagination. I was a bastard, born in Sacramento. She didn't want me, so she didn't give me her name. And she couldn't figure out the man, but thought he was from Colorado, so Colorado it was." I shrugged. There was a silence.

"It doesn't matter, you know," he said gently.

"No, it doesn't." I took a deep breath. "Have I thanked you yet?"

"Not yet."

"Consider yourself thanked."

He smiled and we headed back to the restaurant and hoisted ourselves up on bar stools. In my case it was getting kind of repetitious. I had my money out right away. "First one's on me." He opened his mouth. "And if you don't like it you can drink by yourself." He nodded and greeted the bartender.

"The drinks can wait, Ted. Take a couple of your boys with you and get a good look at the guy in the parking lot propped on a Trans Am. His friends, too, if they're around. I want you to recognize them." Ted looked at Hank, left quickly and came back almost as fast.

"He didn't look too good but I'll recognize him. What happened?"

"He ran into my knee," I explained. The bartender grinned.

"He got a little rough with the lady in the parking lot. Not the kind you want to have around."

"No, we'll take care of it. What'll it be, miss, Hank? The house is buying this one."

"Kat," I corrected, thanked him and ordered an Irish coffee. In no time at all I was licking off a whipped cream mustache again. It was like déjà vu, or instant replay. The evening was beginning to take on a bizarre, other-worldly quality. In the background I could hear Jimmy Buffet singing "Why Don't We Get Drunk and Screw?"

I took a deep breath and a good look at Hank. Hunk is the word that comes to mind, even now. He is well over six feet with dark curly hair, brown eyes and a mustache. His shoulders are broad and he's stocky and well built. Right then he was staring into his drink with a somewhat morose expression.

"I guess breaking up fights in the parking lot on your evening off is kind of like a busman's holiday."

"What? Oh. You did fine on your own, I just helped with the cleanup." He went back to staring at his drink.

"Look, don't feel you have to stick around on my account. I'll be fine."

He shook himself like a big dog and refocused on me. "Sorry, I'm a little preoccupied. So." His mind was clearly flipping through the possibilities for social conversation. "What do you do?" He'd landed on the obvious.

"I'm uh . . . a consultant." It was close enough to the truth. I didn't feel like getting into explanations with a Las Vegas cop.

He looked at me. "On what?"

"Current trends, that kind of thing."

"Like what?"

"Well . . ." We looked at each other.

"You need to change that line, or come up with another story, or tell people to go to hell. Nobody's going to believe it." I nodded glumly. He was right. It was my turn to stare morosely at my drink.

"Is it safe to go now, Hunk, I mean Hank?" I could feel myself blushing.

He looked at his watch. "One more wouldn't hurt." We had one more. This time I had Ted hold the whipped cream. No more mustaches, déjà vu, and altered reality stuff.

When we left Ted told me to come back any time, that he'd see to it that I wasn't bothered. I thanked him but the idea didn't have much appeal.

"We'll take your car and I'll drive."

"Oh, really, that's not—"

"You still don't believe me about those clowns, do you? This can be a rough town, Kat."

"Okay." I shrugged. "How will you get back?"

"I'll have one of the boys on patrol pick me up. This is your car?" he asked in understandable amazement.

"A rental. It was the best I could do."

"You're not from around here, then? I should have known."

"How? My tan's good."

"You're a little too wholesome, not slick enough." Good. The fresh fruit, vegetable, and yogurt routine was paying off. That and vitamins and exercise. I smiled complacently.

"Where are you from?"

"Sacramento."

He looked almost interested. "I have a sister there." So then I tried to look interested.

"Are you here to gamble?" He couldn't quite keep the contempt out of his voice.

"No, business. I really am a consultant."

"I won't ask, save you another bad lie on your conscience. Where are we going?"

I told him. We took off on a route that defied logic, reason, and mileage. I believed him when he said it was impossible for anyone to follow us without him knowing. He delivered me and the canary to my door and politely waited for me to enter. Then he checked the room for intruders, asked if he could use the phone for his ride, and was off. He left me with a polite handshake and a card, and told me to call him if I had any trouble—he'd be only too happy to blah, blah, blah. I changed my mind about the hunk. Hulk, maybe. He didn't smile enough to be a hunk.

It was after one when he left. I was wide-awake tired with all that caffeine pumping through my veins and I decided to call Charity. She would have gone to bed hours ago, but what the hell, this is the woman who comes over in the middle of the night whenever she feels like it.

"Wake up, Charity, it's long distance and I need some information."

"Huh, who, wha . . . Kat?"

"You guessed it. I'm hot on the trail and I need some more clues. What's Sam doing now?"

"How should I know? Kat, for crying out loud!"

"Not *right* now. In general and at work?"

"I don't know. You know I never paid much attention to that. I think he's got a project over in North Natomas, or was it South Natomas," she said vaguely. "Or, I just don't know, maybe he finished that."

"Holy cow, Charity, can't you pay any attention to the nuts-and-bolts details of life?"

"Kat, that's not fair! Anyway, the answer is, no, I can't. I really can't. I'm busy solving other people's problems."

"There's no rule that says problem-solvers can't sharpen their own pencils, notice what their soon-to-be ex-husbands are doing, and solve their own problems."

"Boy, are you in a bitchy mood."

I sighed. She was right. "You're right, I'm sorry. Some guy tried to mug and rape me and it sort of spoiled my evening."

"Kat!"

"I'm okay. I came out of it a whole lot better than he did, and was escorted home by a knight in rusty armor."

"Kat!"

"Relax, Charity. Is there any way you can find out about Sam's business dealings? Not just in the Sacramento area but all over California and Nevada, too?"

"I can try. He never said anything about Nevada."

"The money's somewhere, maybe there—just check it out as best you can, okay?"

"Okay, and Kat, are you sure you're all right? I'm worried. Maybe I should—"

"No, I'm fine, just tired. Call me tomorrow. Here, write down the number." I gave it to her.

"Be careful, Kat."

"I will," I said. More famous last words.

It was all I could do to drag my clothes off and brush my teeth before I fell into bed. Probably I would have slept into the day after tomorrow except the damn phone rang.

Dear Charity,

Is it okay to tell lies, not big ones but little ones that make people feel better or make your life easier?

White Lie Lil

Dear Lil,

It's okay, but it's not right. You and your conscience will have to work it out.

Charity

"Morning, sunshine, just checking up on you."

"Who is it?" I asked stupidly, my brain fogged in like the Sacramento airport on a winter morning.

"Joe."

"Joe. Oh, Joe, did you find out anything?"

"Not yet. Will do by the end of the day. How's about you come out for dinner with the wife and me tonight? We'll catch up on the day and figure out the next step. Bring your suit, too, we've got a pool."

"Great, I'd love to. Joe, do you know a cop named Hank Parker?"

"Yeah, good man. How'd you run into him?"

"Tell you later. What time's dinner and where?" He told me. I yawned and stretched and decided to get up and get going, then went back to sleep for another hour and a half. No problem, nothing was going anywhere real fast. I tell myself that kind of thing all the time. It's more comforting that way, I guess.

As I was eating breakfast I looked through the paper again for a mention of the dead girl. Still nothing. I wondered whether a violent death in Las Vegas was that insignificant, or whether the clubs could put a lid on the news.

I got out Deck's card and stared at it. Not much information there, not much help. It didn't mention New Capital Ventures either, but he had. I wondered how much Deck could tell me about it all. Would, not could. I wondered how far I could push friendship. To hell with it. Too much wondering. I stuck the card back in my wallet and decided to deal with it later. Wouldn't hurt to know more first, either.

I got my map out and marked the residential area I wanted to cover, quite a bit of driving. The canary's air conditioner might or might not be up to it. I didn't head right out to the marked area but drove around, wanting to get a feel for suburban Las Vegas and especially for the developments next to the New Capital Venture land. It was definitely high-income housing. The lots were big and beautifully landscaped, the houses were spacious and luxurious, the kind that probably had swimming pools out back. I could easily comprehend the conflict of last year. The kind of people who invested in properties like this would only accept more of the same as next door neighbors. There's nothing quite like the tantrums that the rich and influential can pull.

New Capital Ventures' land, as far as I could stake it out, was similar, but desert, undeveloped and beautiful in a harsh, sunbaked, pitiless way. I admired it from the car and the relative cool. Then I drove back to town and started looking for real-estate agents. No problem, they were as plentiful as cactus. I picked a likely looking one gleaming with monied touches and complacency, fluffed out my hair, pasted on a smile and walked into Hanaford Realty.

Several agents came to attention and focused on me as I strolled in. Their looks were too controlled to be called hungry but that's what it was all the same. I smiled and scanned the room.

"Hello." They leaned toward me like plants growing toward the sun, potential money in this case being the attraction. I made my choice and addressed a woman in her forties who was slick, stylish, and made-up to the eyeballs. She looked like a call girl who'd outgrown her profession of choice and regretfully settled for something else.

"May I help you?" Sounded like a call girl, too.

"Oh, I hope so," I said at my phony best. "You see, we're looking for property to buy in this area, and my husband said absolutely not to settle for anything less than the very best." Cherries, lemons and green apples rolled over in her eyes and then the $$$ lined up. I'd never seen anything quite like it before.

"We're thinking of building ourselves," I continued to lie unabashedly. "I drove out Loma Linda and I think that's the prettiest area. Why, I stood there at the end of that little dead-end street and gazed out at the countryside and my heart went pitty patty, pitty patty." I patted my left breast prettily and hoped I wasn't overdoing it. "I'm a poet," I added, absolutely and to my chagrin, unable to resist overdoing it.

"So," I gushed, "what I want to know is how do I find out about buying some property out there and how much would it be? Charlie says, 'Get the best, but don't spend too much,' and I say, 'Oh, what the heck, Charlie, we're only young once.' You see." I lowered my voice confidentially, "Great-aunt Milla died and she left us, well she left us a bundle to be honest, and I'm sure she'd want us to spend it and have a good time, aren't you?"

I beamed on them, and they all nodded. I stood there smiling and waiting; they stood there looking a little dazed. "About that land?" I suggested. Vera, I found out her name later, snapped into shape.

"Let's get out a map and check it," she said, and we did. I showed her Loma Linda and "that darling little dead-end street," and then plunked my finger down in the heart of New Capital Ventures country. "Here, I think. We don't want to be too close to our neighbors and we definitely want acreage." I smiled a dazzling smile.

"Definitely." Vera smiled back. She seemed a bit hypnotized.

"So will you find out for me?" Vera allowed as how she would, maybe even in a couple of hours if I wanted to stop back. I did. We all did another round of smiles and then I glided out of the office the way I imagined a rich, hopeful, young woman would. The heat tried to push me back in the building but I fought my way out.

I had some time to kill so I dropped in on a few other realty offices and chatted people up on property values, nice parts of town, rate of growth, and contractors and developers. If folks have the time they love to talk, to tell you things. If you ask nicely it's harder to get them to stop than to start. It's embarrassing sometimes—I get mortified at all the personal details—but it doesn't seem to bother them. And it is a help in my business.

The climate had changed when I got back to Hanaford Realty. An arctic wind had moved in and apparently I was no longer a member in good standing of that sacred group, The Great American Buying Public.

"Hi," I said as I breezed in. "Hey, what did you find out, Vera? Any chance of my—"

She shook her head. "No. However we do have some lovely sites that I could—"

"No. What do you mean no? No, never; no, not right now; no, not until the price is right; what kind of no?"

"A no no," stammered Vera, obviously not adept at the nuances and subtleties of the English language.

"Nonsense. Who owns it? We'll offer them a lot of money," I added briskly. "Everybody may not have a price, but it is a reasonable working assumption."

"I'm afraid I can't—"

"Who did you say owns it?"

"I didn't."

"Well?"

"I'm afraid I can't—"

"Surely you checked into it?"

Her face froze over slightly, not an unimpressive feat in this heat. It must have been the continuing arctic quality of the room. "I'm very sorry," she said coldly, "but that property is unavailable for purchase at this time. Now, if you would care to consider—"

"I don't believe so," I said, and stood up. I peeled my skirt from the backs of my legs and strode from the room.

This was something to think about. The news that the property was unavailable was hardly a surprise; the arctic frost surrounding the subject was. I stopped at a phone booth, looked up the address of the main library and headed on over there. The reference librarian knew exactly what I was talking about and was as helpful as a roomful of Girl Scouts.

"Oh my, yes, there was quite a flap about that zoning issue. That incident ruffled everybody's feathers and made the fur fly for days." I accepted her mixed zoological metaphor with equanimity—enthusiasm, even. I've been known to mix a metaphor myself. "Let's see, spring of last year, I do believe." She flipped competently through her newspaper files. "Here, try this." She settled me down in front of a microfilm machine. "Check the front pages, of course, then the city pages and the editorial section. You'll find plenty of coverage." I read and took notes for several hours until my brair felt almost as crossed as my eyes and both matched my mood, also cross. Microfilm is not company one chooses to keep. I thanked the librarian for her help and was on my way out when another thought occurred to me.

"Has there been an election since the uproar?"

"Why, yes, there has."

"Did it affect any of the people and factions involved in this?"

She looked at me thoughtfully for a moment. "Why, it did at that."

"Might things be different today if they voted on the same issues?"

"Hard to say but they might, they might at that." I thanked her again and left.

Back at the Pink Flamingo I had a cold soda, showered off the day's sweat and grime and plopped down on the bed to think. Some thinking. I woke up just in time to get dressed for dinner. Nothing fancy, Joe had said. I slipped a low-backed yellow-and-white sundress over my head, buckled the belt, rummaged around for my sandals and a swimsuit, and started out. There was a little tingle of anticipation inside me. Food, good company or news, it was hard to tell which; I didn't really bother to try.

The phone rang just as I was closing the door. Damn. I answered it, of course. Once set in motion the high-tech-communications network possesses its own mad magic and compulsion, if not logic.

"Kat, I'm glad I caught you. I've tried to get you several times today."

"Hi, Charity, what's up? What did you find out?"

"Nothing and yet something. That doesn't make sense, does it? Kat, I don't like this, not one bit. I went to see Sam at his office today. Most of the time he's just rude and won't talk but today he seemed almost glad to see me. It was, well, kind of like old times, like good times. We went out to lunch and—"

"Did you find out anything?" I knew where this road led—nostalgia and tears—we'd been down it many times. I didn't mind, it's hard getting over lost love, I just didn't have the time right then.

"No, not really, like I said before. He's working a project in North Natomas, or was it South? Whatever. And maybe a project in Roseville somewhere near the bypass between I-80 and 65."

"Charity." I was feeling slightly impatient.

"I asked him about Nevada and business there and he changed completely. He almost yelled at me in the restaurant. It was embarrassing; everyone started staring. He asked me what I was goddamned talking about and said he had no goddamned business there and anyway his goddamned business was none of my goddamned business. Kat, his words were angry and mean and awful, but his eyes were scared. I'd never seen him like that before. What's going on?"

"I don't know yet. I just have bits and pieces, not the whole picture. You were right, though—whether or not he lost money at the gambling tables he still had quite a bit to invest in real estate down here. At the moment the land is apparently worthless, although political maneuvering could change that. I've got the land-ownership proofs you need. Do you want me to stop here?"

"Could that land be turned back into cash?"

"I doubt it, not as things stand. Or maybe for ten cents on the dollar but not for two-hundred-thousand dollars. The two-hundred-thousand depends on the political maneuvering. It's more complicated than I can explain right now."

She sighed. "Can you stay, then? See if you can figure out how to get the money back. A deed to half of Sam's worthless land in the desert doesn't get me anywhere. That bastard!" She started to wail again.

"Charity, I've got to run. Why don't you go to a movie? You know how that always cheers you up."

"Oh, Kat, life isn't that simple, you know."

"No, but—"

"But what?"

"Have popcorn *and* a candy bar." We hung up on a laugh. It wasn't like Charity to be that fragile. She's usually full of beans and snappy comebacks. Of course some chapters of life are tougher than others. I was heading for a pretty tough chapter myself though naturally I didn't know it at the time.

Dear Charity,
One night a friend told me this awful, horrible, sad story. I didn't know whether to cry, or say something, or scream and run out of the room. What do you do in a case like that?
Baffled in Birmingham

Dear Baffled,
Think of your friend, not yourself. Why not just say, "Oh, I'm so sorry, and I wish I could help"?
Charity

I liked Joe's wife, Betty, right away. She was short and solid and looked like her heart was filled with warmth and her refrigerator with fresh vegetables.

"Come in," she said, shaking my hand, "you're Kat, of course. The boys are out back floating in the pool—or in their margaritas," she added reflectively, "since I'm sure I heard the blender going again. Come on out to the kitchen with me, will you, while I just finish up the salad?"

"Boys? I thought Joe said your children were all grown."

"Oh, yes, ours are. Didn't Joe tell you he was inviting a friend?" I shook my head as Joe walked in.

"Betty, have we got more limes? Kat, you're here. Great. Have a margarita. You know Hank?" A gorgeous man in swim trunks loomed into view. I didn't recognize him at first because he was smiling.

"Hunk—Hank," I corrected myself quickly and hoped no one had noticed, "my knight in rusty armor. Hi, and thanks again." We shook hands, smiled at each other and retold the previous night's story for Joe and Betty. I tried to make light of it but I could see that they were worried, and Joe was upset that he'd left me there. Hank was calm and soothing, and somewhere in all that I got mesmerized by the patterns the dark curly hair made on his chest, around and around and . . .

"A margarita, Kat?"

"Hmm? Oh, yes please. No salt, lots of lime." I shook my head slightly to clear it and offered to help Betty with the salad. She wouldn't hear of it but invited me to talk with her while the boys, as she called them, barbecued.

"Hunk, huh?"

I blushed.

"A Freudian slip?"

"Betty, sometimes I think I was born with my foot in my mouth. I can get both in without trying real hard." She laughed.

"He is a hunk. Single, too. And you?"

"Yes." I thought I spoke in a low key, noncommittal manner but I knew by the way she looked at me that I hadn't pulled it off.

"That bad?"

I nodded. "It was. I'm almost over it now."

"Good. Salad's done." She stuck it in the refrigerator. "I'll grab that plate of hors d'oeuvres. If you'd like to put on your suit the bedroom's down there." She pointed. "See you outside in a minute."

It was wonderful, once I got outside, to swim. I did laps for a while and then just lay on my back and floated. It was a beautiful evening, calm and tranquil, especially since my ears were in the water and I couldn't hear anything. When the world exploded next to me I went down with a sputter and came up with a nose full. Hank was grinning at me.

"As a kid I did the best cannonballs on my block."

I blew water from my nose into my hand and hacked and wheezed in a most unbecoming fashion. He was still grinning. I splashed him in the face and dove, swimming the length of the pool underwater. By the time I got out and dried off Joe was dishing up the barbecued chicken and hollering at us to come and eat. It was good, down-home, simple food, chicken and corn, salad and garlic bread. I ate so much my stomach started to puff up a bit more than usual over my bikini. I'm a little chubby but not too bad, and fortunately not stupidly vain about it. And I work out. Dessert was strawberry shortcake and I ate it without a qualm, even considered seconds.

After dinner we lay back in our lounge chairs along the pool and looked up at the first stars. The silence was companionable. I could hear crickets singing and a last few birds twittering as they settled down for the night. That and the quiet slurp of margaritas. It was very nice indeed.

"You first, Kat," Joe said.

"Does Hank know what's going on?"

"Yeah, I filled him in."

"Okay. Won't take me long, I didn't find out much."

I reviewed my day at the real-estate office and the library, and my talk with Charity. "And my toe still hurts," I added. Hank chuckled; then it was quiet again for a while.

"Joe, Hank, do either of you know a guy named Deck Hamilton?"

"Bad news."

"How the hell do you know him?"

They spoke at the same time. I sighed and my heart sank. I wasn't real surprised to hear it but I wasn't pleased, either.

"Tell me about him."

Hank spoke first. "He's got a considerable police record, more arrests than convictions, I'd bet, mostly for being in the wrong place at the wrong time, strong-arm stuff, suspicions we can't nail down. He's a pretty ugly character, Kat." Hank sounded grim. "The word is that he's an enforcer and an occasional hit man. I have no trouble believing that. None at all. He's not someone you should have anything to do with."

"Joe?"

"I can't add to that except that he's known for playing fair and standing by his word. You square with him and he will with you."

"Kat." Betty said, sounding worried. "You don't have anything to do with him, do you?"

I sighed again. I badly wanted to talk about Deck and my suspicions, but I couldn't. I couldn't figure any way of bringing it up without involving Deck somehow and that was out of the question. Joe and Hank had been kind and helpful to me and maybe some day I'd call them my friends; I hoped so. Still, we were talking press and police, and Deck and I were friends, friends from way back. I sighed again.

"Kat?" Betty asked.

"Am I involved with him? Yes and no." "Involvement" was a tricky issue. Thoughts of the dead girl crossed my mind then. Was I involved there? I wanted to bring that up but didn't. Joe and Hank jumped on me too fast.

Joe exploded. "Goddamn, girl, I thought you had more smarts than that."

"Me too." Hank's voice was quiet and sounded disappointed.

"Oh, lighten up you guys. We went to school together. I haven't seen him since I was fourteen or fifteen and that was close to twenty years ago. We bumped into each other at the airport. He'd changed so much I didn't even recognize him, and wouldn't have except for the Katy."

"Katy?" Betty asked.

"My nickname as a kid. There's hardly anyone around who

knows me by that now. My little sister called me Katy. She died when she was three." I reached for my margarita.

"I'm sorry I jumped on you," Joe said. I nodded. "But he's not a good person for you to know. Hank's right." I nodded again.

"That's what I told him. It was the kitten and, and never mind—" I broke off lamely. "Tell us about your day, Joe."

"I didn't learn a thing, but what I didn't learn was damned interesting." Joe whistled tunelessly for a bit. "I know Vegas and the people in it pretty goddamned well. I know how to tap into information, on the record and off, and I couldn't find out a blamed thing. Somebody's sewed up this town tighter than a canoe. People who would usually talk, or tell me to go to hell, are saying nothing and saying it real scared."

"Who did you talk to?"

"City councilors, planning board members, developers, people with their ear to the ground and ass for sale. No one's got anything to say and they say it fast."

"Don't they know anything, or are they scared? And why?" I asked.

"There are guys in this town with a reputation for playing hardball," Hank answered me. "They ask you nicely and offer you money the first time. The second time they threaten to rape your wife or little girl, or break your son's arms. People will risk their own safety for a principle sometimes, but not their family's, not if there's anything else they can do."

"Is that it, Joe?" I asked.

"I don't know, damned if I do. I hope not."

"Is it possible that the zoning issue could come up again on this land?"

"Damn well looks that way, doesn't it, but I don't know that either. I'll find out, call in some favors, ask some more people." He shook his head. "I don't like it. Damn right I don't." We all sat in silence for a while.

Betty got up. "I'm going to put on some music. Coffee, anyone?" We agreed to it and the sounds of big band and the smell of coffee percolated back to us. Hank and Joe talked shop for a while. I sat on the edge of the pool, dangling my legs in the water and humming along with the music. After coffee Betty yawned and stretched.

"Hank's practically family, so I don't have to apologize to him for going to bed early. You make yourself family too, Kat. Stay as long as you like and help yourself to coffee, more margaritas, strawberry shortcake, whatever you want. Swim, the noise won't reach the bedroom. Stay the night if you want to, Hank often does. He'll show you where the sleeping bags are if you want one." She yawned again, gave me a hug, kissed her boys and exited.

We sat in the dark not saying anything. Usually that's uncomfortable. Sometimes you can do it with old friends, sometimes not. When you're quiet and it feels right it is as though the world's in balance and there's nothing to worry about. The deepness of the silence takes over and peace drifts through your mind, and if you're lucky, and it lasts long enough, it sifts on down to your soul. Joe said good night and then Hank and I sat in silence, but it was different. We were saying nothing and saying it real loud. Hank must have felt it, too. He took my hand and pulled me up with him.

"C'mon, let's go for a swim."

"Last one in's a rotten egg." I gave him a quick backward push that sent him off balance and dove in, beating him easily. I surfaced and he came up beside me.

"Hunk, huh?"

"What are you talking about, Hank?" I was blushing, but it was too dark to see. He laced his hands across my back and pulled me through the water, leaned toward me and kissed me softly, gently, not macho and hard. My hands were on his chest in that dark, thick, curling hair. I shivered and pushed him away. He let me go at once and I lay on my back, floating, looking at the stars and trying to figure out how I felt about all this.

After a while I got out and sat by the pool, letting the soft evening breeze dry me. He pulled himself up out of the water and sat next to me.

"I've got to go," I announced.

"Why?" he asked. I couldn't think of an answer so I didn't answer, and I didn't go.

"Stay," he said. "I'd like it if you did. Let's talk for a while."

"Okay."

"Would you like a brandy?" I nodded and he went to get them, handed me a heavy old snifter. We sat in silence again for a while but it was quiet silence now, not loud silence.

"Tell me about your sister," he said finally. I started to feel sad. He reached out and patted my knee gently, then let his hand stay there. I let it stay there, too, and thought for a bit. I hadn't talked about her in a long time. Finally I took a sip of brandy and started.

"I was nine when she was born and twelve when she died. Ma didn't want her; she didn't want either of us. Ma called her Sis or Cissy, short for sister, I guess. I don't even know if she had a real name. Ma would never say." I started to cry and wiped my nose on the back of my hand, just like I used to when I was a kid.

"I took care of Cissy most of the time since Ma couldn't be bothered. If she wasn't working she was drunk. I worried about Cissy a lot when I was away in school but she was a good baby. After school I'd stay home and my friends would come over or I'd take her out with me. We were always together. I made dinner and put her to bed and, often as not, she'd sleep with me. She had a lot of nightmares. No wonder.

"People always thought that taking care of her was too much for a twelve-year-old kid, but that wasn't it at all. She saved me, taught me how to love and care the way our mother never did. I would have grown up hard and cold inside without her." I paused for a long time, started and stopped, and finally lugged along like an old car on a cold day.

"She died . . . I loved her so much . . . she died . . . I thought my world would fall apart."

I was crying again. Hank put his arm around my shoulder. "Ma missed the funeral. She was drunk, of course. I never forgave her for that, not that she noticed." My voice was very bitter, I knew it was. I'm still bitter and Ma is dead now, too. I'm the only one left."

"How did she die?" Hank had his arm around my shoulders still; it was warm and heavy and comforting.

"Pneumonia. I knew she was sick and I begged Ma to call the doctor but she was drunk and paid me no mind. I finally called a neighbor lady and she took Cissy to a hospital, but by then it was too late. They wouldn't let me see her in the hospital. I was too young, they said. Rules, they said. I cried and pleaded but they said no and that the child needed her mother, where was her mother? Ma was drunk. Cissy died without me and all alone. I never saw her again."

Hank hugged me tightly to him. "The night she died I had a dream. In my dream she got out of her bed and crawled into mine like she often did. She snuggled up and put her arms around my neck and said, 'I love you, Katy, always and forever.'"

I had stopped crying and felt drained and empty. I slid out from under Hank's arm and swam, swam for a long time. When I came back Hank was still just sitting there. I floated in the water and rested my cheek against his knee. His fingers stroked my head and played in my hair, straightening out the tangles. "Poor children," he said at last. "You didn't blame yourself, did you Kat?"

"I did at first but the neighbor lady, who was kind and grand-motherly, made me talk to her and explained things to me. She told me to come over for cookies and milk whenever I wanted. And I did. Not for the cookies, but for the talk and understanding." Hank's hand was like a caress on my head. I sighed and shivered, the breeze was cool on my bare back.

"Out of the water," he said briskly, "you're getting cold. I'll go get you a towel." I clambered out and dripped until he came back and wrapped a huge soft towel around me. Then we sat in the yard, away from the house, on a white wrought-iron love seat that looked like lace in the moonlight. The brandy and the towel and something about Hank were making me feel warm again.

"You have a story, too, don't you?" I said finally into the silence.

"Don't we all?"

"A sad one?"

"Aren't they all?" He sounded very bitter, more bitter than I am, even about Cissy. His must be more recent.

"No, they're not." It was my turn to put a hand on his knee and his to let it stay there. His knee was hard and muscled. He covered my hand with his big one.

"Tell me about it." I turned over my hand in his and we sat holding hands in the moonlight like two lost kids. I waited patiently for him to start talking.

Dear Charity,

Someone I love very much died and I'm mad at the whole
world. I'm mad at people who are happy, and at people who
still have the people they love, and at everyone who is alive
when she isn't. I'm mad at everything and everyone and I can't
bear it. I know it's not right but I can't help it. Please help me.

Lost in Lovelock

Dear Lost,

You cry and cry and cry and finally, when the hurt is washed
away a little, you start over again. Love doesn't end with death
and there are others you will love.

Charity

"I'm a widower. Did you know that?"

I shook my head. "I don't know anything about you except
you're a cop. And you're nice," I added. He seemed not to hear.

"She died two years ago." The pain was still alive in his voice.

"Oh, Hank, I'm so sorry."

"It should have been me."

"You can't say that; you can't know that."

"Yes," he said, "I can, and I do. It was a car bomb and it was meant for me. She was late that morning and her car wouldn't start so I told her to take mine. I had a day off and I figured I'd work on her car later. Later," he said bitterly, "later. The world stopped for me when I heard the bomb go off. I knew what it was right away. I knew she didn't have a chance but I prayed as I ran through the house that I was wrong, that it was a gas main, a car backfiring, that it was anything but what it was."

"And," I said gently into his long silence. His hand was gripping mine tightly. Suddenly he let go.

"It was what it was, and she was dead. Instantly. I never got to say good-bye either. At least you had that dream." His voice was husky and heavy. "I dream that she's alive, laughing and happy, and just as I reach out to touch her I wake up in an empty bed reaching out for nothing."

"I'm so sorry," I said softly, but I don't think he heard me.

"I can't forget."

"Sometimes the heart takes a long time to heal." I reached out for his hand and held it between mine. It was cold and I tried to warm it. "Hank, you don't blame yourself, do you?" It was odd, the questions that night. It was as though we took turns playing the same parts.

"Yes," his voice was harsh.

"Hank, no."

"I'm a cop, Kat. Someone was trying to get me for a job I was doing and I knew it. I should have thought, should have seen it coming. I—" His voice ran down and he put his head in his hands, his elbows on his knees.

"No, you're human, Hank. You can't see everything, know everything. You've got to stop this, to forgive yourself and start living in today, not in the past and in guilt and could-have-beens."

"Goddamn it, what do you know?" His voice was harsh and cruel and I felt my face go white in the moonlight. "Kat, I'm sorry. God, I'm sorry." He put his head back between his hands, started to cry. I put my arms around him and held on so he wouldn't shake himself apart.

"I never cried," he said at last. "They say you're supposed to."

"Yes."

"I'm tired and this seat is making prints on my ass." He got up and fetched two sleeping bags, spread one out on the lawn and another on top of us. We curled up together like lost children who have finally cried themselves quiet. I fell asleep right away.

The sun was shining brightly and the birds going crazy when I woke up. It was still cool but the day's promise of heat was there. Hank was gone. I stretched out lazily in the sleeping bags and yawned. I had slept dreamlessly and everything seemed far away, Cissy, Hank's wife, Sam and Charity, Deck, Las Vegas. I tried to float off into never-never land again but then the sun disappeared and there was Hank, dressed and handsome, standing over me.

"Awake?" He smiled. "Betty has coffee and juice, scrambled eggs and Danish, hot and waiting. If you're ready to get up I'll put away the bags." Reluctantly I crawled out. His hand rested briefly in the small of my back. "Thanks, Kat."

"Ditto." We smiled at each other and I ambled into the house.

At breakfast we tried to make a plan, which was difficult as nobody really had a good sense of what to do. Or, more accurately, there didn't seem much that we could do that would be real effective. Hank was intrigued by now, against his better judgment no doubt, but join the crowd. He, like Joe, was going to ask around, run out a few hints and see if anybody played clue. Betty had left for work already. That left only me twiddling my thumbs.

"I'm going back to Sacramento to see if I can find out anything from Sam. Charity didn't, but then that was to be expected. Also, she didn't have the information I do." That was it, I couldn't come up with anything better. Except Deck, but there was no point in discussing that with these guys. I already knew their thoughts on the subject. I knew mine, too, and knew that I was going to talk to Deck soon, but not now; not just yet.

"I don't know," Joe said, slurping his coffee after heaving about six teaspoons of sugar into it.

"Aaak, how can you drink that sugar slop, Joe? What a waste of good coffee." I wasn't exaggerating; it was disgusting.

Hank grinned. "He usually dunks a sugar donut in, too." We shook our heads sadly while Joe sat in dignified silence.

"If you two connoisseurs of good taste are through, perhaps we can continue." We allowed as how we were through.

"Kat, if you clue in Sam that something's in the works, will he blow the whistle here?"

I thought it over. "I don't know, he might. He doesn't do well under pressure, emotional pressure at least, I don't know about work problems. Mostly he just stuffs everything inside and when the total accumulation reaches explosion point he blows. It can be impressive, I've seen it. Anyway, would it matter?"

"Might help. Since we don't have much else going it could bring something out in the open. A clay pigeon is better than no pigeon and, who knows, they might shoot at it. It's worked before," Hank said.

"Okay," Joe said, "it's a helluva plan but we don't have much to work with, that's for sure. Kat, when are you going?"

"As soon as possible. I'll go check out of the motel and head for the airport. Can I use your phone to call about flights?" Joe nodded.

I came back to the table with the news that there was a flight out at 11:15, and that I was on it. Hank said he had to get to work and took off. I walked him to the door.

"Glad you're coming back, Kat. How about dinner one night?"

"Sounds good."

"Kiss you good-bye?"

"Okay, Hunk." It was intentional this time. We kissed good-bye and my heart did a little flip-flop. Back in the kitchen I had another cup of coffee with Joe, or rather I had coffee and he had coffee-flavored sugar.

"Here's a key, Kat. We've got room and we enjoy your company, so skip the motel and stay with us."

"Joe, I couldn't." I made myself say it, a token protest; I didn't feel it.

"Sure you could."

"Okay, thanks. Sounds great."

"I'm taking off. See you when you get back. Don't do anything foolish."

"Not me," I said, and hoped I was telling the truth. After Joe left I debated for some time whether or not to call Deck. I was having a hard time with that one and wondered why. I wondered all the way through another cup of coffee, but still no answer. I gave up and decided to put off calling him until I got back. Procrastination felt like the path of least resistance, if not the better part of valor.

I left the car at the airport, although the thought of turning it in was an awfully tempting one. Recalling the rental process balanced it out, and I resisted the temptation.

The flight was uneventful except that I was surrounded by a lot of depressed-looking people. A woman behind me was crying softly, and her husband was trying to shush her. Busted gamblers on their way home. At least they were flying. I've seen families standing by the roadside with their luggage and Dad with his thumb out.

I was one of the first people off the plane and glad to get out of there. It's always good to come home, even for just a day.

I picked up my beat-up Bronco in the long-term parking lot and headed out, deciding that I'd try to catch Sam on the way home. He might not be in his office, but if I called he definitely wouldn't be. Sam and I never were friends. We used to try to be cordial for Charity's sake, but, now that that doesn't matter, we've dropped all pretense.

I parked on Fair Oaks Boulevard in front of Sam's office and looked around to see if I could spot his car. I was in luck, a silver Corvette was parked down the street. Sam is the classic example of male mid-life crisis in action and operating at the lowest, most mindless level. I always pointed that out to him, which is one reason we didn't get along very well. I breezed into the office. Sam was sitting alone and staring broodingly at the wall. Promising.

"Sam, old buddy, I'm glad I caught you."

"Oh, for God's sake Kat, whatever you're selling I'm not buying. I wish you and Charity would leave me alone," he said almost petulantly.

"This doesn't have anything to do with Charity. Well, not much," I amended. "And you'll be interested. A lot of people are interested in New Capital Ventures." Sam snapped to attention. "See, I was right. You're interested."

"Like hell I am."

"Sure. That's why you sat up four inches straighter, turned red and started swearing. You'll never make undercover agent or con artist, Sam, don't even try. A third grader could read you like a Sesame Street rerun." Sam sputtered and turned even redder. "In fact I don't think you should play with the boys down in Vegas. Out of your league; they're major and you're bush."

Unasked, I took a chair across from Sam's desk, sat back and waited confidently for the explosion. I didn't have to wait long. After the explosion I waited, with less confidence, for some kind of coherent remark. That took longer. Finally he established to his satisfaction that I was a stupid, conniving, low-down, meddlesome bitch on wheels (but not in a pretentious silver Corvette, I threw in, unable to resist; that set him off once again), and we got down to business—my business, that is. His business, as he made abundantly clear, was to get me out.

"Get the fuck out of here," were his exact words.

"Do you think it's wise to throw me out without knowing what I know? Think about it, Sam." Another red flag to the bull. Sam is not great at cognitive reasoning and hates to be reminded of that fact.

"What the fuck *do* you know?"

"Tsk, tsk, Sam, language."

"Don't push me too far, Kat."

"If you think this is pushing, Sam," I leaned forward, elbows on his desk, "you're a fool. I've got stuff on you and *push* is not the operative word, *bury* is." He turned a little white and tried not to look nervous. It didn't work. He swallowed hard a couple of times and I watched his Adam's apple bob up and down. Funny, in all these years I'd never noticed how prominent it was.

"What have you got, Kat?" he asked finally in a subdued tone.

"You first, Sam. What have you got going down there?"

"The hell with you!" he said with more spirit. "If you think I'm going to tell you anything without knowing what you've got, your head's sprung a leak." That's Sam, too, real handy with a homey metaphor. His point, however, was well taken.

I examined my nails for a while and let him sweat. Then I stared at the ceiling. I was just going back to my nails when he started to yell.

"Just ordering my thoughts, Sam," I said in an injured voice. "Okay," I continued hastily, as he was sputtering again, "I know you didn't lose money in Vegas like you said you did. On the contrary, you invested it in real estate—a sensible investment, but only if the zoning is such that the property can be developed.

"Unfortunately the zoning at present does not allow for such development, nor is the community apparently in favor of it since just such a proposal was turned down last year.

"Fortunately you are working with business associates in New Capital Ventures who have not only bought a lot of land but apparently think they can solve the zoning problem to their satisfaction.

"Unfortunately their methods are not always on the up-and-up and strictly legal."

"That's not—" Sam stopped himself.

"Not what they told you? They left out a lot in what they told you, Sam. I'm not a betting person, and I'd bet on it."

"Don't be stupid, Kat." Sam tried to laugh heartily but it sounded so awful that even he knew it. He shut up and stared at me with bleak eyes.

"There's more and it's worse. I was only interested in the

beginning because Charity asked me to look into it and protect her financial interests in the divorce. Then I stumbled into this. There's a reporter from the Las Vegas *Review-Journal* on it now. Maybe the police are next. Maybe the IRS. I'd be willing to bet on another thing, that the IRS would be real interested in money skimmed off casino operations and invested in real estate. I'd be willing to bet that a lot of people would be real interested in this. Who are these guys anyway, Sam?"

"Go to hell."

"Do the names Jim Browning and Al Torrents mean anything to you?"

"Go to hell." He was nervous; I couldn't tell if the names had made him more nervous.

"How about Don Blackford?"

"Go to hell."

"Well—" I stood up and brushed my sleeve off the way they do in the movies, God knows why, "I've taken up enough of your time. Be seeing you."

"Kat, wait." There was a desperate note in his voice. I paused and turned around to face him.

"What?"

"Let's talk some more. Maybe we can make a deal, work things out. Maybe—" He was whining and playing for time and what I knew. What I knew was that he wasn't going to tell me anything more.

"Too late, Sam." I shrugged. "Maybe you could make a deal with the IRS." I walked out, not bothering to look back. I didn't have to. I knew what he looked like and, even though it was Sam, it would have made me feel bad. I had a notion we were going to be shooting pigeons soon.

Dear Charity,
 I work and strive and plan and nothing turns out like I expect. I can't stand it and it's not fair. What do you think?
                                        Mad in Milwaukee

Dear Mad,
 I think that life is neither predictable nor fair. Learn to roll with the punches.

                                                Charity

I thought I'd be real pleased to get home and stay there, but sometimes you fool yourself and that was one of those times. I was glad to be home for about an hour and a half. Then I got restless. I worked in the yard and watered—things get wilted fast in the valley heat—read my mail, washed my clothes and twiddled my thumbs. Finally I called Charity and suggested that we meet for dinner. We settled on Fat City in Old Sacramento at seven o'clock.

You never know about parking down there, but I lucked out and was early. Mike, the bartender, is a friend of mine (the network again), so we were shooting the breeze and having a good time. I was working around to hitting him up for information, but first we had to catch up on social stuff, on the ins and outs of friends' lives.

I was about ready for another beer when Charity arrived. It took her a while, it always does, to decide what to drink. She finally settled on a strawberry daiquiri—I haven't been able to break her of the frou-frou drink habit. I had another beer. Charity looked a lot calmer than when I'd last seen her, but she was still hyper. Seeing her made me think, once again, that on looks alone she is the last person you would except to be an advice columnist. She is short and round with fluffy blond hair, bangs, and large blue eyes in a serene Madonna face. In the looks-are-deceiving department she's right up there. Not that I look like a private investigator, whatever that looks like.

"Well?" Charity asked breathlessly. She always sounds breathless even though I have never seen her move fast or really exert herself. "Well, what have you found out?" Mike tactfully moved down the bar and started washing glasses.

"Sam's in trouble, Charity. He's gone into business with some highly questionable guys down there. If there's anything remotely legal about the setup I'd be surprised."

"Sam wouldn't do that."

I stared flatly at her for a moment. The depths of self disillusionment never cease to amaze me.

"Charity, he's a jerk—a greedy, money-hungry developer. Why wouldn't he be involved in something like that? It would be just his style, up his creek, down his alley."

"You never liked him, Kat."

"No, but that doesn't mean I'm unrealistic about his character. I think Sam would do anything he could get away with."

"He would not."

"You amaze me. You're the one who said you were sure the bastard had siphoned off bundles of money. And he had! He was trying to cheat you and you had to hire me to track it down and prove it. What's the matter with you, Charity? Get a grip on reality."

"I don't want to see him get in trouble, and I don't want to be the cause of it."

"You're not the cause, he is."

"I am if this all comes to light because of what I asked you to do."

"No, that's not the way it works. He's responsible for his actions and his life. When you get involved with illegal stuff you take the risk of getting caught. That's not Sam's biggest problem, anyway. His problem is that he's involved with a very unscrupulous set of characters and he's in way over his head."

"Kat, I want you to stop all this right now. I don't want to get Sam into trouble. I know it's irrational but that's the way I feel."

"I can't stop it."

"You have to," she wailed.

"I can't. It's gone way beyond you and your divorce, Charity. Now a reporter on the local paper is interested. This is hot political stuff and it's simmering away. If it boils there's no way you or anyone else can keep the lid on. Don't even think about it."

"What will happen to Sam?"

"I don't know; I don't particularly care. He's small fry—maybe nothing much."

"Oh, oh, oh," she moaned.

"I don't get it, Charity. How can you write a column where you dish out great advice day after day and be so clueless about your own life?"

She looked at me like I was nuts. "*Because* it's my own life. Did you know that psychiatrists have one of the highest suicide rates? Plumbers probably have stopped-up sinks. Tailors wear suits with holes in the underarms, garbage men don't take out the trash, tax accountants are late paying their taxes." She stopped for a breath, but I could see that she was just warming up and was good for a bunch more stuff like that.

"Okay, I get your point. Do you get mine?"

"No," she said obstinately, but I knew she did.

We had dinner. It was not one of our more congenial meals, and that was as much my fault as hers, I know, but I just couldn't feel sympathetic about Sam. I wanted Charity to see the whole picture, to see that these guys were messing around with lives, laws, and principles in a big way. I guess that's a lot to ask someone to see. No one wants to admit that their soon-to-be ex-husband is running with the wrong crowd, is maybe even one of the bad guys. I spared a thought for the headlines and grinned.

Charity caught me and asked in a hurt tone what I could find to smile about. I made the mistake of telling her. "I can see the headlines now: 'Well-known Advice Columnist's Husband Arrested in Las Vegas. Scandal Grows.' Hmmm. All the national scandalmonger magazines will cover it, too. Right down their ugly alley. 'Why wouldn't she give *him* advice?' 'What drove him to it?' and 'Will her readers believe her now?'" Charity kind of paled.

"Oh, my god, Kat. I never even thought of that side of it. I could lose my column!"

I snorted. "Fat chance. More likely you'll pick up a couple million more readers. In the ad biz they say that even bad press is good press. It's all in the name-recognition factor." She wasn't listening.

"That's one more reason, Kat, why you've got to stop."

"I can't, Charity," I said, trying to be patient and explain once again. "Things have a life, a momentum of their own. You may set something in motion with a single small act but once started it's out of your control, marching to the beat of a different drum, stuff like that." Which made me think.

"Charity, do a Thoreau."

"Huh?"

"Thoreau. *Walden*, you know."

"So?"

"Find a pond and go into retreat for a while. I'll call you when it's all over."

"Really, Kat, the things you come up with. With a degree from Berkeley I'd think you could do better. Don't you see—I can't just hide. Oh, Kat, I'm so worried." She wrung her hands fitfully, scrunched up her face, and looked like a kindergartner about to cry. "What am I going to do?"

"Wait and see," I said, but I sounded more philosophic than I felt. Actually, I was asking the same question and coming up with the same answer. A blank stare from the universe. I'd gotten nothing from Sam and so I'd pushed, and pushed hard, and now we'd see if that created action.

"Go home, Charity, get some sleep. I know this isn't turning out as you expected but I'm doing my best for you, I really am." That seemed to calm her down, though it was cold comfort for me. I knew from past experience that doing my best was no guarantee of anything. I am always shooting for truth, beauty, love, and happiness, and coming up with stale popcorn, wormy apples, clichés and confounded hopes—and they are not the stuff of which my dreams are made.

"I guess I'll have another dessert." Charity signaled to the waiter. "You?" I shook my head. "The chocolate mousse was excellent but this time I'll try the amaretto cheesecake." She sighed happily. Food is one of the things that brings a sparkle to Charity's eyes and puts meaning in her life. Which is fine; it's cheap and easy and beats drugs, alcohol, and other forms of deranged, antisocial behavior. I watched fondly as Charity packed it away. Then we parted for the evening. Charity went home; I went back to the bar to talk to Mike.

It was slow at the bar. Mike bought me a drink, I bought him one, and we talked.

"Working hard, Kat?"

"Mmm, and not getting anywhere much either. I've got a hot story, Mike. I know it's there and right now all the alleys are blind. The leads promise big and deliver slim to none."

"Story? You still writing?"

"Some, although that's not my interest in this. I'm trying to track something down for a friend. Mike, who do we know in construction, preferably a developer?"

"Jolie's going with Ted Kramer of Kramer Construction. Have you met him?" I shook my head. "Nice guy. Hope Jolie stays with him for a while." I hoped so, too, but neither one of us thought it was likely. Jolie has all the nesting instincts of a butterfly.

"Does she still cocktail here?"

"Sure, she's working tonight, just on a dinner break now while it's slow." Mike left to make some drinks. I waited and thought about things, but mostly waited.

"Kat!" Jolie gave me a big hug. She's just like her name, bouncy, beautiful, and full of sweet cream and charm. "What's up? Mike said you had a question."

"I'm doing some research. I need to talk to a developer and—"

"Oh, you've got to meet Ted then. He's great, nobody knows more than he does," she said proudly. Jolie's passions may be brief, but they're intense and partisan. "He's out of town now but he'll be back tomorrow. We're going to have dinner. Could you join us?"

"Uh—"

"Let's meet here for drinks at seven thirty and we'll figure it out then. How does that sound?"

"Great. Will Ted mind?"

"Oh no, he thinks everything I do is wonderful." She beamed happily and I felt wistful and a little sad that I didn't have someone who thought everything I did was wonderful. Realistically, especially considering the things I do, it isn't likely, but it is a nice thought and I indulge myself with it now and then.

"Whoops, we're getting busy. Got to get some drinks out. Tomorrow, Kat."

"Tomorrow," I agreed. I thought about having another drink but decided to call it a day. It would be good to sleep in my own bed. I could sleep late and it would be a day to kick back since I was staying over to talk to Ted.

In the morning I resisted the temptation to vacuum and dust, not too difficult, and worked in the garden for a while. I picked a bunch of tomatoes and peppers and a zillion almost-out-of-control zucchinis to take back to Betty. I'd been right about the warm heart and the refrigerator full of vegetables. After that I called friends, one a lawyer, one a tax accountant, and posed "hypothetical" questions about skimming, racketeering, IRS penalties, and so on. They were interested and helpful; neither was taken in by the "hypothetical." Both were strongly of the opinion that I should hang around with a different crowd of folks, an opinion that I was rapidly coming to share.

I was on time, but Ted and Jolie were already at the restaurant when I arrived. They welcomed me warmly and had a drink in my hand almost before I could sit down. Jolie was right—Ted was great, and I hoped it would work out for them. He had eyes like fudge chocolates and a smile that fit right in with them. Somebody came over to the table to talk to Jolie, and Ted focused on me.

"How can I help you, Kat?"

"I'm working on something that involves Sam Collins and I wonder what you can tell me about him?"

"That's a little general."

I nodded. "Deliberately so. What's the scuttlebutt, Ted? What's his reputation in the business? Would you work with him? Is he reliable?"

"Just between you and me?" I nodded. "No, I wouldn't work with him. He's always been known as a guy who had an eye for a good setup and could make the most of it. He wasn't adverse to taking risks, but they were pretty closely calculated. He did well."

"Past tense?"

"I think so. Lately he hasn't been calling the shots well at all. He's taken some big risks and lost. Either his eye or his judgment is way off. He's still lining up work but he's riding on his reputation and it can't last. I'd guess he's pretty hard pressed right now. He may pull it off, but it's going to take some doing. I wouldn't put any money on it."

"Is he honest?"

"Again between you and me?" I nodded. "Yes and no. In construction he builds to code but cuts corners. The end result is shoddy but not immediately apparent. There are men—people," he corrected himself and winked at me, "that I'd make a deal with on a handshake. He's not one of them. I couldn't throw him far, and that's how much I trust him."

"If you heard that he was embroiled in a project that involved illegalities, undue pressure to change zoning regulations, that sort of thing, would you be surprised?"

His eyes narrowed. "Yes and no. Before I think he would have kept his nose clean—from expediency, not necessarily integrity. Now, I don't know. No, I guess I wouldn't be surprised."

"Hey, you guys, aren't you hungry? I'm starving. Let's get a table." I started to leave but they would have none of it.

"C'mon, Kat," said Jolie, "it'll be fun." And it was; it was good to push the uglies out of my mind. Tomorrow would come soon enough.

Dear Charity,
  If you make everyone promise not to tell, can you keep a secret?

Quiet as a Mouse

Dear Quiet,
  No. If more than one person knows about it, it's not a secret.
Charity

Tomorrow came and I was on my way back to Las Vegas. This time it didn't feel so bad. This time I had friends to look forward to. I also had an optimistic feeling that I could wrap up everything neatly and cleanly in, well, maybe not a flash, but soon. Which goes to show how well I call things.

I picked up the canary at the airport, moribund and recalcitrant as ever. It was noon and I had six hours to accomplish something before dinner at Joe and Betty's. Six hours that was either too much time or not enough. I stopped at a pay phone and called Joe at the office.

"What's new, Joe?"

"Kat, you back in town?"

"Mmm, just got in. I'm at a pay phone wondering which way the ball is bouncing."

"Every which way and off the wall. The land under question has been rezoned. It happened in a quiet meeting, no publicity, no opposition, no nothing. They accomplished overnight what they couldn't get done in a major uproar last year."

"Is it on the up-and-up?"

"Procedurally, yes. Who knows what went on behind the scenes?"

"Any guesses?"

"From the people involved the vote should have gone pretty much the same as last year. The political makeup of the planning board and city council hasn't changed significantly."

"But the voting pattern did?"

"Three people changed their position. It ran through with votes to spare."

"Were they leaned on?"

"That's my guess."

"Got the names, Joe? I think I'll do some checking around. Home addresses and phone numbers, too, if you have them."

"Hang on." I listened patiently to a buzz on the telephone wires and a typewriter clattering in the background. Someone swore, the phone took a crash, and Joe was back.

"Kat, you there?" I agreed to it. "Here you go. Start with these. These are the likely candidates for weak links." He gave me three names and addresses. "You know this business as well as I do, but watch your step." He was silent for a moment. "And the toes you step on."

"Yes." We both thought about it. "See you at dinner then, Joe."

"Yeah, Kat, see you."

I fished around to see how much more change I had. Enough. I plunked some in and called Deck.

"Yeah." It was a hard, gravelly voice that sounded like sandpaper on rusty iron. I dispensed with the formalities.

"Deck there?"

"Nah, who wants him?"

"Kat."

"Business?"

"Yes."

"Most days you can find him at the Glitterdome around five. In the bar."

"Thanks." I hung up.

Nice guys Deck hung out with. Early Cro-Magnon was what it sounded like. I left the phone booth, grabbed a city map out of the car and headed across the street to a small restaurant. I chugged a glass of water, ordered a BLT and a green salad, and got out my notebook and the map. It didn't take long to figure out where the planning board members lived, or how to get there. I made a few notes and then ate. That didn't take long, either.

It was the heat of the day and the canary and I were stressed being out in it. The air conditioner was holding up, but only marginally. The first house I found was in a nice middle-class neighborhood, the kind with landscaping, pets, and small kids. The houses were mostly ranch-style wood painted beige, cream and tan. An awful lot of Las Vegas is sand-colored.

The pink stucco with the number I was looking for was an exception, but not notable. I parked the car in the shade of a cottonwood and walked up the path. There was a small Buick in the driveway, but otherwise the place looked deserted. Somewhere down the block a kid yelled and a baby started to cry. The silence around the house was complete. The curtains were drawn.

I rang the bell. No answer. I knocked. No answer. I knocked again and gave it a couple of minutes before I started down the walk. Halfway down I turned and looked back in time to see the curtain shift and fall into place. I walked back and knocked again.

The door opened about six inches and a small pale face peeped out.

"Mrs. Phillips?" I was surprised. It was unusual to see such pallor in this part of the country.

"Yes." Her answer seemed almost a question, as if she were as unsure about her identity as I.

"My name's Kat Colorado. I'm an investigator. May I come in?"

"I don't know. I—"

"I won't take much of your time."

"What do you want?"

"I'm doing a survey," I lied cheerfully, "on how people's attitudes toward development is changing. Your husband is a member of the planning board and I wonder if you could comment on—"

"No," she whispered, and her face did the impossible and got paler. "I can't. Please go." She shut the door quickly and I heard a dead bolt slide home. One down.

No one was home at the second address but I lucked out at the third. A cheerful woman in shorts and a halter top answered the door.

"Come on out back," she said, "I got a bunch of kids in the pool and we can't afford a law suit." I followed her bare feet and switching pony tail through the living room and into a messy kitchen. A cat looked up warily from where it sat on the kitchen table finishing up a tuna sandwich. The tuna can was still on the counter, the knife in the mayonnaise jar. A fly buzzed it happily.

"Out here," she said, opening the back door. "Watch your step." We walked out into the shimmering afternoon heat and the cacophony of children.

"Lemonade?" She shoved a glass into my hand before I could answer. I thanked her.

"Ma, Billy's got the ball and it's my turn, you said. You said!"

"Billy, give Carla the ball. Here, catch." She flicked a Frisbee expertly at a small brown head bobbing in the water. It looked more like a seal's head than a child's. "What's on your mind?"

"Mrs. Hellman—"

"Call me Lorie."

"Lorie. I think something funny is going on and I've come to ask you about it." She looked puzzled. "Your husband's a member of the planning board?" She nodded. "He just voted on something yesterday, voted differently from the way he did last year. Do you have any idea why?"

"No," she shook her head. "Billy, stop that and give Carla the ball. Steve never talks about work at home. I have enough to do with the kids and, well, I admit I'm not too interested anyway. Maybe you can ask him, he's due home early today."

I nodded and right on cue someone, Steve I assumed, walked through the door.

"Honey, this lady—" she looked at me.

"Kat," I said, "Kat Colorado."

"Kat wanted to know about some vote."

"Last night's," I said.

"Why?" he asked, "and who the hell are you?"

"Honey!" Lorie sounded shocked and surprised.

"Well, who are you?" He poured himself a glass of lemonade, but too hard and too fast, chucked in the ice, and the lemonade splashed over the lip of the glass.

"I'm an investigator."

"You can get the hell out then. I've done nothing I need to explain to anyone."

"Honey!" Lorie bleated. We both ignored her.

"I don't think you've done anything, Mr. Hellman, I think somebody else has. What did they threaten you with? Or was it your family? What did they say they'd do if you didn't play ball? Were they going to put pressure on you at work, hurt the kids, rape your—"

He went white and then purple and then he shouted at me to get out. The kids got silent. Even the water in the pool stopped splashing. I knew from his face it was no good trying for more. I put the lemonade glass down and thanked Lorie. Then I got out.

Lorie stood there in stark relief in the sunlight, looking sick and lifeless. I felt bad about it. This was a circumstance in life she hadn't known about and hadn't needed to know. Now she would. I looked at her before I left and said I was sorry, but I don't think she heard me. Life had slapped her in the face and she was trying to deal with it. I walked back through the house. The cat had finished the tuna and left, but the fly was still buzzing. I let myself out.

It was a long shot, but I stopped anyway at a phone booth at a minimart. Even with the door open the heat lapped at me in waves. I could feel the sweat starting in little rivulets down my back. The phone rang five times; I decided to go for ten. Finally a pale whispery voice answered.

"Mrs. Phillips, Kat Colorado here. Don't hang up," I added hastily. "I know your husband and maybe you, too, have been threatened. If I can get a little more information on these people maybe I can do something about it. I promise not to involve you in any way." I was speaking into total silence, but the line hadn't gone dead. "Mrs. Phillips, I'm coming over. Please let me in so we can talk for a few minutes."

I hung up and made straight for the minimart and a cold soda. Then the canary and I revved up and headed back to the pink stucco and pale Mrs. Phillips.

The house looked just the way it had before, the Buick in the same place, the curtains drawn and still. I rang the bell and waited, unsure. It's tough to call it when people are afraid—fear changes normal responses. The door opened and Mrs. Phillips whispered at me to come in. She led me through the house and into what looked like a den that nobody lived in or used. Every room I saw was dark and silent, curtained and somber. We stood in the middle of the den and in the smell of dust and dead hopes.

"What do you want?" she whispered.

"May we sit down?"

She raised an arm helplessly, then shrugged and sat down, barely perched on the edge of her seat like a skinny albino bird ready to take flight.

"What did they threaten you with?" I asked softly.

"What do you mean?" the question was almost a sob.

"You're not the only one, you know; they threatened others. What did they say to you?"

"They didn't say anything to me."

"Your husband, then."

"They said—" I leaned forward into the pause. Even in the silent room her whisper barely carried. "They said that if he didn't vote the way they wanted he should make sure his life insurance was paid up. They said that it was too bad that his wife was going to be a widow and an invalid. I'm not sick," she moaned slightly and started to cry.

"Do you know who they are, their names?"

She shook her head. Her tears were as silent as everything else about her. "Does your husband know?"

"I don't know; he'd never tell me."

"Would he tell me?"

"Oh no! You mustn't ask him, you mustn't let him know I spoke to you. He'd kill me." Her hand covered her mouth and her eyes widened in horror at what she'd said. "I mean, he'd never forgive me. You mustn't let him know I spoke to you. You mustn't."

"No," I said, "I won't. If I talk to him I'll say nothing about our conversation."

"Would you go now? Please?"

In spite of myself I pitied her, as afraid of her world inside as she was of the world outside. I thanked her. Her frightened eyes and pale face stayed the same. "Don't worry," I added lamely, knowing that she would, and that nothing I could say would make any difference. She trailed wraithlike after me as I walked through the house and let myself out. I heard the dead bolt shoot home as soon as the door shut behind me.

It was almost five o'clock and I considered heading for the Glitterdome and trying to pump Deck. It needed to be done but I had no heart for it now. I was hot, grubby, and tired. And I felt slimed by the ugliness I'd confronted. Thoughts of the Riders' swimming pool and a margarita shimmered in my mind like a beckoning mirage. Once again I looked for a pay phone. Ma Bell was doing okay on me today.

"Betty, it's Kat and I'm on my way over. What can I bring in the way of groceries and supplies?" Betty laughed; it lifted my .spirits immediately.

"Not a thing. Come on over and jump in the pool."

"But—"

"No buts about it, I'll see you in a bit." I was too hot and tired to argue, and anyway she'd hung up. I don't know my way around Vegas very well so I got piled up in traffic a couple of times. I tried to stay mellow, but it was hard. The radio conked out in the middle of the Stones' "I Can't Get No Satisfaction." By then I was past surprise, almost past irony.

Betty greeted me at the door with a warm hug and a big smile that got even bigger when she saw the sacks of vegetables I'd brought from home. We carried everything into a kitchen that already smelled good and made me feel that life might be worth living still.

"A cold drink, a nap, or a swim?" she asked. It was a tough call but I opted for a swim.

"I put all your things in the back bedroom," Betty said, "it's got a bathroom. You make yourself at home." The phone rang. She turned to answer it and I headed for the bedroom to change.

"Kat, it's for you."

I sighed—it's never over till it's over—headed back to the kitchen and picked up the phone.

"Kat, it's Charity. It's over, everything's fine. You can come home now."

"What? What's over? What are you talking about?" I said, having trouble taking it in. The phone was a wall model, but by stretching the cord I could just reach a chair at the kitchen table. I sank into it.

"Isn't it wonderful, Kat? Everything's fine!" Charity's voice was light, bubbly and frothy, like just-poured champagne.

"Slow down, Charity. Tell me what's happening." Betty pulled a beer out of the fridge and looked a question at me. I nodded gratefully and reached across the table for it, twisted the top off and took a long swallow.

"Sam called me. Kat, he said you came to see him and you weren't nice at all. I wish you wouldn't be like that." I bristled at the unfairness of it, but then I let it go. Fuck 'em if they can't take a joke. I noticed I was ripping the label off the beer bottle and made myself stop. "Anyway," she continued, "Sam said he was sorry he tried to pull such a shabby trick on me, and that he was going to make it right."

"Seeing is believing."

"Don't be so bitchy. He called me from Vegas and said he'd talked to his business partners, explained that he was in the middle of a divorce and that he'd have to get his two hundred thousand out right away. He said that they were a little disappointed but perfectly nice about it. Isn't that wonderful?"

The fact that the answers in Charity's column are short and to the point is an editor's triumph. Really she's a top-division qualifier every year in the "Run-on Sentence Semi-finals."

"So, isn't that wonderful?" she prompted me again.

"Peachy."

"You're being bitchy again."

"Charity, I don't believe it."

She snorted, which in Charity is a sure sign of annoyance. "Are you calling Sam a liar?"

"It's not over till it's over, Charity, and it's sure as hell not over. Not here."

"Maybe not, but what do I care about that? Sam's out and I'm going to get my money back."

"Do you have a check in your hand?"

"Not yet."

"So it's not over. And you're not home free."

"I can't believe how petty you're being." She sounded disgusted. "Thank you for your help, Kat, and I won't need you any more. I guess I never did, really, everything's worked out so nicely. Anyway, just send me the bill."

....

We hung up and I sighed, reminding myself that this was why I didn't like to work for friends. I then finished methodically ripping the label off my beer bottle.

"Bad news?" Betty asked sympathetically.

"Good," I answered, "if it's true. I just don't think it is."

Dear Charity,

Do you owe something to somebody after they die? How much does a promise mean and how important is it to make things right?

AKA in Folsom

Dear AKA,

You owe it to yourself to do what is right. The rest of the world will never know or care. Do you?

Charity

The front door slammed and Joe walked in. "See the paper today, Kat?" He reached out and gave Betty a hug.

"Not the *Review-Journal*. I read the *Bee* on the plane. Which reminds me, have you noticed anything in the papers about a girl murdered in the bathroom of the Glitterdome a couple of days ago?"

Joe looked both distracted and puzzled. "No, why?" I opened my mouth to answer. "Never mind. Read this." He tossed a paper on the kitchen table and pointed out a brief item on the front page.

Building Site Accident

In a freak accident, contractor/ builder Sam Collins, 35, of Sacramento, Calif. plunged to his death this morning from the sixth floor of a downtown building site. Collins was . . .

There was more but I didn't bother. I was too shocked. In my mind I could see a figure sprawled on the ground. Sixth floor. It wouldn't have been a nice sight. Other pictures of Sam flashed into my mind, all of them alive and vital. I shivered.

"Was it really an accident?" I started to say, but the words wouldn't come out. I cleared my throat and tried again. My voice sounded funny but at least it worked.

"Looks pretty straightforward, Kat," Joe had a concerned look on his face. "I know it's odd but don't be making something of it that's not there. Accidents happen."

"So does murder. Why would he have been there in the first place? No reason. He doesn't have a job going down here."

"No reason that you know of. You said the other night that Sam was never one to tell you anything."

"He was part of the setup, Joe. Remember what Hank said—when you can't think of anything else to do, throw out a few clay pigeons and see if anyone shoots. I called Sam's bluff when I saw him in Sacramento. I scared him. I was trying to—trying to flush him out. And there's more you don't know. Charity just called and took me off the case. She said Sam was down in Vegas and called her yesterday to say everything was all right, that he'd made a deal with New Capital Ventures to pull out, no problem." I paused and took a deep breath. "But suppose it wasn't that way? Suppose what Sam told Charity and what happened are two different things? What if Sam came down and shot his mouth off about vote fixing, skimming, IRS problems, and wanting out? What would happen?"

Joe frowned. "Exactly. What would, or at least could, happen is an accident. The last thing they would want now is publicity. Sam's not the kind of person you can trust to keep his mouth shut."

Betty had the paper and was reading from it. "It says he was with the foreman and the owner of Trainor Construction. They were consulting with him on the project. They said he walked too close to the edge, even though he was warned, and then he stumbled. It happened fast and they couldn't get to him in time, they told the police."

"Ed Trainor?"

"What?" Betty looked up from the paper.

"Is he the owner of the firm?" Betty read some more and verified it.

"He's one of the investors who bought a sizable chunk of land in the partnership with New Capital Ventures."

Joe and I stared at each other for a bit. "Okay," he said, "let's look into it. I'll get onto the reporter who covered it and see what else I can dig up but I doubt we'll prove anything. So far the police are calling it an accident."

I put my head in my hands, a sick feeling washing over me. I could see Sam's Adam's apple bobbing furiously up and down as he talked to me the other day, nervous and scared. Some of the responsibility for this was mine. Betty came over and put her arm around my shoulders.

"You two stop it now, at least until after dinner. Kat, you haven't had your swim and there's plenty of time still. Hank's coming over later and we'll go over it again."

I sat in the chair feeling like shit. "Maybe I set Sam up for this, talking the way I did. Maybe if it weren't for me he'd be alive."

"Stop it, Kat." Joe grabbed my arm and shook me hard. "You know better than that." I wanted to believe him, but I didn't. Except for me Sam would be alive.

"Oh God, what about Charity? She thinks that everything's okay, that Sam's alive. Why hasn't anyone told her? How could she not know? Someone on the wire services is bound to pick it up. Why haven't the police told her? I've got to call her." I was babbling. I knew it, but I couldn't help it. I was shaking too.

"Slow down, gal," Joe said gently. "You're not going to be a big help to anyone like this. Can you call a friend or relative of Charity's, and find someone to help out?"

I took a few deep breaths. "I'm okay now," I said, and we all knew I wasn't. I called Charity, her mother, her sister, and her best friend besides me. No answer anywhere. Finally I left a message to call me on Charity's answering machine, and then wished for about the hundredth time that day that I'd stuck to my policy of not working for friends. I put my head back in my hands.

Betty pushed and bullied me out of the chair and down the hall to get my suit on. "If you're not out here in five minutes I'm coming after you," she called. I was grateful for it. I made it in four and swam for a long time. Then I sat by the pool and listened to more of Betty's big band music, smelled Joe's barbecue and contemplated painting my toenails hot pink—the kind of minor distraction that sometimes helps me cope.

I didn't hear Hank come up behind me. He ruffled my hair and looked hot and handsome. I tried to shape up fast and suck my tummy in. He caught me out and laughed.

"I don't like skinny, fragile little things," he said. I smiled, but it was weak.

"What's the matter, Kat?"

"Charity called to take me off the case, Sam's dead, there's evidence of—"

"Whoa, slow down, honey. If it's that complicated, wait until I get into a suit and grab a beer, okay?" I nodded and he rumpled my hair again. I was going to have to break him of that habit, my hair rumples all too easily on its own. I drifted inside and plopped myself down at the kitchen table. Eventually we all ended up in there, Joe, Hank, and I sitting at the table or moseying around getting in Betty's way.

"Okay, Kat, spit it out," Joe said. "Take it from the top so Hank gets the whole picture." I took a deep breath and slugged half a beer.

"It will make more sense if I backtrack and start with what happened in Sacramento. I dropped in on Sam on my way home from the airport. He was not pleased to see me, not that that means anything. He never is, was." I gulped.

"I told him I'd tracked down his real-estate investments and that I knew he was in with New Capital Ventures. I painted the whole picture for him, including the probability of illegal pressure to change the zoning. I threw names at him and told him that the deal smelled dirty from every angle and that it was probably largely financed by money skimmed off the casinos. I said there was a reporter working to blow it open, that there could be a leak to the IRS, that he was way out of his league.

"I scared the shit out of him," I finished.

Betty put a large bowl of corn chips, and guacamole and salsa on the table. We all dove in.

"Salsa's hot," Joe warned. I swallowed a giant mouthful, sweating and panting slightly. He was right; it was hot. Then I finished up the Sacramento end of the story by recounting my conversation with Ted Kramer.

"Ted struck me as sharp and reliable. If he says Sam's business is, was, on the downhill slide, I'm inclined to believe him." I paused to wipe my forehead. The salsa was blister-raising hot. "What I don't believe is Charity's story, although she obviously does. She called earlier to take me off the case saying that Sam was here in Vegas and had arranged to get his money out with no problems and, like a good Boy Scout, was bringing it all home.

"Sam couldn't afford to lose two hundred grand, not now. My guess is that he didn't handle it very well; he usually doesn't, didn't, I mean. He might even have been stupid enough to start blowing around the information I'd given him on skimming, illegal pressure and so on."

"He wouldn't be that dumb," Hank said.

"I wouldn't rule it out."

Hank shook his head and we finished up the guacamole and salsa. Betty put out some kind of a sour cream dip with little bits of red and green floating around in it. It looked fairly revolting but tasted great. I can eat a lot of chips when I'm frenzied and upset.

"Two hundred thousand is nothing in an operation like this, Kat," Joe pointed out.

I agreed with him. "That wouldn't be the problem, the problem would be Sam's lack of discretion. Somebody's putting a premium on silence." And I told them about my afternoon: about Hellman, who'd gotten so angry and defensive; and about poor, scared, little Mrs. Phillips, a pale shadow in sunny Las Vegas.

By now I was starting to feel sick. Maybe it was the corn chips and dips, but I didn't think so.

"It wouldn't have been that difficult for them to get Sam over to the hotel construction site. Sucker him along a bit, you know—hey, want you to see what we're doing here, be interested in working with you another time—that kind of stuff. Sam would have played along until he got his money. From there it's easy. It's a big construction site, busy, noisy, no one paying any attention to three guys on the sixth floor. Two witnesses say it's an accident and Sam's not saying anything. End of chapter. End of problem. End of Sam."

"But it *could* have been an accident," Betty pointed out reasonably.

"Maybe, but I don't think so. Can you check on the police reports and autopsy, see if there's anything there, Hank?"

He nodded.

"Dinner's almost ready," Betty announced.

I got up to change into shorts and a T-shirt and then joined everyone at the table. Dinner was great: steak, pasta and spinach salads, and a zucchini dish with bread crumbs, cheese, and spices.

"Kat grew the zucchini," Betty said. Hank looked impressed, and I leaned back in an aw-shucks-it-was-nothing kind of way—which of course was true. A five-year-old with a stick, a seed and a watering can could grow zucchini—the original, no-talent, guaranteed-gratification vegetable. Hank obviously didn't know that, but who was I to burst his bubble?

"Tomatoes are good, too." Joe shoveled a couple in and Hank looked even more impressed. Tomatoes are the runner-up to zucchini in the no-talent, guaranteed-gratification vegetable department. Sunflowers are third. (I always go for the mammoth ones that top out at fifteen feet. They have a personality, too, which is nice—their faces follow the sun.) I didn't say any of this, definitely a tactical error. I would have been on a lot safer ground with vegetables than with what followed.

"I think I'll go over to the construction site tomorrow," I announced, "see what I can find out. I've decided to put myself back on the case."

Betty made a face that was all worry lines and furrows. "If it wasn't an accident, Kat, that's not a very safe thing to do, is it?"

Joe snorted. "That's an understatement."

"Leave it to the police, Kat. We're equipped to handle this kind of thing and you're not." Hank said it unnecessarily harshly and it got my contrariness up.

"So far we're working on the assumption, probably correct, that the police accept it as an accident. That's one definition of handling, I guess."

"I'll look into it, I told you. Meanwhile it would be a good idea for you to stay out of it."

I tried to count to ten before I answered but I only got to three—a bad sign. "You do your job and I'll do mine," I said.

I didn't like the way the conversation was going, but we were caught up in it. I didn't want to fight with Hank but neither did I want him telling me how to handle my job. Men who give me orders don't score a lot of points on any scale of mine.

"It's a dangerous situation, Kat," Joe said, but in a worried way, not a telling-me-what's-what way.

"Yes, it is, and I'll act accordingly." I stood up from the table. Our wrangling had ended everybody's appetite for thirds. "If you'll excuse me, I need to check in with my answering machine."

I waited for the call to go through and thought about tomorrow. I wanted to go to the construction site, and I also wanted to see Deck. It was time to tie a few things down. I had a bunch of messages but only two had any bearing on this case. One was from Charity.

"Tell me about Don Blackford?" I asked as I sat down at the table again. The silence was complete.

Dear Charity,

I don't mean to brag but lots of times I see just what's going to happen. Nobody listens to me and then, when I point out that I told them so and they should have listened, they just get mad and walk away. What should I do?

Always Right

Dear Always,

Don't kid yourself, you do mean to brag. Everybody has to learn the hard way at some point, and that's their way, not your way. You should spend more time minding your own business.

Charity

The silence at the table was the heavy, unending, and unbreakable kind. I looked at faces and waited it out. Betty's was white and strained. Joe's was blank. Hank looked like something out of a Hieronymus Bosch painting. We sat there for a while until Hank finally asked why I wanted to know.

"There was a call from him saying he'd like to meet with me. I was introduced to him at the auction preview."

Hank started to speak, stopped, struggled with something and then started again. "I seem to be telling you what to do a lot, Kat, and you're right, it's not my place, but . . . but don't have anything to do with him. He's a ruthless businessman who gets what he wants. He also has an eye for women and a reputation for using them and throwing them away."

I started to speak, then changed my mind. There was something about Hank.

"There's a lot between us. I was after a couple of boys in his organization when Liz was killed. I could never prove it, God knows I tried, but he's the one who was responsible." Hank stood up, pushed the chair back and left the room, taking what little comfort remained with him. We sat in silence for a while.

"Is it true, Joe?"

He nodded. "Nobody could prove it, and Hank wasn't the only one who tried. Hank's got a lot of friends in this town, and in the department. Liz did, too. He's been waiting ever since, waiting for the chance, staking it out. That's most of it, but it doesn't help any that you're the first woman Hank's noticed since Liz died."

"I'm on a case, Joe, not out socializing."

"I know that. Hank does too. And we both know that Blackford dusts anything that gets in his way. His score is good, Kat." We sat in silence for a bit. "Does he know what you're working on?"

I shrugged. "I can't see how he could. He must have gotten my work number from Deck, but Deck doesn't know what I'm doing. Unless—" I paused and let the wheels spin, "unless Hellman or Phillips blew the whistle on me. Still, I doubt that he knows much. There's not much to know."

"Bad assumption, leaves you wide open. You know better than that, Kat."

I shrugged. It was getting to be a routine gesture with me. Joe was right but I didn't have the class to admit it, and both of those things annoyed me. "Either way, it can't hurt to talk to him. He left his number. I'll set up something for tomorrow, lunch or drinks in a public place. I'll stay protected, Joe, don't worry. I'm not new at this."

"Las Vegas ain't Sacramento."

"No," I grinned and decided not to let it get to me, "thank goodness for that. I can't wait to get home to small-time stuff."

Hank came back in the room looking less like a Hieronymus Bosch painting and more like a real person. I considered him warily.

"I'd be the first to admit that I can't see that one straight, Kat, but my issue with him aside, you won't find anyone in town with anything nice to say about him. His rules are the only ones he plays by, and he doesn't play straight, he doesn't play fair. Your buddy, Deck, is a choir boy compared to him."

"I'll be careful."

"Good. Enough said, then." We all made a massive effort to shift gears and move on. We pretty much failed. Then we sat around the table for a while trying to look calm and relaxed. I topped out first, shooed Betty out of the kitchen, and started doing the dishes and cleaning up. Joe went out to the pool with Betty, and Hank stayed to help me.

We did not whistle while we worked, or talk, or relate in any way. It was more fun than a barrel full of monkeys. Hank worked carefully around me and, when he handed me things to wash, made sure our hands didn't touch. I was worn out after fifteen minutes of it. Then he left, which I guess was better but I still felt bad. I talked with Betty and Joe for a while, tried to reach Charity again with no luck, then gave up on that day and went to bed. I couldn't even read; I just drifted into the midnight ozone.

In the morning I called Deck and wasn't surprised when another member of some lower primate order answered the phone. I asked for Deck and listened to the grunt and the sound of the phone dropping. Then I waited.

"Yeah."

"Deck, it's Kat."

"Kat, what's up?" He sounded glad to hear from me.

"How about breakfast, have you eaten?"

"Yeah, but no big deal, I can always eat again."

"Good, tell me where to meet you and how to get there." He did. We arranged to meet in half an hour.

The restaurant was downtown in the old part of Las Vegas but it had the look and feel of a truck stop. The waitresses were cast perfectly—middle-aged, unsmiling and hard. Any hopes they had left were rhinestone and they knew it. Las Vegas is a city for the young and beautiful, or the ambitious and opportunistic. I squeezed my way past a mammoth hostess and looked around. Deck was in a corner booth and well into a cup of coffee. He made as if to stand up but I waved him down and slid into the booth across from him.

"Hi Deck, and thanks."

"My pleasure." He grinned and I believed him, which was a nice feeling. Lately not too many people seemed real pleased to see me.

"Coffee?"

"Okay."

"Ready to order?" The waitress made it sound like it was our last chance for the next hour, or until a shift change. Naturally we agreed; I am easily intimidated by waitresses like that anyway. I let Deck go first while I scanned the menu.

"I better go light," Deck said, "large stack; double bacon, extra crisp; sausage, links not patty; couple eggs sunnyside. That ought to do it."

I sat bemused at Deck's idea of a light second breakfast. I hadn't seen anyone eat like that since chow time with a football team when I was doing a story for the university paper.

"You," the waitress snapped. It was an order, not a question.

"Grapefruit, two eggs over easy, hash browns, wheat toast."

"No wheat."

"English muffin."

"No English."

"Skip it, then."

She snapped her pad closed, slipped it into an apron pocket, then stuck her pen into a bouffant hairdo that I thought had gone out with the Fifties. Maybe she'd had it done then and now wrapped it in a chiffon scarf every night to preserve it, a monument to insignificance and mediocre taste.

"What's up, Kat?"

"Hmmm?" It took me a moment to refocus.

"What's on your mind?"

"Deck, that waitress. There's been a twilight zone time warp and she's been zapped in from the Fifties. I think we ought to do something."

"Send her back?"

"At the very least. Maybe turn her inside out and give her a pass/fail test on manners first."

"You always were sensitive, Kat. Well, not so much after Cissy died. You got harder then." I stared at him. He nodded. "Maybe you were still sensitive, but that's when you started trying to be hard. Like now. But you ought to drop it, it's not really you."

"That was a long time ago. People change."

"Not that much."

"Did you?"

"Change? Not that much. Back then I'd do what I could for you. I would now, too, so what's up, Kat?"

The waitress slapped my grapefruit down and waved and sloshed the coffeepot around. Some of it accidentally hit our cups.

"I'd like to tell you a hypothetical story with hypothetical characters and then ask you some hypothetical questions and see what you think." In other words, nothing was up. I was trying out theories on Deck and hoping to learn something.

"Okay."

"Let's say you have a group of businessmen, most of them in the casino business, who have skimmed off sizable sums and— "

"What's your business, Kat?" Deck asked quietly.

"I'm here investigating something for a friend."

"What's your friend looking to prove?"

"Personal business." My conscience yelled at me. My answer was true but only up to a point, a point I'd passed long ago in including Joe and Hank. Quickly I hog-tied and gagged my conscience, shoved it into a back closet, and slammed the door. I could still hear it—kicking at the door, I think.

"Go on," Deck's voice was quiet, his face expressionless. The waitress slammed our plates down, then came back with the coffeepot and splashed some more coffee around. I started putting napkins out to soak it up. Pretty soon our table looked like a collage, or a relief map in browns and beiges.

"Anyway, these guys have a lot of money to launder, uh, invest, and decide to go into real estate. They form what is probably a dummy corporation and start buying up land, good land with good investment possibilities, but there are a few problems." I cut into my eggs; they were cooked solid.

"Hey!" I looked over at Deck's eggs. His were supposed to be sunnyside and mine over easy. I'm a trained investigator and I couldn't tell the difference.

"What?"

"The eggs, that's what, I'm sending mine back."

"Might as well order lunch then. The cook turns them out however he feels like it. It doesn't matter what you order."

"Why do they bother to ask?"

He laughed. "How do I know? Maybe it's like a lot of things in life where you try to give people the illusion that they're getting what they want, what they order. No point in saying, 'Life's a shit sandwich, and how'd you like that, on white, wheat, or rye?'"

"A shit sandwich? Life's not that bad."

He shrugged. "Back to your story. What are the problems?"

"Zoning. The property they invested in is zoned for purposes other than what they have in mind. However, they reason, and in fact it turns out to be true, with a little persuasion that issue can be resolved. The persuasion does not follow any current guidelines for good manners or legality."

Deck finished his eggs and sausage and poured a pint of syrup on his pancakes. The quality might not be here but the quantity was. I guess it made up for something; I wasn't sure what.

"Go on. I'm listening."

"Let's say an out-of-town investor, strictly small potatoes, gets involved. He's a businessman but not playing it as sharp as he could. Actually he's missing the obvious and coming up with three from two plus two. You get the picture."

"And is he related to your friend with a personal problem?"

"As a matter of fact, yes."

Deck grunted and sopped up the last of his syrup with the last of his pancakes. How had he done that? Damn, I wished I'd been paying closer attention. I'm convinced that there are a number of life's mysteries disguised as everyday problems—making the pancakes and syrup, cookies and milk come out right—and when you get enough of them clear you're home free. I pulled my mind out of the ozone.

"Let's say that this guy, on top of everything else, is about as cool as a rhino in heat. He figures out—"

"Or someone tells him?" Deck gave me a hard stare.

"Yeah, whatever." No point in agreeing to anything I didn't have to. "He figures out that this scheme is not as up-and-up as he's been led to believe. He goes to the man at the top, says he wants out, says why. He's running scared and it's apparent."

"Hmmm."

"Okay, so that day he calls his wife and says everything's fine and he and the money are on the next plane home."

"And?"

"And the next day he gets killed. It looks like an accident."

"Accidents do happen."

"Yes, they do. So does murder."

"How does it occur?"

"He falls off the sixth story of a building under construction." Deck looked at me sharply. "He's with two people, both of whom are connected to the dummy corporation and both of whom swear it was an accident. Of course, it's possible they've got something of a stake in that conclusion."

"What are you asking me?"

"Nothing. Just, if you were finishing the story how would you do it?"

"I'd say it was better not to ask. And I'd get any characters I liked the hell out of the story. Accidents run in patterns, you know."

"What do you know about—"

"Listen to me, Kat, this is not story time. Play this game out and the next story you hear could be a bedtime story before you sleep a long and dreamless sleep."

"What do you know about—"

"Kat!"

"I'm listening—let me finish, Deck, then I'll listen some more—about Don Blackford?"

"You met him through me and I'm not happy with that." He didn't sound happy for sure. "I know him; I work for him. But I don't like him. He's no one for you to have anything to do with."

"He called me."

"So what?"

"I plan to talk to him."

"Why?"

"To try and fill in some of the blanks. He seems to play a role in the story I told you."

"He eats sweet, young things like you for breakfast. Leave town."

"I just want to talk to him, Deck."

"There's no 'just' with him, or with this kind of game. Go home."

The waitress appeared with the check and coffeepot. Automatically I reached for the napkins. Deck paid for the breakfast and waved away my protest.

"I've played the game in this town for a long time. I know when the deck is stacked, the odds so long you don't bother betting. When that happens you go home, and you go home thankful that you saw it and got out in time. There are some games you can't win, some stories you can't finish. This is one of them."

"I—" He cut me off.

"I know what I'm talking about, Kat. I've seen people writing stories like you do. They wrote their own endings, too, but it never happened like they wrote. The ending's always the same, and it always ends with nobody to tell the story."

I hadn't learned anything new and I'd gotten a warning. That's how it goes some days.

"Thanks for breakfast, Deck."

"Yeah, you're welcome." He flipped a couple of bills on the table for a tip. I moved them over so they sat in a coffee puddle and watched them turn dun-colored with considerable satisfaction. We walked out to the parking lot.

"See you, Kat. Next time you come to town, look me up. We've got a dinner in the plans."

"Thanks, Deck."

He put his arm around me and hugged. I felt my shoulders squish up. I also felt guilty at letting him think I was leaving town. I ignored both feelings and headed for the car.

"Hey, Kat." I turned. "What's in a sidecar?"

"Huh? Oh. Brandy, Triple Sec, sweet and sour and lime—with a sugar rim and a cherry. Nobody drinks them anymore."

He grinned and waved and I waved back, at him and at the memories.

Dear Charity,

The other day in the park I saw a small child run over to a huge dog and start pulling its ears. Fortunately the animal was friendly. Why don't parents teach their children to be aware and careful?

Amazed

Dear Amazed,

A lot of parents don't know better. Maybe your letter will reach them. I agree that pulling on the ears of anything bigger than you is a mistake.

Charity

The address was in the paper so I found the construction site easily enough. A huge crane was set in place and working, the hotel up to seven stories now and still climbing. The site looked busy and orderly. No one was just drifting around looking heavenward and waiting for murders to happen. A cyclone fence enclosed the whole area and a double gate stood open for deliveries. I headed in on foot but didn't get very far.

"Hey, you."

The guy was yelling at me over the noise, which was considerable, but even so he had a couple of decibels he didn't need. He had shoulders a yard wide and was one of the most nearly square people I have ever seen.

"You can't go in there," he hollered. "This is a restricted area. Hard hats, too."

"Where is the foreman?" I shouted back.

"Over there, yellow hat, name's Bremmer." He pointed him out to me and then lost interest. I started on over to yellow hat.

"Mr. Bremmer?" He was standing, arms folded, watching a truck unload. I had to shout twice before he heard me and turned.

"Mr. Bremmer, my name's Kat Colorado." He frowned.

"Press?"

"No, I—"

"In there." He pointed to a double-wide trailer. I nodded, then followed him in. The door closed on the noise and the temperature dropped.

"Lot quieter in here. Cooler, too. What's your name again?" I told him. He slouched against a large metal desk which brought him down to about my height and looked at me without blinking. I didn't think seeing me was making his day.

"So what can I do for you, Miss Colorado?"

"I'm a friend of Charity Collins, the wife—widow," I corrected myself, "of Sam Collins who was killed here a day ago." His face changed in some way but I couldn't read it.

"That was a terrible thing, terrible. Sometimes you go a whole job with nothing worse than a hammer dropping on a guy's toe, other times—" his voice slowed down. "We've had a run of bad luck and accidents lately, though nothing as serious as this, no deaths. I run a tight crew so I can't figure how—" he interrupted himself. "You're not interested in that, though. Look, I can't tell you how sorry I am about this. Really sorry." His voice ran down again. I waited. "Did he have any children?"

"No."

"That's something. I always think of my kids when a thing like that happens, wonder what—" He broke off. "Is his wife pretty?"

"Yes."

"What a shame. What a damned shame." I wondered why it was worse to be a beautiful widow than a plain one and couldn't come up with any answers. "Look, anything I can do, but—" he spread his hands helplessly. "They told me not to talk to anybody," he added suddenly.

"They?"

"The company. It's about lawsuits, I imagine. I'm supposed to refer everyone to the company lawyers."

"This is nothing like that, Mr. Bremmer."

"Call me Ollie."

"Ollie. It's just that his wife," I let my voice choke up a little, "wanted to know about the last few moments of her husband's life, what he said and—" I let the sentence trail off.

"Jesus." He gestured to a straight-back wooden chair and I sat down. "Coffee?"

"Thanks, cream if you have it." He poured two cups and put a huge teaspoon of powdered cream substitute in. I shuddered. He handed me the coffee and patted me on the shoulder, thinking, no doubt, that I was overcome. Which I was, but it was the cream substitute, not Sam. I should have gone with black.

"You must have known him, too?" he asked sympathetically. I tried to nod sadly. "Well, how can I help? What can I tell you?"

"We couldn't figure out why he was here. As far as his wife knew, he didn't have any projects going on in this area."

"I can't help you much with that. Ed Trainor owns Trainor Construction and I heard him asking Collins if he might be interested in a job out here sometime. Then someone came over to ask me something so I didn't hear about the job or the specs." He slurped his coffee loudly a couple of times.

"Ed doesn't usually farm out many jobs, although I don't really know what goes on in the business as a whole—just where I'm in charge. I thought I heard Collins say that when they closed this deal he'd be ready to consider another. That's all I caught. Ed's the one you want to talk to but he's out of town for a couple of days."

"How'd it happen that you were on the sixth floor? It was you, wasn't it, you and Sam and Mr. Trainor?"

"Yeah, it was, and I don't have much of an answer to that one either. I got the impression Ed wanted to point out a possible job site to Collins. It's a nice view, not to mention a helluva lot quieter up there."

"Is that the way Mr. Trainor does business?"

He shrugged, and I could see he didn't think so, or didn't think much of the idea.

"There's a lot of guys, contractors, who like to walk a job, see it from all angles just for the interest of it."

"And you?"

"I had other things to do. It was a busy day for me, deliveries all day, order changes, mistakes. I tried to get out of it but Ed insisted, and he's the boss."

"What happened, Ollie?"

"I wish I could tell you—I'm not much help, am I?" he smiled ruefully. "I'd walked over to the south side to watch a delivery coming on in. They were standing on the west side, which is where Collins went over. I was only away for a minute or two when I heard a shout and after that a scream. God help me, I don't ever want to hear a scream like that again." He fell silent.

I nodded dumbly. The blood from my head had all drained out into my feet making me feel light-headed and heavy at the same time. Once would be enough, and I never wanted to hear it either.

"I went running over there. Actually I looked up when I heard the scream but I couldn't see much, the structural beams pretty much blocked my view. I thought I saw arms moving, flailing about, but it was hard to tell and I couldn't say whose. When I got there Ed was standing at the edge. I looked over and saw—well, never mind. It wasn't pretty. I could see someone running for the office to call for an ambulance so I turned back to Ed. He was in pretty bad shape, shaking like a dishrag in a breeze and saying, 'Oh my God, oh my God,' over and over like a parrot with only one line." He paused and rubbed his eyes hard, as if, somehow, that could erase the memory of it all.

"I pulled him back from the edge, one accident was enough, and asked him what happened. He went on being a parrot for a while until I took him by the shoulders and shook him hard. He stopped babbling then but he was still shaking."

"Shock?"

"I guess. I asked him again and he said, 'Ollie, I don't know. I just don't know. We were talking and then he walked over to the edge and stumbled or tripped or something. I tried to get to him but it happened so fast.' And then he started in with the oh my God routine again, so I took him on down to ground level and stuck him in the office with someone. Then I went out to wait for the ambulance. I knew there was no hope but it didn't seem right to leave him out there alone. Someone had covered him with a tarp," he added on as an afterthought.

"Was there anything to stumble on, or trip over, up there?"

"I looked. The police asked that, too. We all went up to check and no, there wasn't, nothing at all. It's a plain slab floor."

"How soon did the police get there?"

"Didn't take the police, nor the ambulance, but five minutes."

"Who did the police talk to?"

"Everyone on site."

"Were you there?" He nodded. "What did they find out?"

"They asked if anyone had seen or heard anything at all."

"And?"

"And nobody had. You see how busy it is, how noisy. I've got a good crew. These guys are working, not standing around with their thumbs up their, uh, excuse me, loafing about."

I nodded. I wasn't surprised at the answer and I was sure the police weren't either.

"Did anything strike you as suspicious, Ollie?"

He frowned. "What do you mean?"

"Could it have been a suicide, for instance?" His face cleared. "Shucks, Miss—"

"Kat," I interrupted.

"Shucks, Kat, you know better than I do, but I'd say not a chance in a million. He seemed cheerful, even excited, about something. If ever a man looked like he was happy to be alive it was that one. I remember him saying something about lunch, too, how he was hungry and where was a good place to go. Those aren't the words of a guy looking suicide in the eye."

"No," I agreed, "no, they're not." How about murder? But I didn't say that. It wouldn't get me anywhere and it would mess up my rapport with Ollie.

"The police were satisfied?"

"As far as I know. They didn't say anything to the contrary to me. After they were done I shut the job down for the rest of the day. Something like that shakes people up and it's better to take a break. It's a gesture of respect, too." He moved his hands helplessly. "You be sure and tell his wife how sorry I am, how real damn sorry."

I nodded. "Did Sam say anything, Ollie, anything at all about what he was doing, about what was on his mind, stuff like that?"

"No, but then he wouldn't. It was just job talk and shoot-the-shit talk. Maybe he and Ed got into something but if so I wasn't around."

"Where did it happen?"

"I can show you. I can even take you up there." I shivered. "No, better not. You can see well enough from the ground. Want to go out there now?"

"Might as well," I said, with my heart sinking a little. I wasn't too pleased with myself for not going up to the sixth floor. I tried to reason that only a fool would do that, but it sounded stupid. Ollie was the last person who looked or acted like a murderer. Ha, said my mind, they're not all wild-looking, like Richard Speck. What about Charles Whitman? He looked okay. Most people don't wear it in their eyes, and on their faces, like Richard Speck and Charlie Manson.

On the way out Ollie grabbed a hard hat for me. "This is about the smallest we have." It was pretty big but I could sort of see out from under it. "This way," he shouted. I nodded and followed him, pushing the hat back. Outside in the mindless cacophony a whistle blew and silence fell around us. Lunchtime. After the noise the silence sounded loud.

"This is where he landed." I looked at a spot on the ground that looked no different from anything around us. "I had it filled in and smoothed over." I gulped and swallowed hard. Of course.

"You can see," he pointed upward, "they were standing up there. There's nothing to break his fall on the way down."

"No." I imagined a figure, arms and legs desperately grabbing at hope and air, then suddenly outstretched and falling through a bright, cloudless summer day. I shivered in the heat. The sun felt warm and welcome on my back.

"What do you think happened, Ollie? A man, especially in this business, doesn't stand on a sixth-story edge and stumble. Most of us, in any business, think too highly of life to do that."

"Damned if I know and damned if I have a better explanation. I agree with you, but I don't see what else could have happened."

"The autopsy will show if he had drugs or alcohol in his system. What was your impression?"

"I'd say no, and I'm pretty good at spotting it. Have to be. This job's dangerous enough without adding a factor like that."

We stood there in the sun with our hands in our pockets for a while. There didn't seem much left to say.

"Well," I said, remembering my earlier story, "I guess I can tell his widow that in his last moments he seemed calm and cheerful, interested in life and a new project." I pushed the hard hat way back on my head and looked at Ollie.

He nodded. "I wish to hell I could tell you more but I can't."

"Thanks for your time, Ollie." I fished in my purse until I came up with a business card that said *consultant*, not *investigator*, on it. "If you think of anything else, anything, please give me a call." He took my card, looked at it carefully, then stowed it in his wallet.

"Sure, but I don't imagine I will." We shook hands and I walked away. I got about six feet before I turned and came back.

"Not my size." I handed him the battered yellow hard hat.

"Look, you be sure and let me know about the funeral, okay? The company would like to send flowers or something. It's not much but—"

I said I'd be sure. I bet Speck and Whitman never sent flowers. I know Manson didn't.

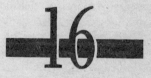

Dear Charity,

What's the proper etiquette for a business lunch? Is it business before pleasure or vice versa?

Asking in Albuquerque

Dear Asking,

Why can't you eat and talk at the same time? Warning: never drink more than two martinis, and never blow your nose at the table. It seems obvious, but you'd be surprised how many people forget.

Charity

Out on the site I'd been cold—sweating on the outside but shivery on the inside, even though I was pretty sure the temperature was well over 105 degrees. Now, walking back to the car, I was hot, hot and very out of sorts.

I could almost hear Sam's scream echoing in the heat shimmers, feel Ollie's mournful sympathy, Charity's bewilderment, Hank's anger and bitterness. Mine, too. Cissy was long ago and I'd dealt with it, but there was Jack. Jack and the piece he tore out of my heart when he left. Hell of a souvenir. It was Valentine's Day too. Hell of a Valentine.

Just before I got to the car I saw the Metropolis, an old-fashioned drugstore. Of course it wasn't really. It was new in the fashion of old, oozing money and conscious charm like a high-class hooker. Through the big picture window I could see a counter with an old-time soda setup. There was even a soda jerk who was and wasn't. He didn't seem to know much about sodas, but he did seem like a jerk. I went inside and ordered a vanilla Coke. Fifties music was playing in the background, The Platters singing "Smoke Gets in Your Eyes." The prices were Eighties. I slugged my Coke down and ordered another one.

Usually I'm satisfied with my life. I like my job. I like the notion of pulling some kind of order out of confusion or ignorance or malfeasance. I only work for people who appeal to me and I like that too, the idea of being a good guy, working for good guys, tipping the cosmic scale a little in the right direction. Today it was dust and ashes in my mouth. Vanilla-flavored. And I could still hear Sam's scream.

When I get like this it helps if I go home and garden. I have a small wood house on a quiet street in an unincorporated area outside of time. There, the world seems to have slowed down. There are horses in the pasture next to my house; goats and chickens down the road. I can forget in the garden or in the quiet house with the beautiful old worn Oriental rugs, the Victorian furniture and the doilies from my grandmother.

There I can eat salad and fresh sourdough bread, drink chilled white wine on the patio as the evening cools down the day. Then the roses let their fragrance drift, the tomatoes smell sweet and pungent as you brush their foliage, and the aroma of barbecue floats wantonly, temptingly, through the neighborhood.

Tough luck. I was a long way from home.

I felt slightly sick from the two vanilla Cokes but, being in the mood I was in, almost had another. Disgruntled and reckless are linked states of mind for me. Not good. Not good at all.

I got up off my Fifties bar stool, which did not twirl so right there you knew it was a fake, and headed for the Fifties phone booth. Yes, Mr. Blackford was in, and who was calling, please? The receptionist managed to sound arrogant and snotty at the same time. She put me on hold and I mentally switched back to the drugstore listening to the Shirelles wonder if someone would still love them tomorrow. Then I looked for Fifties graffiti on the inside of the phone booth. There wasn't any. Naturally. So I sneered, and then shared the Shirelles impression that, come tomorrow, no one would love us. Depressing.

"Miss Colorado, good of you to call." His voice was as smoothly textured as fifteen-year-old Scotch.

"Ms. What can I do for you, Mr. Blackford?" I was cool and businesslike, but I remembered the dimples.

"May we discuss it over lunch? Have you eaten?"

I had to think for a moment. Had I? No, that was breakfast. "Yes and no, in that order."

"Good. Would the Plumed Serpent be all right with you?"

"Sure, although it sounds very much like a restaurant I'm not dressed for." I looked at my white cotton slacks, passable this morning but construction-site dusty now. I knew my face was pink and my hair mussed. My green silk blouse stuck determinedly to me, front and back.

"Nonsense," he said. I could hear a smile behind the words. It was sexy. I bet his dimples were showing, too. "Shall we say forty minutes?" I agreed to it and we hung up. My heart beat a little faster for some reason; that was another way I knew I was being reckless.

The Plumed Serpent was chic and elegant, an interesting contrast to the D.H. Lawrence context from which it was no doubt lifted. Ambience was everything. It was mauve and gray, linen and crystal, an environment in which beauty and power were taken for granted; neon and garishness were of another world. I didn't stick out like a sore thumb, but I didn't exactly fit right in either. That was okay. I'm used to it.

I was on time but he had beat me. The maître d' escorted me deferentially to the table. Blackford looked up from the menu and rose.

"Ms. Colorado, good to see you." He leaned forward to shake my hand. It was a cool, firm grip, but I felt the body heat. Radiation, I thought, not direct contact. It seemed like a contradiction but I didn't have time to think it through. I slid into my seat.

"What will you have to drink?"

I shivered. Hot and cold. I'd been struggling with it all day. I ordered a glass of white wine and he canceled with an order for a bottle of Dom Perignon. I was agreeable, I get very few chances to drink Dom Perignon. Elegantly we sipped champagne and then, inelegantly, I cut through the preliminaries.

"Why are we here, Mr. Blackford?" That was a leading question. I knew why I was here, of course. I didn't have much to go on and I was hoping I could get him to spill something of interest. I didn't know why he was here, or what he wanted from me. He smiled and leaned back. The impeccable cut of his shirt showed his chest off to advantage, a fact I'm sure he was as aware of as I.

"No amenities, no social chitchat?"

"If you'd like. I'd just as soon dispense with it. I'd imagined that was your style as well."

"In business, of course, not necessarily with a beautiful lady." The dimples flashed. I arched my eyebrows. It was a bit thick.

"Am I supposed to play coy now?"

He laughed out loud. "I was—I am—intrigued. I wanted to meet you again."

"And you're a man used to getting what he wants?"

"Why not." It was a statement, not a question.

"What was so intriguing, Mr. Blackford?"

"You underestimate yourself, Miss Colorado."

"Ms. and no, I don't think I do." I smiled. Two can play the dimple game.

He laughed, a laugh far back in his throat and rumbly, and leaned across the table toward me. The radiation was switched on again, power and charm and sex. I felt it drift my way like fog on a Sacramento morning. It had a chill to it, too. I became aware of the waiter hovering in the background.

"What will you have?"

I looked at the menu blankly, trying to snap out of the fog, settled then on lobster salad even though it's always a conscience pricker for me. I can't believe they don't scream as they feel the hot-steam rush and then plunge into boiling water. The waiter poured more champagne and left.

"I am intrigued by a beautiful woman with intelligence and spirit."

His eyes flashed and sex oozed out again, wafting my way. Pheronomes, I supposed, and I wondered if he could turn it off and on like a radio.

"Especially spirit. Most women are compliant; I prefer a challenge."

I wondered what kind of women he knew, then mentally looked around and understood—the best money could buy.

"What is the challenge?" Even as I asked I knew the answer to that one, remembered the eyes of a man I'd known on a ranch not far from where I live. Lefty broke horses. When he was done their eyes were dead, their necks no longer held a proud line. They were dependable then—a three-year-old could have ridden one—but their hearts were gone, their spirits broken.

"A man likes to deal with equals."

"And win."

He smiled. "Of course." His eyes were dark unreflecting abysses. Like Lefty's. He raised his glass and we drank to God knows what and then lunch came. I was happy to eat. It was too easy to imagine the hard hands, the cold steel bit, the relentless pressure.

"What kind of work do you do, Mr. Blackford?"

"Need we be so formal? Call me Don." He said it with considerable charm and grace though he'd turned off the sex. I agreed to the informality with an inclination of my head. "I am an entrepreneur," he finished.

"Interesting. I thought only newspapers used that word—I've never heard anyone actually say it. It's rather vague and nondescriptive, though."

He laughed and his eyes lit up. He did like the challenge. "I own a casino, that's where I got my start. From there I branched out into real estate and other business ventures. To me business is like a woman, hardheaded and strong-minded, wanton and foolish, seductive and alluring. I can't stay away, can't not play the game. Sometimes there is danger and that is even more interesting."

"Danger?" I forked in a succulent bit of lobster. I could ignore its dying screams more readily than Sam's.

"Financial empires are not built with honesty, hard work and playing by Sunday-school rules. Horatio Alger is a myth, a stupidity best ignored, and dangerous if acknowledged. One can waste a great deal of time on such stupidities." He drank deeply and ignored his food. It was a wine for savoring, but he tossed it down. "Winning is everything."

"Do you always win?"

"No one always wins." He shrugged. "I rarely lose," he added cryptically. He signaled to the waiter. Another bottle of champagne appeared and was uncorked without a pop. I can't seem to do that.

"Sometimes, for the fun of it, I take on an apparently doomed venture. Reversing it is a challenge, and the winning that much sweeter."

"Will you give me an example so that I can see more clearly what you mean? For instance I have heard that you are involved with—"

It wasn't just the words, or the eyes, or the hand gesture, although any one of them would have done, would have frozen the end of my sentence. He smiled genially.

"I do not talk business like that. And never with beautiful ladies." I opened my mouth. He shook his head. I shut it again.

So much for that idea. I ate the rest of my lobster instead. The elegance here could be the sugar coating on a pill. I wondered about the pill. Or fudge on a child's mud pie. It looks fine from the outside but . . .

"Will you have dessert? The selection is excellent here."

I shook my head—the fudge mud pie stuck in my craw still—and drank the smooth, chill champagne. He had cheese-cake mousse parfait, which sounded like three desserts but was only one, priced no doubt like three.

After that we didn't linger. I was not much wiser than before, but considerably fuller. Blackford paid by scrawling his signature across the bottom of the check; then we threaded our way out through the quiet tinkle of silver on crystal, which is how lunch for the rich sounds. His hand cupped my elbow, making that one spot hot and tingly. The rest of me was still cool and shivery. I welcomed the desert heat as it hit me in the face, implacable and smothering but without judgment or malice. It didn't care about breaking my spirit. I gulped in a hot dry mouthful.

"We will have dinner soon, Kat. Do you have a local number?" His hand was still on my elbow, his thumb ever so gently caressing my arm. I felt my face flush. His cool assumption was galling to me. My mind tried to sort it out as my body responded.

"My plans are somewhat indefinite now," I said at last.

He accepted it graciously. "You have my number and I hope you'll call. Any time. It would be my pleasure to show you around."

I thanked him for lunch and we parted. I felt like I had fingerprints on my elbow, clear ones with all their whorls neatly engraved on my flesh. I wanted a swim badly, but knew I was hours away from one.

Second best then. I headed for a phone booth and fished around in my purse for Hank's card.

"Detective Parker, please." I waited for several minutes before his familiar voice came on the line. "Hank, it's Kat."

"Kat," his voice sounded pleased and happy. I started warming up from the inside.

"What are you doing tonight?"

"Nothing much, what's up?"

"Can we go out for milkshakes and cheeseburgers and then maybe go bowling?" Actually I don't even like to bowl but it was the most wholesome, everyday, all-American thing I could think of.

"I don't know about that," Hank sounded distinctly dubious, "but we can do something. Seven o'clock okay with you?" I let my breath out slowly. Right now would have been a lot better.

"Kat?"

"Seven's fine." I lied like a trooper.

"Good, I'm looking forward to it."

"Me, too." We hung up and I walked out into the sunshine and stood on the corner of Maryland Parkway and Flamingo trying to make up my mind what to do next. The light changed three times while I debated the relative merits of calling Joe, trying to track down Ed Trainor, putting pressure on Mrs. Phillips, and going over to Joe and Betty's and sleeping off lunch.

I heard the squeal of tires and then someone screamed. My early warning system was snoozing under the wine and it meant nothing to me.

Too bad.

Dear Charity,

Do you believe in accidents? My friend says that nothing is really an accident, that everything is part of some plan somewhere.

Tilly

Dear Tilly,

Where? And whose plan? Yes, I believe in accidents. I also believe in plans. And all too often it's difficult to tell the difference.

Charity

At the last minute some instinctive reaction reluctantly ground into gear and I jumped back. The pickup truck hit me on the left side and sent me flying. I always hope that even in such extreme moments sound investigative instincts will triumph and I will notice all the important stuff. I'm always wrong. It was a pickup truck and I think it was white. That was what I noticed. Mostly it hurt like hell.

I sailed for about eight feet (I learned later) and then landed on an awning—striped hot pink, wild green and electric yellow. The awning was part of a sidewalk café, not, of course, open to the sidewalk in summer heat, but enclosed in awning and glass.

The awning held for a bit (time is different in moments like those) and then ripped. I slipped through and landed on the table of some very surprised-looking people. There were more screams. I don't think they were mine but maybe they were.

Lunch is served, I said, or maybe I just thought it. There were maybes all around me. Somebody's tomato soup had spilled on my arm and it was warm and red—something white and sharp stuck out of it. I tried to apologize but it came out sounding like a moan. Then I passed out.

> She flies through the air
>   with the greatest of ease,
> That daring young woman
>   on the flying trapeze . . .

My head hurt a lot and I wished whoever was singing that stupid song would stop. It was black around me and I decided to open my eyes. Slowly though, because it felt like I had a jackhammer drill team doing routines on the surface of my brain and the backs of my eyeballs. I did it so slowly that nothing happened. At first I thought I hadn't moved my eyelids and then I realized I had, but it was still black.

"Hey!" I said and the jackhammers moved into fortissimo staccato. The pain bounced off me in waves, steamrollers and dump trucks taking up where the jackhammers had left off. Without meaning to, I moaned. At least that stupid song had stopped.

"Shush," someone said. A cool, dry hand took mine. "You're

in the hospital and you've hurt your head." No shit, Sherlock, I thought, but was too weak to say. "Be quiet and go back to sleep."

"What happened?" I whispered, unwilling to start the heavy equipment operating in my head again. "I want Hank and Joe and Betty." And Cal. Oh damn you, damn you Cal, if it weren't for you none of this would ever have happened. I'd be home raising babies and baking cookies and all that other stuff. I could hear him laughing at me and calling me a liar. Well, maybe not all of it. The cookie part was true though.

"I'm going to give you a shot so you'll sleep."

"Why can't I see?" I tried to pick up my arms to feel my face and eyes. Why couldn't I move my arms either?

"Please," I whispered. I tried to talk but it was only a whisper, "please tell me what's going on."

"Later," the voice said soothingly and the cool hand held mine again, this time taking my pulse. At least I had a pulse and arm, even if I couldn't feel or move them. I felt the shot though.

"Please," I whispered, and then they started singing again.

> She flies through the air
> with the greatest of ease,
> That daring young woman
> on the flying trapeze . . .

I fell asleep before they could sing those same stupid lines over more than three times. Didn't they know my head hurt? The jackhammers were back like a drum chorus. Jack was smiling, Charity was crying, Ollie was shaking his head sadly, Don was laughing. They were all singing like a demented Greek chorus. Hank was there holding his hand out to me.

"Hank," I whispered, "I'm going to be late for bowling tonight, I'm sorry." Then I was out again.

When I drifted back to earth and out of the ozone it was light. The light hurt my eyes unbearably and made me feel great at the same time. I tried to figure out why, and then I remembered the blackness. That was why. My heart made little joyous and free leaps. Cautiously I opened one eye and then the other. Hallelujah, they worked! First thing I looked for my arms, anxious as a new mother to count all the fingers; then I looked for my legs and counted the toes.

They were all there. Ten of each and a brand new cast on my lower left arm. I breathed a sigh of relief that it wasn't worse and immediately wished I hadn't; my rib cage felt bruised. My first rush of elation was wearing off and pain was seeping back in. I decided to moan and see if it helped. Not bad. I tried it again, a groan this time.

"Well, now," said a brisk voice. I'd closed my eyes and didn't bother opening them to see what it was. I could tell it was white with hard, sharp, starched edges. "And how are we feeling?"

"Like warmed-over shit." That cozy patronizing "we" always puts me in a bad mood.

"Tsk, tsk," the white voice said disapprovingly, "that's no way for a lady to talk."

I almost told her to fuck off but caught myself in time. "What happened?"

"There, there, dear. The doctor will tell you everything you need to know." I thought I might still tell her to fuck off.

"What happened?" I asked again patiently. Had I, for instance, really been on a flying trapeze? Was Jack here? Had a comet hit me and then burst into a pink, yellow, and green fireworks display? Was it time for breakfast, lunch, dinner, or bed? What day was it?

"Please," I said again, still patiently, "just tell me—"

"A nice, relaxing shot," is what she told me. I felt it, registered that I still had feeling in that part of my body and then drifted off into the ozone again. Nobody sang this time, thank God. I think I finally told the nurse to fuck off. I hope so.

When I came to again someone was holding my hand. It was large, calloused and warm, not small, lean and cool. I opened my eyes.

"Next time you play bumper cars, do it in a car." Hank smiled at me but his smile was tight, his eyes anxious.

"Okay. Did you bring my cheeseburger and chocolate shake?"

"I forgot." He leaned over and kissed me. Oh good, my mouth wasn't bruised.

"Mmm, do that again, it makes my blood circulate." He did it again several times.

"Just this once I'll overlook the burger and shake. I wanted fries, too," I added, "extra ketchup."

He kissed me again.

"Okay, I'll overlook the fries." We smiled at each other. "Hank, get me out of here. This is not a romantic place and I'm in the mood. Kisses first, then cheeseburgers, shakes and fries." He laughed; his eyes lightened up.

"I don't want anything to happen to you, Kat."

"Me, either."

"Well, how are we feeling now? Better, with our company, aren't we?" I gagged slightly; Hank grinned. "It's time for our shot, if you'll just step outside, sir."

"No," I gripped Hank's hand. "No shots, I want to be awake, not off in Lala Land."

"Doctor's orders," she said brightly.

"Tough shit," I said and meant it. She backed off.

"Now, Kat," Hank said. I glared at him and he backed down, too. Good. It made me feel perkier. "I don't want a shot. I want to talk to my friend; I want information; I want food." I wanted to be kissed some more, too. Especially that. The nurse left.

"Don't be such a tough, Kat."

"I'm not, Hank, I hurt all over. Kiss it and make it well."

"Where does it hurt?"

"Here. And here and here and—"

Joe and Betty walked in just as Hank was kissing a spot somewhere in the vicinity of my left breast. We were both too engrossed and pleased to be very embarrassed about it. Joe cleared his throat by way of announcement. I thought it was a freight-train imitation at first.

"Kat, how are you, dear?" Betty was holding my other hand, what was left sticking out of the cast, and smiling away.

"Hard to tell, they've had me all drugged up. I know I've felt better."

"What happened?" Joe asked.

"Search me, I'm still trying to figure it out." We all looked hopefully at Hank.

"A pickup came down Maryland Parkway, accelerated and went up the curb. It sideswiped you and hit two others, a pregnant woman and a child. Killed them both."

I closed my eyes. Thoughts about Cissy came flooding back. Little ones dead. I don't think I'll ever have children, I can't bear the awesome responsibility of human life, the love and loss and pain. Sometimes even friends and lovers seem too much for me.

"ID on the vehicle?" I asked at last, but kept my eyes closed and wished Hank would hold my hand again. Betty squeezed my fingers. Hank caught my thought and put his hand on top of mine.

"Yes, there were plenty of witnesses. Not much of a lead, though. The truck was reported stolen this morning. We'll probably find it dumped on a back road or out in the desert."

"Description on the driver?" I opened my eyes.

"White male wearing a baseball cap pulled low over his face; he was hunched over the wheel." Hank shrugged. "Not a damn thing to go on, in other words."

I closed my eyes again. "I don't suppose it was an accident."

Hank shrugged again, I'd bet on it. "Too soon to tell, but I'd guess not."

"What buttons have you been pushing lately, Kat?"

That was Joe. I still had my eyes closed and was silent for a while, debating about coming clean. I opened my eyes and saw Joe looking at me hard and Hank waiting in an edgy way. I decided to come clean. It looked like I was going to need my friends.

"I had breakfast with Deck this morning."

"Yesterday morning," Hank said in a grave voice, like he was getting pissed off and not trying hard to hide it.

"Yesterday morning." Time flies when you're unconscious. "After that I interviewed Ollie Bremmer, the foreman at the construction site where Sam was killed. Then I had lunch with Don Blackford."

Hank dropped my hand like a hot brick, roughly pushed his chair back and stood up. He walked over to the window swearing softly and generally doing an imitation of a maddened bull waiting for another flag to wave.

Joe sat down in the chair Hank had vacated. "And that's on top of your interviews with the Hellmans and the Phillips woman the day before. You've had a full dance card, Kat."

I nodded. It was kind of odd, too, I'd always been a wallflower in school. No accounting for popularity and the change of tastes, I guess. Or was I a late bloomer? I liked that better.

"I think," Joe resumed, "that we'd better assume that it wasn't an accident. Too many coincidences."

"At least we know that we're getting somewhere. Someone's paying close attention and getting worried, that's a start."

"That's one way to look at it."

Joe's agreement was dubious at best. Hank started cursing steadily and methodically. He was still staring out the window. Not much agreement there, or it was well disguised.

"But where, I wonder?" I sounded a little querulous and it annoyed me. How lacking in dignity can you get? "I can't think straight, these painkillers are getting to me." I rubbed my head with my good hand. "A B C D E F G. Four times seven is twenty-eight. Eight times nine is seventy-two. Twelve times twelve is one hundred and forty-four. Seems okay but I just can't—"

"Kat, goddamn it!" Hank exploded.

Betty gripped my fingers tightly. "It's only because he cares," she whispered. I looked at Hank's face and realized I'd have to take her word for it. "He's worried," Betty added, still in a whisper. "Actually we all are."

"Worried!" Hank exploded again. He'd stopped being a mad bull and was into volcano imitations. Big deal, I didn't like either one of them. "Worried! I don't think that quite covers it."

The door opened and something small and white bustled in—a nurse, no doubt, followed by something larger, white and authoritarian—a doctor, no doubt.

"What's going on here? The patient should be quiet. What are these people doing in here, nurse?" She gestured helplessly.

"My friends," I explained. "Now, tell me what's the matter with me and then I'm checking out."

"You can't check out." He wasn't outraged, mad, or upset, just matter of fact and definite. It's the kind of thing I hate about authoritarian types. That and the lack of humor. "You've sustained a mild concussion, broken your left arm in," he referred to the chart, "three places, and bruised several ribs."

"Is that it?" I asked. He looked slightly nonplussed.

"That's enough to keep you here for a while."

"Betty, would it be okay if I came home with you?"

"Kat, dear, of course! Don't even ask."

"Thank you. See if you can find my clothes, okay?"

"Miss," the doctor looked at his chart again, "uh, Colorado, you are in no condition to leave."

"Doctor, I'm not sick, just bumped around."

"Miss Colorado, I insist—"

I sighed. "Doctor, I can check myself out anytime, and you know it as well as I do. I don't need to be in the hospital to rest. Betty, how are we doing on clothes?"

She held them up. Show and Tell, with no need to tell. They were a mess. The blouse was bloody and where it wasn't ripped it was cut open. The pants were dirty, bloody, and looked like I'd sat on someone's spinach quiche. I probably had. At least they were in one piece. I looked at Hank and Joe to see if either one of them was wearing a T-shirt. Hank was.

"Hank, could I borrow your shirt til I get home? Please." I tried to smile disarmingly. Hank just stared at me and then he looked at Betty with an I-can't-figure-it-out look on his face.

"Might just as well," Betty said. "We can take good care of her at home. And keep her out of trouble," she added.

"Great, that's settled." I tried to sit up but every muscle in my body protested, making me feel like a giant third-degree bruise. "The Bruise," "Revenge of the Bruise," and "Daughter of the Bruise," all rolled into one. I choked back a groan but a loud gasp got away from me. The doctor smiled in satisfaction, which I thought was small of him, not to mention unprofessional. Some bedside manner. The nurse clucked in a worried, sympathetic way and I liked her for the first time.

"Joe," I finally caught my breath and could talk again, "lend me an arm." Joe slowly hauled me up. I swung my legs over the side, showing a bunch of leg and more besides. Hank didn't even notice, which indicates the kind of state he was in.

"I wish I could come undress you, Hank. The spirit is willing but the flesh is weak."

"Huh? Oh." Hank started taking off his shirt. He was wearing a V-neck tee shirt that showed lots of chest hair. Very sexy.

"The Bible," I said to the doctor, who was looking kind of puzzled, "or don't you know about anything but medicine?" He frowned at me; the nurse tittered, then hastily covered it up with a cough.

"If you boys would wait outside," Betty was shooing everyone out, "we'll be ready in a minute."

I thought a minute was an optimistic time frame but appreciated the concept. "Let's skip the underwear and keep this simple," Betty suggested. Good idea. It took five minutes to coax me into my slacks. I was exhausted and not at all sure that the spirit was still willing. Hank's extra-large shirt was a breeze and covered up the worst of the stains on my pants. Betty rolled up the sleeves about a yard, which brought them to my elbows.

"I don't know about your shoes, Kat," she said doubtfully. One sandal had snapped a heel, straps were broken on both shoes, and white was only a memory.

"Barefoot," I said. "Did my purse show up?" Betty nodded. The nurse brought a plastic bag and Betty tossed my underwear and purse in. The blouse and shoes went in the trash. Holding Betty's arm I tottered out to the corridor where she turned me over to Hank.

I had to sign a release form before leaving. Thank God for catastrophic medical insurance; I'd be sunk without it. On our way out we ignored the stares of the passing public as I snailed along barefoot in my clown outfit. Joe brought the car around to the front door and Hank carried me out. I started to protest until I realized that my feet would fry if I walked. So much for any dignity I had left. I fell asleep in Hank's lap on the way home. So much for manners.

Dear Charity,
At what point can you sign off on a job? Suppose you've agreed to do it but it gets a lot more dangerous than you expected—is it okay to quit?

Chicken Little

Dear Chicken,
You really need to sit down and do a cost/benefit analysis. And yes, it's all right to quit. I hope you look good in yellow.

Charity

"Kat, have you heard? Oh, it's too awful, I can't believe it." I moved the phone away from my ear a bit. "About Sam, Kat? Sam's dead."

She started to cry and I let her run on for a while. I was too weak to interrupt anyway. Betty had me propped up on six pillows, four for my back and two for my arm, and I was about as alert and mobile as the Sphinx. Slightly less, actually. It was a strain to hold the phone.

"Charity, I've heard and I'm real sorry. Are you all right?"

"No, of course not. I mean I know I was going to divorce him, but death—Kat, it's so final." It was hard to argue that one so I didn't try. "Look," there was a long silence and I heard her take a deep breath, "do you think it was an accident?"

"No."

"Do you think it had something to do with the money and the deal he was involved in?"

"Yes."

"Oh my God, oh my God, it's horrible, terrible. Kat, I'm sorry about all those things I said the other day. Will you please go back to work for me? It's not just the money now, it's Sam, too. I feel like I owe it to him." She started crying again.

"Is Hope there, Charity?" Hope is Charity's sister and as different from her as it is possible to be and still believe in monogomy and genetics. The names testify to something else. Fortunately their mother never had a third daughter, though not for want of trying. She, of course, would have been Faith. It was like their mother to get the names backwards.

"She's coming over soon. I thought I'd stay at her house for a few days."

"Good. I don't think you should be alone. Just in case."

"Just in case what?"

"Just in case."

"Don't you think you're being a little melodramatic?"

"Charity, I'm lying in bed with a broken arm, a concussion and a couple of bruised ribs. No, I don't think I'm being melodramatic."

That started her up again and I wished I hadn't said anything. Too late. But then, she needed something to take her mind off Sam anyway. Maybe not something like more trouble, but that was all I had to offer. Finally I got her quieted down to the point where I could hang up. Then I lay there exhausted, wondering where I was going to get the strength to get up and pee.

"Hey, beautiful." Hank was smiling down at me from the doorway. Beautiful? I stared at him. I was black and blue all over, my hair looked like I had combed it with WD-40, and I hadn't shaved my legs in four days. The man was either a few bricks shy of a load or, the happy thought occurred to me, falling hard. I would have enjoyed dwelling on that romantic notion longer but necessity grabbed my attention.

"Hank, could you haul me out of bed? I have to go to the bathroom. Gently," I added as he leaned forward with alacrity. He hauled and I tottered to the bathroom. "Don't go far," I hollered at his retreating form, "I might not make it back on my own." I looked in the bathroom mirror. Big mistake. It was worse than I imagined, which was saying something. Black eyes rimmed my green ones. Not too bad, but not too good. Damn. At least it was a distraction from the stringy mess that was my hair, although that was definitely a bit consolation. I managed to make it back to bed on my own.

Hank returned with a giant glass of orange juice, which I drank in about four gulps. It was wonderful and made me glad to be alive, even though taped together.

"I'm still waiting for my milkshake."

Hank laughed. "You're something else, Kat. How have you survived this long?"

"I don't usually play so rough." Which is true, I don't. "I do legwork for lobbyists, run down corporate histories of potentially merging partners or companies, occasionally find a missing person, that kind of thing."

"Why don't you leave—"

"No, let's not get started on that again."

"Lunch." Betty brought in a couple of sandwiches and a gorgeous fruit salad. I fell on a sandwich in a spirited manner and finished my share in record time. It was egg salad, one of my favorites. Then I eyed Hank's. He forked half of it right over without making cracks about my unladylike appetite. I hate it when men do that. Who wants a person that doesn't like to eat, drink, and screw anyway? Then we started in on the fruit salad.

I felt like I hadn't eaten in days, which was more or less true. A day, anyway, that's what I'd lost in the hospital. Hank took the tray into the kitchen and came back with ice tea, sweet and tart, just the way I like it. Mine had a bendable straw so I could lean back in my pillows.

"Let's go over things, Hank. I feel like mush for brains and I want to get it straight in my mind."

"Where do you want to start?"

"In Sacramento. Charity hires me to track down two hundred grand, which her soon-to-be ex-husband claims he's lost at the gambling tables but she's sure he's stashed it somewhere."

"Which he has."

"Which he has. I track it down to the investment pool of New Capital Ventures. In checking that out we come up with a pattern of under-the-table investments, undue influence on the planning board to effect a change in zoning laws, and the investment of large amounts of money, apparently in cash, leading to the speculation that this corporation is, at least partially, a vehicle for laundering money skimmed off one or more casinos."

"How much of this can you prove?"

I drank some ice tea and thought about it. "Not enough, unfortunately. Not much, actually. I can trace money, cash money and lots of it, back to Blackford's casino, not in his name of course, he's too sharp for that. Given the time and resources I imagine I could establish a direct connection. Lacking both, a tip to the IRS seems a more feasible plan. As to the undue influence on the planning board, I don't know if the Hellmans or Mrs. Phillips would ever talk—they're real scared. The money is going to be easier to prove one way or another."

"Sam's two hundred thousand is nothing in that context."

"Right, so what was the problem there? Judging from conversations with Sam—mine and Charity's—I'm guessing he came to Vegas and blew it. Maybe he said he didn't realize they were strong-arming the planning board, skimming and so forth, and that he wanted out. They never really needed Sam anyway. Probably they just used him and a pool of small-time investors as a cover while they were buying land. At this point his usefulness was nil."

"And he was a threat."

"Exactly." I slurped up the last of my ice tea and made rude noises with my straw. "What do you do with the weak link?" I paused, feeling like a weak link myself, or maybe a missing link.

Hank patted my hand. "You get rid of it."

"Yes. So Sam had an accident on a construction site owned and run by Ed Trainor, whose name and money appears in the New Capital Ventures investment strategy. The only real witness to the accident is Ed. Ollie's there but doing something else."

"If you can believe him."

I nodded. "I've thought about that and I do, or at least I do in the absence of other data. I think he was being straight with me. If he wasn't that doesn't basically alter the situation, he's on the Trainor payroll after all. Sam's murder becomes a definite possibility, I'd say probability."

Hank nodded in agreement.

"Okay, I guess that brings me up to breakfast with Deck. I know how you feel, but we're old friends and I trust him. I ran this by him in hypothetical terms and basically he confirmed what we've been talking about, including murder. He also warned me off. His opinion of Don Blackford, by the way, is the same as yours."

Hank nodded and didn't look real surprised. "Then I returned Blackford's call and he asked me out to lunch. Why? He claims I caught his interest at the auction and he wanted to see me. Now, I know I'm adorable and all that—"

Hank burst into laughter and I sat in injured silence. "Sorry, Kat, you are of course. It's just that now—" He started laughing again. I sat in more injured silence. So much for his "Hey, beautiful," and my theory of a man falling in love. I felt chagrined and put upon and it was all I could do not to pout. Just in time I remembered I was a competent professional and not a dipshit lovesick bimbo.

"To continue," I said in cool, professional tones. His guffaws subsided to chuckles. "It was quite possibly not just my personal charm that interested Blackford but the fact that I was poking around in all this: New Capital Ventures' investment scam, the intimidation of the planning board, Sam's death. We had lunch and I didn't get a thing out of him except lobster salad and good wine." And hot fingerprints on my elbow, I think, but I don't say. It's not the kind of thing to say to Hank.

"Then you're a victim of a hit-and-run accident in which two other people are killed. I think we can safely assume that no one was gunning for the pregnant woman and her child. Either it was an accident or you were the target."

"Yes."

"We now have racketeering, skimming, bribery and intimidation, hit and run, three possible murders, one possible attempted murder. It's adding up."

"So now what, Hank?" I was tired and my mush for brains felt like someone had poured a gallon of warm milk in and then left it to puddle. Not too much was sparking.

"Now I'm going to work. Put it on a back burner and have a nap. I'll see you later." He waved and started out the door.

"Hey," I called him back. "Pull a couple of these pillows out from under me, will you?" He did and I settled down.

"Do you have dark glasses?"

I stared at him. "Of course. Why?"

"Maybe I'll take you out to dinner tonight." He leaned over and kissed me.

"Jerk," I grumbled into his ear. I was too weak to bash him with my cast. He laughed and kissed me again. I fell asleep and dreamt that the Mormon Tabernacle Choir was singing, "She flies through the air, with the greatest of ease . . ." and I was the only one in the audience. It kept getting louder and louder until I woke up, hot and sweaty with my heart pounding. I kicked off the bedspread, took a pain pill, and went back to sleep. I dreamt about more scary stuff but at least I couldn't remember it.

Dear Charity,

I have this nightmare over and over. Something terrible is about to happen and I have to stop it. I don't know what it is, or how to do it, but I have to anyway. Then I wake up all sweaty with my heart pounding. I can't stand it anymore. What can I do?

Sleepless

Dear Sleepless,

I'd eat a much smaller bedtime snack if I were you.

Charity

Maybe it was a dream, maybe not, but I woke up with a picture of the dead girl on the bathroom floor in my mind. I'd been doing a good job of ignoring it for the past few days but I couldn't any longer. Something about it bothered me, more than usual I mean. When I try to push something under the rug for a while and can't make it go away, then I figure I'd better look at it. I wasn't enthusiastic about the prospect, but that's how I figured it. I've learned not to ignore the insistent nudges of my mind.

I reached for the phone Betty had put close to my bed. Hank had left his number there and told me to call him if I needed anything. Which I did—answers.

"Hank, it's Kat."

"Kat, are you okay?"

"Yes, look, if you have a chance could you check on a few things for me?"

It took him a moment too long to respond. I guess I should have talked more about how I was, or asked him how he was. Sometimes I have a hard time with social amenities.

"What's up?" he asked without enthusiasm.

"I'd like to see the autopsy report on Sam. Also," I paused, trying and failing, to think of a diplomatic way of introducing yet another body. I gave up and blurted it out. "A body was found last Tuesday in the bathroom at the Glitterdome, a young woman with her throat cut. Actually I was the one who found her and—"

"You what?"

"I found her and—"

"I heard you the first time."

"Okay. Well, could you please—"

"A body in the bathroom, a thug in the parking lot, a hit and run, can't you stay out of trouble for a minute?"

I sighed. He was working up to a shout and it made my head hurt. In general I felt very put upon. "Hank, be reasonable, there's no way I—"

"Reasonable!" he exploded. Bad choice of words, I thought, my head pounding away. People behaving unreasonably hate to be told to be reasonable. Me too, in fact.

"Hank, calm down—" I sighed as he interrupted me again. Another bad choice.

"Goddamn it, Kat!"

"I have to go, Hank, I don't feel well." I hung up on his roar and reached for my pain killers. I swallowed two as fast as

humanly possible, thankful for the miracles of modern pharma-
cology, then sank back into my pillows. The jackhammers had
returned and were busily working on the inside of my brain and
the backs of my eyeballs. I hate it when I'm not as tough as I think
I am, or think I should be.

I was trying to breathe into the pain and breathe it out, the way
a nurse who was into yoga had shown me—another time,
another hospital, another story—when the phone rang. I felt like
I'd been hit with a cattle prod. So that's what they mean by the
expression, jumping out of your skin. The jackhammers picked
the beat right up. I tried to ignore everything and breathe. On
about the tenth ring I admitted failure and decided to answer. It
took me three and a half more rings to reach the phone. It was
Hank. Surprise.

"Kat, I'm sorry."

"Okay, please don't yell."

"I'm not." He wasn't, I realized.

"Oh, it's in my head then. My head," I elaborated, "feels like
a giant echo chamber with a symphony playing Brahms, a
Dixieland jazz band, and Led Zeppelin, all going for it at once.
And jackhammers. It sounds terrible and I don't feel so great."

"I know, I'm sorry I yelled at you. I've got the autopsy report on
Sam. What do you want on the girl?"

"Name, address, background, job, circumstances leading to
death, suspects, theories. Just the usual stuff."

"Okay, I'll do my best. Anything else?"

"Mocha-chip ice cream. I have to go now, Hank, I'm tuckered
out. Thanks for calling back." I collapsed into my pillows, the
phone cradled in my arm. I figured I'd just rest for a moment
before trying to hang it up.

I made an effort to open my eyes when Betty quietly disen-
gaged the phone from my grip but it felt like someone had poured
superglue on them. She was smiling at me and I tried unsuc-
cessfully to smile back. I felt hot, grumpy, and terrible. Physical
injury does that to you. At first you're just happy to be alive, and
you take the hurt as a fortuitous reminder. Better alive and

hurting than the alternative, you say, and of course it's true. It's amazing how fast you forget that and want to feel good and whole again. That's where I was.

"How are you?" Betty asked. I grimaced. At least the jackhammers had stopped.

"Betty, could you help me clean up? I feel like shit, but at least I don't have to look like it."

"Sure, let's get you out of bed." She hoisted me up and I tottered along behind her into the kitchen. We washed my hair in the kitchen sink and then she wrapped my cast in plastic and stuck me in the bathtub. I soaped up and soaked, even shaved my legs. That was after remembering Englishmen in the colonies and how careful they were to dress for dinner, drink gin, and not go native. If they could do it, so could I. I pulled on shorts and a T-shirt but couldn't tie my shoelaces, so barefoot it was.

It was amazing how much better I felt being clean and out of bed. I even hummed as I hobbled into the kitchen. It was the flying trapeze song, which brought me down a bit.

Betty smiled in approval as I came in, then clucked in disapproval as I offered to help. In two minutes she had me installed in a lounge chair by the pool, drying my hair and feeling glad to be alive.

"Milkshake for the lady."

"Hank!" I popped my eyes open. "Mmm, chocolate, my favorite. How come some of it's gone?"

"Is it? Well, son of a gun. Evaporation, I guess." He winked at me and went back into the house. I settled down to serious milkshake contemplation.

In the next thirty minutes everyone ended up out by the pool. Hank had decided after our phone conversation that I was in no shape to go out for dinner. Wise decision. Instead he had brought the makings for cheeseburgers and a wonderful potato salad. Wise move. I ate too much, much too much, but every bite was good. It's like that when you're feeling thankful to be alive. We had champagne; Hank had thought of that, too. And mocha-chip ice cream for dessert.

Afterward he dumped a stack of paperwork on me.

"Do you want to read it, Kat, or shall I just run through it?"

"Run through it, please. My eyes hurt when I read." Betty got up and started fussing with the dishes. She's not fond of gory details. Who can blame her? The three of us moved from the kitchen back outside into a warm, inviting evening.

"There's nothing surprising in the autopsy report on Sam. He was in good health with some signs of alcohol and cigarette abuse." I nodded. "There were no signs of drugs or alcohol in his system at the time of death. There were no signs on his body that were inconsistent with the fall, with one exception: a medium-sized bruise in the small of his back."

"Not inconsistent with a push," I added.

"But nothing you can prove either," Joe finished.

"Exactly." We sat in silence for a minute and listened to the birds calling and settling down for the night.

"And the girl?"

"What girl?" Joe looked at me and I flushed. Hank put a stoic and unreadable face on as I explained; Joe shook his head. "For a new kid in town you sure get around." Hank continued his recitation.

"Her name was June Daly. She was twenty-five and in good health, was employed at Temp Express, a business that supplies temporary office help. She was in considerable demand as she knew typing, shorthand, and the major word-processing programs. Two years ago she moved into this area; never been married or had a child, lived with a female roommate in north Vegas. Didn't have a lot of close friends. No known enemies, nobody she was currently dating, no indication why anyone would want to kill her."

"Family?"

"Father dead, mother in a rest home in L.A., no brothers or sisters."

"Recent jobs?"

"Nothing that checked out in any way. She worked a lot for a local computer company, several small businesses and so on. It's all in here."

"Her roommate couldn't help?"

"No. She didn't seem real cut up, either." I winced at the metaphor but Hank didn't notice. "The roomie is a cocktail waitress and said they hardly ever saw each other. June worked days and she worked nights."

"Thanks, Hank. It seems straightforward enough but it's been bothering me, I don't know why."

"A young woman with her throat cut is enough to bother anyone."

"Yes, I guess that's it." But it seemed like there was more, more than just the picture of red blood and white tile and that horrible smile gash in her throat. Tomorrow I'd look through the reports. It was early still, not yet ten o'clock, but I was fading fast. I said my goodnights and wobbled off to bed.

"I'll give you a while to get settled, then come say goodnight," Hank called after me.

I used up my last energy reserves brushing my teeth, washing my face and getting out of my clothes. I was almost asleep by the time Hank got there.

"Good night, sweetheart," he said, leaning over and kissing me.

"Sweetheart?"

"Sweetheart," he said firmly and kissed me again. I kissed him back and was out, a nice way to go to sleep.

20

Dear Charity,

Is it possible to be an innocent bystander? Were there innocent bystanders in Hitler's Germany? Were we innocent bystanders in the Vietnam war? Is anybody who's anywhere really innocent?

Concerned

Dear Concerned,

If a tree falls in a forest with no one around, does it make a noise? We'll never know, and we'll probably never know about innocent bystanders either. Truth and innocence are not only relative, they're extremely hard to define or prove. Hope this helps, though I doubt it.

Charity

In the morning I felt a whole lot better. I woke up early and had breakfast in my bathrobe with Joe and Betty before they left for work. I refused to let either one of them stay with me or come home at lunch to check on me. I was fine, I explained, and could take care of myself perfectly well for the day. Also, I wasn't going to be there. I didn't mention that.

I had a shower, which took me a long time because of the cast and got dressed. With dark glasses on I didn't look bad at all. It was nine o'clock and I figured to catch Allyson, June's roommate. Cocktail waitresses who work night shift are rarely up early. I went through the reports Hank had brought and found out where Allyson lived.

The apartment building was nice enough if you like modern, nondescript and boring, which I don't. It was two stories high and surrounded a courtyard with a pool and palm trees. Each apartment had its own outside entrance off a shared balcony walkway. I stood in front of apartment twenty-three and rang the bell. It was on the fourth or fifth ring that the door finally opened and an unfriendly face looked out.

Allyson's disheveled prettiness was marred by the petulant expression on her face. She stood there having a hard time tying the sash of an old terry-cloth beach robe that had seen better days. Her long legs and arms were bare, her face smeared still with last night's makeup.

"What the hell do you want?"

"Sorry to bother you. My name is Kat Colorado and I'm looking into the death of June Daly."

"Police?"

"Private. Her friends and family would like to take it a little further than the police have so far."

She sighed. "Okay, what the hell. I guess it's the least I can do for the poor kid. Anyway I'm up now. C'mon in and I'll make some coffee."

The place was fairly tidy but every shade and curtain was pulled. After I bumped into an end table and a foot stool I took my dark glasses off. Allyson walked into the kitchen, snapped on a light and pointed to a chair.

"Jesus, what happened to you? You look like I feel."

I gave her an amended version of the truth. "Car accident."

She put water on to boil and started rummaging around in the refrigerator. "Damn, I thought I had some milk. Black okay?"

"Fine."

She went to the cupboard and got out cups, instant coffee, and what looked like four-day-old powdered-sugar doughnuts. The sugar didn't look powdery anymore, but moist and gummy. All this she dumped on the kitchen table. Presentation was evidently not her strong suit.

We settled down to breakfast—I passed on the sugar doughnuts—and talked about June. I covered most of the ground the police had without coming up with anything more than they did. Rats.

"Any particular job she worked recently that she seemed more involved in than usual?"

Allyson frowned; her lipstick smear made a kind of double grimace. I waited hopefully, mentally counting chickens before they hatched—a bad habit of mine.

"Well, there was one, not that she got excited, mind you, because she never did. It was her way to stay calm and uninvolved all the time. Not like me." She launched into a long description of her excitable nature. Gently I tried to steer her back. When that didn't work I opted for the direct approach.

"About the job she seemed to be a little more involved in than usual?" I prodded.

"Oh, yeah. Well, she was working for some guy in the real-estate business. His secretary had quit in a hurry and left quite a mess behind her, or something like that. She talked about him more than she usually does, said he was a planning board member and an important person. That's all I know."

I let my breath out slowly, newly hatched chicks happily cheeping away in my consciousness.

"Did she ever mention the guy's name?"

"No—yes—maybe." The cheeps faded a bit. "Wait a minute, it was something like hill, mountain, Hillman, something like that."

"Hellman?"

"Yeah, that could have been it."

"Was she personally involved with him, do you think?"

"You know, I did think that. Want another cup of coffee?" I shook my head. "Me, I have to have about six cups just to wake up."

"Why?"

"I dunno. Used to be I could get going on three or four but now—"

"No, I mean why do you think that she was personally involved with him?"

"Oh. A couple of nights we got home about the same time. Ordinarily she never stays up until two or three in the morning. She is, I mean was, an early to bed, early to rise type. Anyway one night she was all flushed and sort of mussed up, the way you look when you've been at it for a while with a guy. I kidded her and she blushed and stammered around like a high-school kid. I even asked her about it but she wouldn't tell me much. I kind of figured that the guy was probably married, the way she wouldn't talk. Anyway," she said with a yawn, "I wasn't interested enough to bother with it, to tell you the truth. She wasn't a very interesting person, you know. Nice, but not interesting."

Pitiful epitaph. And she was a lot less interesting now—except for one thing. The why. Why had she mattered enough for someone to kill her?

I thanked Allyson for her help, gave her my number in case she remembered anything else, and took off. Poor little June Daly. Did she know too much, talk too much, or was she just in the wrong place at the wrong time? Was she tied in with the mess I was working on or was it just a coincidence? Were sun spots acting up, would we have another dry year, and would the 49ers make it once more? I didn't have answers to any of it.

I thought about Hellman, too, the jerk, stepping out on loving, pretty Lorie and that rat pack of kids. I hate it when men are bastards like that. But was he enough of a bastard to kill June?

I was driving aimlessly around doing what passed for thinking when I decided I needed a phone. Public phones are like cops, they're never around when you need one and always there when you don't. I finally found one with half a phone book. Fortunately it was the half I needed. Feeling like a heel, something that happens too often in this business, I called the Hellmans' house. Lorie answered, not sounding as bright and chipper as a few days ago, but then who was? Not me. Not June. Not Sam.

I asked politely for Mr. Hellman and when he, of course, wasn't there, asked for his office number. I called the office to ascertain that he was in and available, checked my map again and was off.

The receptionist's office at Sagebrush Realty was a busy place, though it did not look to me as though anything much was getting done. The receptionist seemed harried and pointed me in the direction of Hellman's office. Cubicle would be a more apt word. It had the bare minimum: four walls, a door, a desk, and two chairs. He was engrossed in paperwork so I leaned in and knocked on the open door.

"Steve Hellman?" He looked up and frowned. Probably trying to place me. "Kat Colorado." He reddened and started to rise. He'd placed me.

"Get out of here."

I smiled my sweetest smile. "Okay, and when I leave I'm going to the police. I'm sure they know June Daly worked in this office, but I bet they don't know about your affair and I think they'll be interested."

The red turned white as though he was being slowly dipped in starch. The white crept up his neck, chin, and jowls, and finally obliterated the dark patches where his hairline was receding. I hoped Lorie was watching his cholesterol and blood pressure, or preparing for an early widowhood.

"May I sit down?" I asked him. He sagged weakly into a chair. I took that for a yes and sat.

"Isn't this cozy?" I asked. He stared at me blankly. Not much bottom to him.

"I didn't do it."

"Didn't do what?"

"Anything. Kill her."

"Who did?"

"I don't know."

"I think you do."

"No, I . . . I don't have to tell you anything." I shrugged. "Who the hell are you anyway, a cop?"

"No, I'm private, looking into it for friends of the family."

"She didn't have any friends or family. I—"

"You should know," I finished. "I imagine that she didn't have many affairs, but she had one with you, was still involved with you at the time of her death."

He stared miserably at me. "Poor kid," he said finally. "She had so little. I only wanted to bring a little happiness into her life."

I choked back a retort. Married men make me sick with their sanctimonious justifications. He spread his hands out palms up, as if to ask for my understanding and forgiveness. The thoughts of his manly endeavors had made him all red and hearty again.

"Instead you got her involved and killed. Did she even know?"

"What do you mean?" He was getting pale again.

"Did she know what you were mixed up with and how it could include her, or was she just a marked lamb marched off to the slaughter?"

"I don't know what you're talking about," he whispered.

"Don't kid around with me, Hellman. I looked up your voting record. You've been the swing vote on a lot of issues, issues involving development, zoning changes, variances granted, that kind of stuff. You've been sitting in developers' pockets for a while. The New Capital Ventures deal was nothing new to you. But this time you held out for a while. Why? More money?"

He stammered incoherently.

"That was it, wasn't it, more money? You threatened them with not playing ball if they didn't raise the stakes. Did you suggest that you could get the others on the board to go along with you? Did you try to play big guy? What did you do?"

He gnawed a knuckle miserably while I talked, stared at his desk, at the wall, everywhere but at me.

"It wasn't the money." I snorted. "No," he shot me a glance. "It wasn't. I just got tired of it. I got tired of the phone calls telling me what to do, and how, and when. I got tired of—"

I was getting tired, too. "Didn't anyone ever tell you that you can't change boats midstream?" He stared at me stupidly, that chunk of folk wisdom zipping right over his head. "Didn't you know you couldn't back out of a deal with these guys?"

"I thought—"

He stopped, probably couldn't remember what he thought, and I could see how he would have a problem. "I thought—" He stopped again.

"Did they warn you?"

"Huh?"

"Did they tell you what they were going to do?"

"They just said they expected business to go on as usual. They sent me—" he broke off.

"The money," I finished, and he nodded unhappily.

"Yeah, I was going to send it back but it was a tough month and we'd just put in the pool and—"

"Jesus, Hellman," I exploded, "don't you know anything? You weren't planning on delivering the goods and yet you took the money?"

He was gnawing his knuckle again. "I didn't know what to do. And then—"

"Did they warn you?" He gnawed away. "Did they?"

"They said I'd better cooperate."

"Who said?"

"They did."

"Name names."

"No, I can't." Or won't, I thought, but it wouldn't have done any good to press him. He was too scared.

"They said you'd better cooperate or what?"

"What do you mean?"

"Don't be such a goddamn fool, Hellman. What did they threaten you with?"

"They said . . . they said if I didn't cooperate my girlfriend wouldn't like it."

"Did you warn her? Did you do anything?"

"I didn't talk about that kind of stuff with her. She didn't know anything about that. I didn't want her to worry. I—"

"You make me sick." I felt sick, too, and my head was hurting again. Hellman was playing with paper clips on his desk blotter.

"After she was killed did they say anything?"

"What do you mean?"

"You know what I mean. Answer me."

"They called and said they hoped I cared more about the health of my wife and kids than I did about my girlfriend."

"And do you?"

"I voted for it." He looked at his hands.

"Do you sleep well at night, Hellman?" I got up and reached for the doorknob.

"Wait a minute. Don't go. What are you going to do? You're not going to the police, are you?" He struggled to his feet. "Look, I can make it—"

"Worth my while? Bribery is a crime."

"I didn't say anything," he said sullenly.

"They cut her throat, Hellman, from ear to ear. Did you make it worth her while?" He sank back in his chair and I walked out.

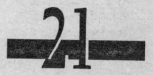

Dear Charity,

My mom says that girls should let boys look like the smartest ones, because that will please the boys and get girls lots of dates. What do you say?

Not So Dumb

Dear Not,

I think it is a great idea if you like dumb boys and want to look dumb yourself. Your mom probably thinks blondes have more fun, too.

I think you should be who you are.

Charity

In the books and movies private eyes always tough it out to the end. Maybe they're drunk on Jack Daniel's, thrown out of a car at forty miles an hour and dragged a hundred yards, but they still lurch away to solve the crime, eat, drink, and screw all night. I figure the big difference between them and me is audience. They have one, I don't. I decided to head for Joe and Betty's and climb into bed with whatever I could find to eat and watch soap operas until I fell asleep. Later I'd figure out how to tough it.

I slept straight through the afternoon until dinnertime. It was great, no dreams, nobody singing choruses of the trapeze song. I woke up, not to the frantic beating of my heart, but to the quiet sound of voices in the kitchen. I lay there for a while, listening without hearing. There was a tap on the door and Betty came in.

"How do you feel? You look rested. Hank's here and wants to know if you'd like to go out to dinner. Mexican food, I think he said."

I perked up. Mexican food is one of my favorites. "I'll have a shower, get dressed and be right out," I said. And I tried, but *right out* is relative. Time takes on different dimensions with a cast.

I struggled into a pink, drop-waist cotton dress with short sleeves and a layered skirt. It looked great with the high-heeled white sandals I no longer had; I dug out some flat ones. I looked good except for the black eyes and the unzipped zipper in the back of my dress that I couldn't manage. The black eyes I couldn't do anything about, the zipper I let Betty handle.

"Pretty as a picture you are, Kat," Joe said with old-fashioned gallantry. I laughed, remembering how, as kids, we used to put black eyes on the models in the slick magazines. Some picture. Joe smiled, thinking I appreciated his compliment, which I did. Betty asked me if I wanted beer or wine, and Hank pulled me down to his wide, solid lap and hugged me gently around the middle. I said wine and leaned back against him, felt a scratchy cheek rub against mine. It felt fine.

"You look a lot better after a day of rest." He hugged me again. "Smell good, too, like lilac and lavender. How old-fashioned. Perfume?"

"Hand lotion and actually—"

"Reminds me of my great aunt. I guess not many women wear perfume these days."

"I don't know. More men do, though." I made a face. "It gives me a headache and it's expensive. If I'm going to buy expensive alcohol-based items I'd rather drink them than wear them."

Joe guffawed. "Atta girl, Kat. Who says common sense and femininity don't go together?"

"Not me." Hank said and hugged me again.

"No." A moral dilemma was hanging over me—how I'd really spent my day as opposed to how I'd reputedly spent it—so I couldn't concentrate on a topic that ordinarily I find gripping. "Look, I—"

"The fashion changes," Betty said. "Thank God. Remember Twiggy? That look wouldn't fly now. Now we extol physical competence and fit bodies as well as mental competence and common sense. Women aren't admired for being helpless, dumb and incompetent, and it's about time."

"Some of us have always appreciated those things." Joe pinched Betty's ample rear end. She fondly swatted his hand away.

"Are you strong, Kat, do you work out?" she asked me.

"Yes to both. I can run five miles, swim two miles, move pool tables by myself, and leap short, squat buildings in a single bound. I can also talk tough, drink shots of Wild Turkey, and eat very hot Mexican food."

Hank hugged me again. "Mmm, my kind of gal."

"Look," I started again vainly, "there's something—"

Betty chuckled. "And now we think competence and strength is beautiful in a woman. Just imagine the Chinese binding women's feet or the Victorians taking out ribs and deforming their bodies with those hideous whalebone corsets. It was in the name of femininity, but what it really did was make them helpless, dependent, and unfit." She made a face. "Fortunately things are different now and men are attracted to strong, proficient women."

I snorted.

"Don't you think so?"

"No," I said.

"Yes," Hank said.

"Well, yes and no," I qualified. "Some men, but they are more the exception than the rule. Or they like it in theory, but they wouldn't want to know one, or work under one, or have their brother marry one."

"You know too many of the wrong men," Hank said.

"Yes."

"But we could change that."

"Yes." He kissed my ear and it made a loud smacking noise somewhere inside my brain.

"I'm extremely attracted to strong, proficient women, especially ones with casts and black eyes," Hank said.

"Good, because I'm starving."

"Finish your wine and we'll go."

"I'm pacing myself," I explained, "and also I want to talk about some things." I took a deep breath. "I had a couple of interesting conversations today."

"On the phone?" Betty asked.

"Actually I went out for a bit." I tried to sound nonchalant.

Hank started to laugh. "Of course, what else?"

"I thought you liked strong, competent women?"

"Yes," he said, but he said it in a different tone this time. I hugged his arms. Even good men don't get there overnight.

"Who did you talk to?" Joe asked.

"Allyson, the dead girl's roommate. She didn't have a lot to add to what she told the police. Except for one thing, and that made the trip, the instant coffee and the stale sugar doughnuts worth it." My comment was greeted with expectant silence, which I briefly relished. "June was having an affair with Steve Hellman, the planning board member who cast one of the key swing votes."

Betty sighed. "Poor girl, poor, unsuspecting girl." I could feel Hank's body go rigid under me. I think, without realizing it, he was metamorphosing into a cop. Like a werewolf in a full moon, he couldn't help it.

"Then I went to see Hellman." Hank got even more rigid and Joe frowned.

"I badgered him into a corner. Not difficult," I added. "Underneath his tough-guy act he's a wimp, a wimp running scared."

"They can be dangerous," Hank said.

"I know."

"Like a cornered rat, not so much for what they do, but for what they can make happen."

I nodded. I'd seen it before too. Mothers will fight to protect their young and there's nobility in that. Rats won't fight for anything but themselves. Since the human ones have few values or ethics they are also unpredictable. Dangerous, as Hank said, and nothing noble about them.

"He admitted he was on the New Capital Ventures payroll though he couldn't, or wouldn't, name names. He said he wanted out though he took the money. A man's got to pay for his swimming pool somehow, you know."

"Smart boy." The sarcasm in Joe's comment was unmistakable.

"Yes. It gets better. They told him that if he didn't play the game by the agreed-upon rules his girlfriend would be sorry. So he waffled some more of course."

"Did he tell the girl, or do anything to protect her?"

"No. After her death he got another warning. Play ball or the wife and kids are next."

"Why is it always the innocent who suffer?" Betty asked in a thin, plaintive voice.

"Not always, but too often," I said.

"I can't sit on this, sweetheart," Hank said. His body was still rigid under mine.

"No, of course not, I wouldn't want you to." He relaxed a bit, probably afraid I'd disagree, but if the police could wrap this up it was fine with me. Until then, though, I wasn't ready to bow out.

"What next?" Joe asked, and I said, truthfully, that I didn't know. If you don't take names you can't kick ass and that's what we were missing, names. Names and facts. Or maybe it was the connection between them.

We had facts: Hellman was on the take; Phillips and his wife had been threatened; a girl was dead—Sam too; New Capital Ventures was buying up real estate on the QT. We had names: Blackford for one. He had my vote, but so what? What we didn't have were connections. I sighed inwardly. The police would look at it again now. Maybe they would get names, facts, connections. They were good at that. Good at kicking ass, too.

"What next?" Hank said. "We eat. Hungry?" he asked me, standing up and plopping me on the floor.

"Starving. I could eat a horse, saddle and all."

"That's what Joe says," Betty mused.

"Yes, I took a page out of his book." I smiled.

"I might not bring her back," Hank said, taking hold of my hand and walking me out. I smiled again.

Dear Charity,

Do you consider it vitally important to serve exactly the right wine with the right food? Is that an etiquette essential?

Vintage Yuppie

Dear Vin Yup,

No. I consider it vitally important to invite the right people. They will cheerfully eat and drink whatever you place in front of them.

Charity

Hank opened the door to an old Mustang, the kind I always imagined in the song "Mustang Sally." The white paint was new; so was the tan upholstery. It was great and I told him so.

"I worked on it a lot after Liz died. It kept me off the streets and out of trouble." I reached out and touched his cheek.

"Where are we eating?"

"At my house." That made me nervous. He glanced sideways at me. "You don't look too pleased."

"Can you cook?"

He laughed. "Is that what's worrying you?" I nodded. "Of course, can't you?"

"Yes, but not well. Scrambled eggs, tacos, spaghetti. Mostly I eat out of a carton—yogurt, cottage cheese, stuff like that."

"Fortunately, while women were scurrying out to the corporate arena and body building, men were scurrying into the kitchen and learning to cook."

"Some men."

"Yes."

"Did you always cook, even before Liz died?"

"Always." He thumped his belly. "I love to eat and I love to cook."

"Lucky me." We smiled at each other. He drove the rest of the way mostly with one hand; with the other he held my hand on his knee. I started to feel funny inside and it wasn't just hunger.

Hank lived on a quiet street with a lot of cottonwoods and cactus. It was an older part of town, the houses were set on good-sized lots. His house was in the Spanish adobe style with a red tile roof. We entered through a small courtyard enclosed in an adobe wall with a wrought-iron gate. In the courtyard a fountain splashed and sang; there were lush flowers and greenery every-where. It was like something out of a romance novel. I loved it and stammered out incoherent words of praise. Hank laughed at me.

"I love it too. It's my one indulgence. The rest of the landscaping is in drought-resistant natives, rock gardens, that sort of thing."

"Fish?" I caught an orange-and-gold gleam in the pond. "Hey, what are their names? Can you tell them apart?"

"Oh yes, fish have personalities, though not real interesting ones. You can name them, I haven't. Come inside."

He tugged my hand gently. "We'll sit out here later."

The house was cool, quiet, and peaceful. Then the black

tornado hit. Hank thumped the dog's sides, held its head and talked to it while it tried to wiggle and waggle itself into a state of ecstacy.

"Kat, this is Mars. Mars, Kat is a friend."

The dog acknowledged me with a look and a sloppy lick. He was big, mostly black, and probably mostly black Lab.

"After the planet, the god, or the candy bar?"

"What?"

"Mars."

"First it was mostly after Mars, the Greek god of war." I nodded. "A buddy gave him to me right after Liz died. I tried to refuse. I didn't want any consolation then, anything between me and the blackness."

"But he wriggled right in and wouldn't go away."

"Yes."

"And made it better?"

"Yes."

"And is it still the god?"

"Getting closer to the candy bar." He grinned and reached out for me, started nibbling on my ear.

I slid out from under his arm. "Which way is the kitchen? Time to feed you. And me, too. What smells so good?"

"Sauce for the enchiladas. I started it earlier."

"Homemade?" I was awed.

"Of course. A glass of wine? Come choose."

But I stayed in the living room and looked around. It was simple and lovely. An old fireplace, Mexican and Indian rugs on wooden floors, and matter-of-fact furniture in earth tones. There was a bleached bighorn skull over the mantle, a print of a Georgia O'Keefe on the wall, and a bunch of beautiful blue pottery. I was entranced.

"Red or white, Kat?"

"What?"

"Wine."

"Oh, I'll come see." I tore myself away. "Hank, it's beautiful."

"Yes, if I didn't have something peaceful to come home to I'd have to stop being a cop. It was better when Liz was here but Mars and I get by." He paused. "You're the first woman I've invited over."

"I'm honored."

He smiled. "Red or white?" He pointed to several possibilities on the Spanish tile counter. It was an eccentric offering, to say the least. I looked at him thoughtfully. "You don't drink much wine, do you?"

"Is it that obvious?" I nodded and we laughed. "There's champagne in the refrigerator. Let's start with that. That's always good."

"Mmm, always."

We toasted, at first to nothing in particular, just with our eyes, and then to new beginnings.

"Can I do anything?" Hank had put on a record, jazz—I don't know anything at all about jazz but I liked it.

"You can make the salad."

I tried but after I banged my cast twice and my head once he made me stop.

"I'm not usually this uncoordinated."

"You pour the wine, I'll do the rest."

I poured more champagne and then wandered around and looked at his house while he made enchiladas and we talked.

We had chicken and sour cream enchiladas and cheese, onion, jalapeño, and olive tacos. They were so good that I stuffed myself and almost asked for the recipes, forgetting that I probably couldn't make them anyway. There was a rice dish and a green salad, too, both delicious beyond belief.

"There's dessert, or do you want to wait?"

"Wait," I said, "and I want to talk and see if we can figure this out."

"Okay." He sighed. "But only for a while. Then we drop it."

"All right."

"Let's start with what you know."

"I know that Sam was involved with New Capital Ventures and somebody killed him. I know that pressure was put on at least two planning board members to vote for a zoning change essential to New Capital Ventures' plans and that June was killed as a warning to Hellman to stay in line. I know that Deck didn't seem surprised at any of this and that he warned me off. I know that there's a connection between gambling interests, Don Blackford's in particular, and New Capital Ventures."

I paused for a breath. Hank was alert and attentive listening to my litany. Mars snoozed at our feet. "I strongly suspect that there's skimming and laundering going on and that New Capital Ventures comes in handy there. I know someone tried to kill me, presumably because I'm poking around in all this. I know a lot, Hank, but I can't prove a damn bit of it."

Hank nodded and stacked the plates.

"Even if Hellman or the Phillipses would talk, which I doubt, there still wouldn't be proof. There's nothing on the girl's murder, or Sam's, or the hit and run, and it's unlikely that anything will show up."

"Hard to say."

"Do you think it will?"

He hesitated. "No, I guess I don't, not unless we get a tip."

"So now what?"

"We play wait and see for a while."

I shook my head. "No good. Better to flush them out."

"What did you have in mind?"

"I'm still working on it." Nothing, in other words.

"Don't get any ideas about playing decoy. You're not a cat, you don't have nine lives."

"No." I said it innocently and agreeably enough but he looked at me suspiciously.

"They tried to kill you already."

"Yes."

"Kat, I don't want anything to happen to you."

"Me either. I'll be a Kat amongst their pigeons."

"No, you're the pigeon, a pigeon amongst the cats, and it's not a happy thought."

I could only agree. In fact the idea made me shivery. I decided to change the subject.

"Shall we do the dishes?"

"They can wait." I didn't protest. Housework of any kind, dishes especially, is low on my list of priorities.

"Let's go outside."

Hank poured more champagne and we went into the walled adobe courtyard where the moonlight danced and the fountain sang. It seemed like a long time that we sat there, talking, laughing, kissing some. We sat in silence for a while and then Hank spoke.

"Will you stay here with me tonight?" He didn't touch me when he said that. He wanted me, I knew, and wanted me to want him, but only for the right reasons.

"Yes." I didn't touch him when I said it either, but afterward I leaned into the arms he held out for me.

"If I'm not careful—" I stopped, tongue tied for the first time in two and a half years.

"We'll be careful—about health, babies, everything."

"About love?"

"No, not about that."

Hank put an arm around my waist and stood up, pulling me with him. I could feel the muscles in his body, strong and hard. I wanted him as much as he wanted me. A lot. Because of the cast he had to undress me. Once I almost hit him with it. We didn't care. We didn't get much sleep, and we didn't care about that either.

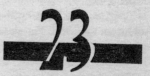

Dear Charity,
  My history teacher keeps talking about people who have the "courage of their convictions." What does that mean? It sounds old-fashioned and stupid to me.

Al in Ohio

Dear Al,
  It means that you're brave enough to live, or die, for what you believe in. Nathan Hale died for his country, Joan of Arc for her God. We don't hear about it very much anymore, but that doesn't mean that it's old-fashioned and stupid. I think we could use a lot more courage and conviction.

Charity

I woke up that morning with my head on Hank's chest and his arms around me. My good arm was under me and my plaster cast was partly on the bed and partly in the thick, dark hair of his chest. I lay there for a while feeling shy but good, then I shifted a little and started to wriggle out. Hank's arms tightened on me and he made a low sound in his throat, all in his sleep. I kept wriggling. He opened his eyes.

"I'll be right back," I said, and he smiled and nodded sleepily. I went to the bathroom and then to the kitchen for a glass of water. Mars kept me company and we watched the first rays of the sun come up over Sunrise Mountain, pink and beautiful with the promise of a new day. I was chilly by the time I crawled back into bed. Hank pulled me into his arms and warmth and started kissing me, making me shiver from the heat, and the pleasure, and from the hands that slid over me and caressed me. We made love for a long time. The sun had come up then and we smiled in the new light.

"What do you want for breakfast?"

"Mmm." I stretched out luxuriously and then rolled over to flop on Hank again. Regrettably I miscalculated.

"Ouch, goddamn, Kat. What the—" he broke off and looked at me wordlessly, one hand rubbing the spot on his head I'd just whomped with my cast.

"I missed," I whispered. "I'm sorry, I was trying to hug you and I'm not real good with this cast yet. Are you okay?"

"Nothing time won't cure. You can stop whispering now."

"Oh," I said in a normal voice. I hadn't realized I'd been whispering. "Here, let me—" Hank dodged out of my grasp.

"Not a chance, sweetheart, you don't know your own strength."

"I could just kiss it," I said persuasively.

"Just kiss it?"

"Yes."

"Okay."

"Where? Here?"

"Lower."

"Here?"

"Lower."

We started laughing and it was a time, a long time and a good time, before the subject of breakfast came up again.

"Omelets, waffles, French toast, what'll it be? I'm hungry, sweetheart, and it's time to get up."

"I'll make breakfast."

Hank looked dubious and rightly so.

"No, really, I'm *good* at breakfasts," I lied cheerfully, wanting to impress him. "It's my best meal. Pancakes are my specialty." I lied again.

"Sounds great. Let's go have a shower."

Hank held my cast out of the shower curtain with one hand and soaped me with the other. I got mostly clean and not too wet on my plaster arm. I left him singing in the shower and pulled on my underpants and one of his T-shirts. I couldn't manage anything else without help.

My adopted grandmother used to say that great cooks can use their imagination but everyone else should use a cookbook. I would be the last person to argue with that, but, since I couldn't find a cookbook, I decided to wing it. How tough could pancakes be? I whipped out the batter, found juice and fruit for a fruit salad, and boiled water for the coffee I couldn't find. Then I set the table.

"Looks good, smells good," Hank said appreciatively, looking at me. He leaned over, smelling all clean and soapy, and kissed me. I started to hug him but he backed off. "Uh oh, a cast and a spatula, armed and dangerous." He stood where I couldn't reach around at him and nibbled at the back of my neck. "I'm so hungry I could eat a horse."

"Saddle and all," I finished. "Make the coffee, would you? By then the first batch of pancakes will be ready. Where's the maple syrup?"

The pancakes were round, puffy and impressive. They looked a little different, odd different, but smelled good. I watched complacently as Hank shoveled in the first bite. He started off with relish but his enthusiasm diminished with each bite.

"Er, what's in here, Kat?"

"Why? Don't you like them?" I felt my voice getting a tad defensive.

"I didn't say that, I just wondered what was in them."

"Oh." That made me feel better. After all, cooks should be willing to share recipes and trade secrets. "They're fruit pancakes," I explained. "Instead of milk I used OJ. Then I added pineapple preserves and a bit of strawberry ice cream."

"Strawberry ice cream in pancakes?" he asked in a weak voice.

"Only because of the strawberry, the fruit motif, you see. I thought it was a nice touch," I admitted, proud of my ingenuity. "What do you think?"

Wordlessly Hank handed me his plate. I could understand. Words often fail me at a critical moment—in the contemplation of art, or in the appreciation of culinary delights. I cut out a largish wedge, sopped up the syrup and forked it in.

The ice cream sogged the middle of the pancake, the OJ seemed thin and watery, and the pineapple preserves were lumpy.

"Hank, it's horrible and I wanted everything to be so special." I sighed.

"Honey, it's special already, breakfast doesn't matter. And it is memorable." I looked at him suspiciously. He was struggling with his expression.

"Hank!"

"I'm sorry, Kat." He started laughing so hard the tears ran down his cheeks. "I think we'd better just start over." I stood in injured and dignified silence. He picked up the plate and whistled. Mars came trotting in with expectant ears and wagging tail. Hank put the plate down and Mars wolfed up a doggie-sized gulp.

"See, Mars likes them," I said triumphantly, gloating too soon as it happened. Mars's tail stopped wagging, his ears drooped. He looked at Hank with a reproachful expression on his face, then left the room.

"Oh." I stopped bragging and got droopy, too. "Oh well."

"How about if I make French toast?" he asked, giving me a hug.

"Okay."

"You made my day long before breakfast, Kat." He smiled at me and I felt better. I felt better knowing I wasn't going to have to eat those pancakes, too. Instead I had two and a half helpings of French toast, to keep my strength up, I told myself, and to get better fast.

"Remember what I said last night about trying to flush them out?" I remarked finally, when I quit stuffing my face long enough to talk.

"Mmm."

"Hank, are you listening?"

"Mmm."

"I'm going to paint myself red, white, and blue and stand naked in the streets. What do you think?"

"Mmm."

He wasn't listening. Reading the newspaper at the breakfast table and not listening must be genetically linked to the Y chromosome. I whistled for Mars and offered him the last bits of my French toast. He looked at me with interest and suspicion and sniffed carefully before he ate. I sighed loudly. No response. I sighed again. Mars left the room; he was no dummy.

"What do you want to do today, honey?"

"I want to talk to you."

"Okay, fire away." He turned back to the paper.

"And I want you to listen."

"Mmm."

I sighed again and drifted off to the bedroom. Then I drifted back with my bra on but undone and holding my sundress. "Hook me up, Hank." I sat on his knee. Subtlety was not going to work while he was reading the newspaper. He didn't hook me up. He flipped my bra off and reached around to cup my breasts and started nuzzling and kissing me. Enlightened and aware men like Hank always insist that they're attracted to you more for your mind than your body—then things like this happen and you wonder. Obviously awareness is relative.

"Can we talk now?"

"Talk? How about later? Kat, let's—" I sighed.

"Hank, I need to talk to you."

"Okay, honey."

"Hook me up, you're not concentrating." It was his turn to sigh. He hooked me up, good start. Then his hands caressed my belly and played with my nipples which, traitorously, got hard. I turned around and sat facing him astraddle on his lap. He leaned back as my cast went by, which was a good thing. It might not quite have cleared his chin otherwise.

"Mmm, Kat, how about—"

"I think I have a plan, Hank."

"Me too." His hands cupped my bottom and squeezed.

"Hank, it's behavior like this that gives men a bad image."

He looked a little stricken, then stood up, set me down, readjusted his pants around the bulge and headed for the coffee pot.

"More coffee?"

"Please."

He poured us coffee and sat down, all business except for the bulge.

"What kind of a plan?"

"To flush them out. It came to me last night in an in-between moment." He frowned and I smiled inside. "They wouldn't have tried to kill me if they weren't worried, if they weren't unsure of just how much I know and can prove. I can use that to my advantage. The longer I sit tight hoping for a break, the clearer it becomes that I have nothing to move on." Hank opened his mouth. "Which is true, of course, so that's where the rumors and/or statements come in."

"Such as?"

"Such as statements from the police that you have 'a promising lead' or 'a new witness' on one or more of the murders. It would be best if it involved me. I figure Joe could start circulating the same kind of stuff. In this town it shouldn't take long to get around. It's a bluff, but maybe somebody will do something, preferably something stupid."

Hank looked unenthusiastic in the extreme. Throwing shit out and hoping that it will hit the fan is not a technique entirely unknown in the investigative field but it's not one that routinely gets top billing either.

"What other choice do we have?" I asked, pleaded almost, hopeful that he, anyone, would come up with something better.

"I don't know, Kat, I'll think about it." He looked like a cop again and the bulge had gone down. "I'm sure as hell not doing anything that sets you up, so forget about that."

I decided not to mention the other plan I had. I climbed into my sundress, had Hank zip me up, and went looking for my sandals. I came back to find him staring morosely out the window. It was not promising.

"Kat—"

"I know."

"You don't," he said angrily. "How can you? After Liz—"

I knew it. Damn. "I'll be careful."

"I care about you. After Liz—"

"I care about you, too. And about me. I'll be careful."

There wasn't much to say; we both stood and stared morosely out the window. I was the first to break the silence.

"Take me back to Joe's, Hank."

"All right."

We went the scenic route and Hank showed me things but it wasn't fun. The air was tense, stretched between us like taut rubber bands waiting to snap. Finally we let the silence be. It made the time long and heavy and the drive slow. It was with relief that I saw the little yellow car in front of Joe and Betty's.

"It wasn't just a one-night thing for me." Hank didn't look at me as he spoke. I put my hand on his knee.

"I know. Not for me, either."

"Don't play it alone, Kat."

"All right." I took a deep breath. "I promise," I said, hoping I could keep that promise, knowing that I would try. We kissed. I got out of the car and headed for the house.

There was ice tea in the fridge. I started on that and decided to call Joe, tell him what I'd told Hank and ask for his cooperation.

"What do you think, Joe?"

"I don't think it'll work."

I sighed.

"Do you?" he asked.

"No."

"Those boys didn't fall off the turnip truck yesterday. Unless they're running dumb and scared it's going to take more than that to smoke them out."

"That's why I have a backup plan." The silence was ominous. "Joe, you there?"

"Yeah, just waiting with bated breath, Kat."

I ignored the sarcasm. "Oh. Good. I thought I'd go see Ollie, do some plain talking. I figure information will flow through channels pretty fast after that."

"You're setting yourself up, aren't you?"

"Not exactly, though I am hoping that someone will get in touch with me."

"Could well be. In fact I suspect they will. If they do, it won't be a bozo in a pickup. This time it will be someone who knows what he's doing. Forget the clay pigeons. This is sitting-duck time."

"I'll get back to you, Joe," I said, and hung up before he could say anything. I hate it when nobody shows any enthusiasm for my ideas. It makes me cranky, too. The phone rang for a long time right after that but I was too busy struggling with zippers and buttons to answer. Anyway, why bother answering when you're through talking?

Dear Charity,

Do you believe in making sacrifices for good causes? There are so many: dying whales, threatened redwoods, ozone with holes, starving people, battered women, abused children. Where do you start and what do you do? I feel so confused and helpless.

Helpless in Tucson

Dear Helpless,

You start where you are and you do what you can. If everyone picked one cause dear to their heart—it wouldn't matter what—and did something, this world would be a different place. Figure it out: 5 billion people + time, energy and money = change and hope.

Charity

The construction site was as busy as before but this time I walked in unchallenged. I didn't see Ollie right away, but at a distance and with everyone in hard hats, that was no surprise. I kept my eyes open and headed for the trailer. I was almost there when a hard hat detached itself from a group and waved. I waved back and sat down on the trailer steps to wait. It was hot and I hoped it wouldn't be long. It wasn't.

"How you doing, Cathy, isn't it?"

"Kat."

"Yeah, that's right. Damn, just like me to make a fool mistake like that."

"Not so fool. Pretty close."

"Yeah. What can I do for you?"

"I came to talk and let you know about the funeral. You're pretty busy now, though."

"Yeah. I can give you a few minutes." A semi roared by and the crane started up again. I felt the dust settle on me. "What happened to you, kid?" He pointed at my arm and shouted over the racket.

"Long story. Can I buy you a beer after work? I'll tell you that and more."

"Sure, best offer I've had today," he said, grinning.

"Name a time and place."

"Hey, Bremmer, where you want this shit?" a beefy-faced guy with a semi and an attitude problem yelled.

"Five o'clock, Diamond Lil's." He pointed vaguely. "You can't miss it."

"I'll be there." He smiled at me and then faded into the dust, like the Cheshire cat, as another truck roared by. I waved at the retreating grin and headed out, first for the car, then for a mall.

I'd bowed to the inevitable and decided to go shopping, which I loathe, but the accident had taken its toll in clothing and business here was running longer than I'd expected. I picked out a pair of white slacks, a blouse, a full-skirted sundress (elastic waist, no zipper) and a pair of high-heeled sandals. All credit card, some of it expense account.

I smartened up and changed into the new dress and sandals in the ladies' lounge at one of the casinos. It was an improvement, dust and dirt not generally being regarded as a cosmetic enhancement. The dress was bright and short and with my cast I looked attractive in a rakish, devil-may-care kind of way. I pulled my unruly, curly mop of hair back and jammed it into a clip. Then I slapped on a dab of makeup and a smile and was ready to face the world.

After that I had two hours to kill, which I did at the blackjack tables. Playing conservatively and unimaginatively I accumulated eighty dollars over the next hour. Naturally it went to my head and then I lost a hundred in twenty minutes. Taking it as a cosmic clue, I gave up, stowed my stuff in the trunk of the car, and headed for Diamond Lil's.

The bar was cool and dark with historical (albeit inaccurate) pretensions. The cocktail waitresses were supposed to look like nineteenth-century bar girls but they missed it. Instead they looked like they had bought their push-up bras, corsets and garter belts from the same slightly sleazy mail-order outfit. Most of them seemed to have the same hairdresser, too, one who was partial to ringlets. At least it was a change from the usual Vegas showgirl.

I sat in a booth and ordered a draft. It wasn't a long wait before Ollie slid in across from me.

"Better bring me one of those," he said to the waitress.

"Better bring him two," I said. He grinned.

"Good idea. So Kat, what happened to you?"

"Car accident. Sent me to the hospital, too. I missed the funeral, which is why you didn't hear from me." He nodded. "Instead of flowers I know the family would appreciate a donation to Sam's favorite charity." I paused as the wheels spun in my brain. "Save the Redwoods." Ollie nodded but looked a little puzzled. I smiled. Saving natural things was the antithesis of what Sam held most sacred: wanton destruction of the environment for developer gain.

Ollie finished his second beer and I signaled for another round.

"Ollie, I haven't been entirely candid with you." He raised his eyebrows and managed to convey interest and speculation at the same time. "I represented myself as a friend of the family and, while that is true—Charity Collins is one of my closest friends—I am also a private investigator and here on business."

Ollie started laughing. "Why doesn't that surprise me?"

"I have a devious look?"

"No, but I guess I figured there was more here than met the eye." He smiled. "And I was right. What are you looking into?"

"Charity figured Sam, her soon-to-be ex-husband, had lifted two hundred grand out of their joint accounts and invested it here to beat the California community-property stipulations. I came down to check it out. He had. It was in a financial investment corporation called New Capital Ventures. Heard about it?"

"No, should I have?"

"Your boss, Ed Trainor, is a big investor. So is Don Blackford. So are a bunch of other small investors and a number of top-level casino names."

"Why do I need to know this?"

"Humor me for a bit?"

"Okay," he said, frowning.

"I looked into New Capital Ventures. Their financial probity is highly questionable. I'm a jump away from proving it's a front for laundering skimmed money. Their political integrity is also questionable. Another jump brings us up to payoffs and the intimidation of city officials in a rezoning proposal that allows for the investment of the above funds."

Ollie finished the pretzels and I signaled for more.

"I don't want to hear this shit."

"I think you do. People like that have a way of involving everyone around them, including those working for them. Innocent and stupid doesn't cut it." We sat in silence while the waitress set out the pretzels and tidied up.

"Go on," he said finally.

"The intimidation has gone past name-calling and threats. Four people are dead."

He looked at me, startled. "Dead? But what—can you prove it?"

"I can link it up. One was the girlfriend of one of the city officials I mentioned. He was wavering. They told him to play ball or she'd be sorry. He didn't play fast enough, and she was. Not for long, though," I added reflectively. "I don't imagine she had much time to think about it. It doesn't take long to die when your throat's cut."

Ollie was busting up pretzels aimlessly in the bowl. He kept it up until they looked like rabbit food.

"Go on."

"After I made waves a guy in a stolen pickup truck tried to run me down. I got away with a day in the hospital, a busted arm, sore ribs and bruises. A pregnant woman and her four-year-old daughter died."

"Shit." Roughly he pushed the pretzels away; they scattered across the table. The waitress came scampering over. I ordered another round, skip the pretzels.

"You have children, don't you?"

"Two girls." He stared at me. I nodded. The waitress plunked our beers down.

"Then there's Sam. He found out that everything wasn't on the up-and-up and panicked, came down here and started shooting his mouth off. In a crunch Sam was no good, he'd wet his pants. A company like New Capital Ventures can't afford a weak link, especially one shooting his mouth off."

"You're saying Ed—that it wasn't an accident—that . . ."

"Yes, that's what I'm saying. Murder is the word."

He stood up abruptly. "Excuse me. Restroom." I hoped he'd come back. I thought he would. Ollie loved his little girls and that was as good a reason as any. It took a while but he came back.

"It's not right, I know it, but I hate you for telling me this."

"I understand," I said, and I did. I'd felt that way before. "But innocence and ignorance don't help. It won't protect you or your family."

His big calloused hands clenched and unclenched. I watched the knuckles go from red-brown to white and back again. And I waited.

"You're telling me this for a reason. What is it?"

"I want your help."

"I'm not going on the line. I'm not brave like that, not much where I'm concerned and not at all where my family's concerned. Maybe it should be different but, I dunno, it's not."

"It shouldn't be different. That's the way we all are. Still, helping stop them is part of protecting your daughters. The pregnant woman and her daughter who were killed?" He nodded. "Think how he felt, the husband and father."

He was silent for a while. "Okay. What do you want? I'm not saying I—what do you want?"

"I can't prove what I've told you. The people who could prove it are too scared to do so—for reasons like yours, good reasons. I want to beat the bushes, rock the boat, raise some hell. That's where I need you. I want you to pass this on, maybe go to Ed Trainor pissed at the crackpot talk this PI from Sacramento is blowing around. Run it all past him."

"You're taking a chance."

"What do you mean?"

"On me."

"Yes. I am."

"Why?"

"I think you're okay; I think you care about kids, yours and other people's; I think you care about an honest job for a decent wage. I think you'll send a company contribution to Save the Redwoods even though you probably don't believe in it."

"Did Sam?"

"No."

His laugh cracked out painfully, like a bullwhip on edge. "Actually I like redwoods. And kids." I waited. "That's not the only chance you're taking."

"No."

"If they killed Sam, they could kill you."

"Yes, they could."

"And?"

"And I don't think they will. I'm also very careful."

"It's still a chance."

"Yes."

"Aren't you scared?" He looked genuinely interested.

"Sure, but I don't have a family to worry about. And I care too. About kids and redwoods and principles. And money. This is how I make my living."

"What do you want me to do?"

"Talk. I'd like all of what I told you, except for this last bit, to get back to them. I want the shit to hit the fan—just protect yourself."

"I'll have to leave Trainor Construction."

"Not right away. Protect yourself."

"What will I do?" For a big man he looked helpless.

"I've got contacts in California if you want to relocate. Give me a couple of days' notice and I'll set things up."

He looked at me bleakly. "I never figured to be a Boy Scout."

"No. Life just works out that way sometimes. I don't know how much of it we can figure out."

"What do you think happens next?"

"I think the shit will hit the fan and fly. I know I'll be watching."

We finished our beers and left separately.

Dear Charity,

Sometimes it's hard to sort out the real and important things. I know a lot of people who think it's drugs and drinks and fantasy, but that can't be it. I don't think it's Rolex watches, fancy cars and vacation homes in Tahoe either, although I sure would like a 'Vette. A red one. 1990. I don't think it's knowing the right fork to use and going to the right school and having the right name. What is it?

Puzzled in Peoria

Dear Puzzled,

Love and learning.

Charity

For two days nothing happened except that I ran up a lot of phone bills to my answering service in Sacramento. Hank and I had dinners and fun together and I got a lot better at maneuvering my cast in close situations. Just as well. No need for us both to have black eyes, though mine were fading nicely. I got restless, too, and cranky. I get that way. I tried not to show it and didn't fool anyone.

Thursday morning at ten-thirty Steve Hellman called. I wasn't too excited about it but I was curious.

"I've got to talk to you."

"I'm all ears."

"No, not now, not on the phone."

"Name a place."

"There's a coffee shop on the west end of town." He gave me directions. "Be there in half an hour. I'll meet you in the parking lot."

"Okay." The phone went dead in my hand and I replaced it thoughtfully. Was it clay pigeons or bullshit that was flying? Hellman was right in the middle of this but I didn't think he had the balls to bail out, or to do the right thing—a concept that had probably died years ago in the wake of the expedient. I thought about it more as I drove through town, and the hotter it got the more cynical I became.

I was a few minutes late but it didn't worry me. Let him sweat. I drove into the parking lot, looked around for his tan Buick, pulled up next to him and got out. He made frantic gestures and when I didn't respond rolled his window down two or three inches.

"Get in," he croaked.

"No dice."

He looked puzzled. "Your car then?"

"Inside."

"No, I can't risk being seen with you." His face gleamed unhappily behind the window. His eyes looked scared and like a rat's, a cornered rat's, little and shifty. Not pretty.

I shrugged. "I'm going in for a cup of coffee. You've got ten minutes, then I'm leaving." I walked off. I didn't feel like playing games with him and I was wary enough to be careful.

The coffee shop was done in late chrome and early plastic.

Someone had obviously gotten a great deal on plastic plants and flowers. There were vase arrangements at every table and huge planters and hanging pots that clawed and pulled at me as I walked by. It was the Venus-flytrap concept of decorating. Dust was thick on the plastic leaves and puffed into the air when I brushed against them. I sat in a back booth and looked around for a waitress.

Hellman was scared to come in, but, I was betting, reluctant to leave without accomplishing what was on his mind. I figured two minutes would have him inside. He made it with thirty seconds to spare, the waitress hard on his heels. We ordered coffee and I sat back and waited. It was his show.

"Jesus, why couldn't we talk in the car?"

"Relax, there's no one in here, Hellman." He looked around, at the old man at the counter and at the two teenagers drinking Cokes at a table. "You afraid of kids and old people?"

"I just don't want to be seen with you."

I shrugged. "I don't much like spending time with you either, so let's get to it."

"You don't think much of me, do you?"

I shrugged again.

"Do you?" he insisted.

"No, I don't."

"I guess I can understand that."

"Can you?"

"You think that votes shouldn't be bought and sold." He leaned across the table and his face got all red and fat. I was reminded for a minute of the Porky Pig cartoons I watched as a kid but then it faded. "Well, don't you?" I shrugged. "And maybe I agree with you. Well I do, but life isn't that easy. It isn't that simple." Porky peeped out of his fat face and red eyes again.

"It's not just votes and money. A woman's dead because of you, Hellman, and your wife and children are threatened."

"And me too, what about me?"

"I don't care much about you, remember?"

"Well I do." His voice got high, squeaky, and stuttery. I

watched in fascination. How did Porky here ever manage to sell real estate? The waitress arrived with the coffee and his whining trailed off. When she left he resumed.

"When I was a kid everyone always picked on me. I—I was a fat kid and they made fun of me. I swore to myself that when I grew up I'd be someone. I'd show them. I'd make something of myself." Spittle had gathered in the corners of his mouth. He stopped talking and took a big slurp of coffee. The cup clattered as he set it down.

"Well, and I have. I have a nice house with a pool, a beautiful wife and kids—"

"A dead girlfriend." His face flushed bloody and mottled but he ran right over my interruption.

"A good job with a respected real-estate company and a position on the planning board."

"Which you've sold out." He didn't seem to care.

"Well, what if I have? That's life, you know, life and business."

"You're a rat, Hellman, a rat, a whiner and a sellout. And a woman's dead because of you." He didn't hear me or care that time either.

"I thought it would work out, but Lorie doesn't like me now. Everything I've worked so hard for is slipping away. Everything. And I won't have it." His voice rose again.

I shrugged. "The 'This Is Your Life' routine is touching, but I could care less. Let's get to the point. I've had enough coffee and your company bores me." I didn't have a watch to look at or I would have. I don't wear one, never have.

"I want to make it right again." I waited. "Lorie said she'd leave me if I didn't. Look, if I tell you everything can you keep me out of it? The company said they'd transfer me to another state. We could get another house, another pool. Lorie said she'd leave me if I didn't." He was starting to babble.

"Tell me."

"And you'll keep me out of it?"

"I don't know, I can't promise anything. I'll do my best."

"Lorie said—"

"I know. Talk."

"More coffee?" The waitress smiled and held up the coffee pot invitingly. In the background plants waved in the air conditioning and the dust resettled.

Hellman jumped and knocked over his empty cup. Caffeine and stress overload—obviously he didn't need any more. I nodded. She poured me a cup and left.

"Not here," he hissed, "not now."

"Why not? Let's get it over with."

"No." He paused. "And anyway I don't have everything with me. I've got documentation. I'll give it all to you," he said, now an eager, fresh-faced little Porky Pig. "Names, dates, amounts, everything. Everything. Lorie said—"

I sighed. "I know. When?"

He wasn't listening. "Everything. I—"

"When, Hellman?"

He stopped. "Later."

"Where? Here?"

"No, oh God no, not twice in a row, not here. I'm afraid, you know. They won't like it but Lorie said—" He broke off, reached into his pocket for a card and scribbled an address on the back. "It's—you just go out—uh . . ."

"I can find it. What time?"

"Four. Be there at four. And come alone. You promise?"

"Cross my heart and hope to die." He looked at me suspiciously. I smiled.

"Okay, four. See you." He got up and stumbled away from the booth.

"Hellman."

"Huh?"

"You forgot to pay for the coffee. It's your party."

"Oh." He took a couple of ones out and tossed them on the table. The waitress came by with the coffeepot so I had another cup that I didn't need and thought about the situation. It made some sense but it didn't add up.

Dear Charity,
What do you think about all the nonsmoking areas? They're
not really fair to us smokers.

Addicted

Dear Addicted,
Who cares? I think they're great.
Charity

I had nothing better to do for the next couple of hours so I
decided to check things out. Looking at the map told me that the
address Hellman had given me was in an exclusive part of town.
Driving there made it definite. They weren't houses out there,
they were estates, with huge lots, some of them with walls or
wrought-iron fences. The one I was looking for had no walls but
plenty of landscaping. It also had a Sagebrush Realty sign
announcing it was For Sale planted in the front lawn.

It was an imposing white house set well back on the lot and it looked empty. No curtains, no tricycles, no garden hoses. It was a good place for a clandestine meeting, a good place for a hunter, but not for the hunted.

I got out of the car and walked up to it, gazing around in an interested manner like the prospective buyer I wasn't. I checked out the house, tried to get a feeling for the inside layout, and walked the grounds. Houses have yards, estates have grounds. There was a fountain, a koi pond, a rose garden and shrubbery. No pool. The garden was pleasing but old-fashioned, the kind that takes a lot of money and work to keep up.

I took mental snapshots of it all, then lined up the pictures on the pages of my mind. Later I could flip back and forth and pick out the ones I needed, if I needed them. Then I drove out of the neighborhood by a different route. I'd learned the hard way that it's a good idea to have several exit visas. It was a lesson I'd only needed to learn once and didn't want to repeat.

It was one o'clock by the time I got back to the house. I headed for the refrigerator and made a tomato, avocado, onion and cheese with mayo on rye, then shoveled it in with a glass of ice tea on the side. The wolf in my belly went back to his cage. I changed into my suit and went out to the pool to do a few laps, holding my cast out of the water. I've been told since I was a child: "Always wait an hour after eating," and "Never, never, never swim alone." But I did, and I didn't die. There was satisfaction in that. Afterward I lay in the sun grilling my epidermis and courting melanoma when the phone rang. I didn't recognize the voice at first, which is unusual for me. Nerves, fear, and excitement change a voice's tone and timbre.

"Kat Colorado?"

"Yes."

"It's me, you know, uh—"

I snapped to it. "Steve Hellman."

"Don't say it, for God's sake!"

"Calm down, Steve, and tell me what's up."

He moaned. "Please. Oh God. Look, I can't make it at four.

Nine-thirty tonight instead. Everything else is the same. Don't tell anyone. Come alone. Oh God."

He hung up on me. It was hard to imagine anyone less suited to the cloak-and-dagger aspects of life. I considered the time change. At nine-thirty it would be dark. Then I debated telling Hank and Joe—while backup would be helpful, interference would not. I called Hank and left a message. I left a note for Joe too, explicit but not detailed, and then I decided to scram before everyone caught up with me and the interference started.

I dressed sensibly, my new white pants, a navy blue T-shirt top and Nikes. If I'd had dark pants I would have worn them, on the easier-to-sneak-around-in-after-dark theory. I left my purse at home, stuffing the few things I'd need into my pockets. I tucked my .38 Smith and Wesson Chief Special into the waistband of my pants, then bagged my large-size T-shirt over it. At five I left the house and went in search of a meal. I wasn't that hungry but I figured it was a good idea. A lot of things are better done on a full stomach. After that I went to the library for a couple of hours and tried to read. When it was time to go I was still on the same page.

I had no trouble finding the place again. Out of habit I parked the car down the block and walked. Nobody was around to see me, or to wonder about me slipping through the shrubbery, where first I listened, then I prowled. Everything looked just as it had that afternoon. Nobody was on the grounds, I was certain of that, and reasonably certain that the house was clear too. I settled down out of sight in a clump of bushes to wait for Hellman.

He was late, nervous, and alone. Either he hadn't seen my car or hadn't recognized it. I watched him pace on the porch for a while and then slid out of the bushes and across the lawn to meet him. He didn't hear me coming and jumped and twitched when I called out.

"Holy shit!"

"Aw, shucks, I bet you say that to everyone."

"You scared me. What the hell do you think you're doing sneaking up on me?"

"I wasn't sneaking. Why are you whispering?"

"I'm not whispering," he whispered.

I shrugged. "Okay. Give me the stuff. Let's get it over with."

"Not here. Inside. We're supposed to be viewing the house." I hesitated. It was smarter to stay out in the open. "Inside where no one can see, not here on the porch with all these lights. Come on."

What the hell, I thought, humor the paranoid delusions of a coward. He stepped up to the front door and fumbled in his pocket for the key, almost dropping the manila envelope he had under his arm. Finally he managed to swing the door open.

"After you." He tried to be gracious but didn't quite make it. I stepped in and knew right away.

I heard nothing and saw nothing, but I smelled the cigarette smoke, fresh, not stale, and close. I ducked and twisted, tried to scramble out the door. I didn't make it. A thick arm wound around me, pinning my arms to my side and straightening me up. Another arm closed around my neck. The door slammed shut on Hellman's white and frightened face.

I was conscious of a rough sleeve and the acrid smell of tobacco smoke as it filled my nostrils. The smell faded as hands slipped around my neck, cutting off air and life. Lights sparkled in front of my eyes and then it started going dark. I clawed at the implacable hands at my throat with no effect. This is my last breath, I thought, and it's cigarette smoke.

What a bummer.

Single guy wants fun gal for good times. Must love sports and have sense of humor. Aries preferred. Reply box 2002.

"Goddamn, Katy, why didn't you say something? I almost . . . I could have . . . why didn't you say something?"

"I couldn't," I croaked. "You were choking me."

"Oh. Yeah."

A wave of nausea washed over me. I put my hands on the thick pile carpet where I sat, slowly lowered myself down and waited for it to pass. Deep slow breaths, I thought, and filled my lungs with blessed air. The pile pressing against my cheek was soft and rough at the same time and I marveled at it. I breathed in the sharp, chemical scent of rug shampoo and marveled at that, too. Everything was a marvel, life especially.

"Are you all right, Katy?" The voice was worried, concerned, tender, even.

"Almost. Maybe you could get me a glass of water."

"Oh. Yeah, sure." He padded off. I heard the sound of steps

and then running water. I still felt sick but it would pass. I was okay. I was alive. I heard his footsteps coming back and then his voice.

"How did you know? You did, didn't you, you tried to get away?"

"I smelled the cigarette smoke. I'm not a smoker, Deck."

"Yeah, I forgot about that. That was stupid. Can you sit up? Come on in here."

He helped me up and led me into the living room where we sat on a window seat in a bay window. I sipped my water slowly. The chlorination was heavy and I could smell coffee residue in the styrofoam cup. It didn't matter. I was alive.

"Why, Deck?"

"I didn't know it was you."

"Why anyway?"

"Boss's orders."

"That's what you do?"

He twisted his big hands, lit a cigarette, and wouldn't look at me.

"Yeah, that's what I do. Some of it, anyway." I digested that.

"Why me?"

"I don't know the specifics since I didn't know it was you. But you're still here in Vegas—you didn't clear out and go home like I told you—and that means you've been kicking up dirt and making trouble?" He looked at me and I nodded. That's what it meant, all right. "That's reason enough right there."

"The boss?"

"Don Blackford. Want some more water, Kat? You don't look so good."

"Not now. Where's the bathroom?" He pointed.

"Want help?"

"I'll be okay." And I was, after I threw up twice and bathed my face in cool water. I rinsed out my mouth and wished I had some aspirin and Tums and, what the hell, I wished my childhood friend wasn't a killer. I sat on the toilet seat for a while with my head in my hands before I went back out and joined Deck in the window seat. He had another glass of water for me and a flask.

"What is it?"

"Cognac. Drink some." I did and I remembered Alice in Wonderland drinking from the bottle labeled, "Drink Me," little knowing her reality was going to change. Mine wasn't, whatever I wished, or drank. Deck put an arm around me and hugged. I leaned gratefully into his bulk and warmth but the smell of cigarettes made me feel sick again.

"Got any Life Savers, Deck?"

"Gum." He fished around in his pocket and handed me a package of bubble gum. I fired up two slices and masticated and thought. It's easier for me to think while chewing. I can understand why cows have that peaceful look on their dumb bovine faces as they chew their cud.

"You've burned your bridges now, haven't you?"

"What?"

"When I don't show up dead you're in for it."

"Yeah."

"What are you going to do?"

"Leave town. Start over."

"Can you do that?"

"Sure. Why not?"

"I mean, can you get away with it?"

"Done it before."

I blew some bubbles and popped them. The first and second weren't much but the third was impressive. I looked into its pink opalescence and tried to read the future. It popped too soon.

"Tell me about the overall structure, Deck."

"What about it? You pretty well got it taped out, Kat. New Capital Ventures was set up to launder money in a real-estate scheme. Then they needed a couple of areas rezoned so that was set up, too."

"Sam Collins?"

"He lost his cool and threatened to blow the cover, so he had to go."

"The hit and run?" Deck's eyebrows went up as I explained.

"I don't know for sure, it's not my department, but I'd say that was set up, too. Kill you, or warn you off. Either way it'd work."

"But the woman and child?"

Deck shrugged. "You try not to, but it happens." He was twisting his hands again. The knuckles cracked. I reached for the cognac and slugged some down.

"What about Ollie?"

"Ollie?"

"Ollie Bremmer, the foreman at Trainor Construction."

"What about him?"

"Did he . . . was he the one who . . ." my words stumbled off.

"No, he's not with us. Trainor. It was Trainor." I was glad about that.

"Then there's Hellman."

"Yeah. He's on the payroll. He set you up today." I nodded. It was the most likely possibility. I should have paid more attention there, bad call on my part.

"And the dead girl?" Silence. "In the bathroom."

"What about her?"

I thought about things. "Was that you?"

"Yeah." His knuckles cracked. I remembered the kitten from long ago. "Kat, hey, I don't think about it like that. It's just a job that needs doing."

I tried not to think of it like that, too, but I couldn't. She was so young. I could still see the dark hair and the red blood spilling across the white tile floor. And I could have been dead, face purple and eyes bugging out. I'm pretty young, too.

"How did you do it? Wasn't it risky in a public bathroom?"

He shrugged. "Nah, I slapped an out-of-order sign on the door. I followed her in. I had a raincoat and gloves on for the blood and it doesn't take long to slit a throat. When I left I took the sign off the door. It was easy." There was a note of pride in his voice at a job well done. I shivered inside and took another sip of cognac. Then I blew a bubble.

"Did you know her name or anything about her?"

"No. It wasn't important. That stuff doesn't count."

"Did she?"

"What? Count?"

"Yes."

"No."

I blew another bubble. "Are you leaving tonight?" I asked finally. There didn't seem to be anything else to say.

"Yeah."

"We'd better go." We stood up.

"Back door, back way."

"Okay." I didn't question it, and I followed Deck. I had no problem believing that he knew the layout better than I did. Not that it mattered now, except for what the neighbors would think, and I didn't imagine they would notice.

Deck unlocked the door and we slipped out. I shut it behind me and heard the latch click into place. For a moment we were dark silhouettes against the light house and then Deck started to move. I didn't recognize the popping sound at first.

"Fuck!" Deck grabbed me by the wrist and jerked me away from the house and into some bushes. Branches lashed across my face as he hauled me to the ground. Crouched over, he moved rapidly behind the cover of a long, dense hedge. I followed. We made no noise. Neither did the other guy. The gun hadn't made much either.

"Who is it?" I barely breathed the words into Deck's ear as we paused; I pulled my gun out of my waistband.

"One of Blackford's boys."

"Why?"

"Backup man in case I fuck up. Boss must have had his eye on me."

"How many?"

"One is standard. Have you got a gun?"

"Yes."

"Will you use it?"

"Yes."

We were silent for a while, then I felt Deck's hand on mine. He pushed a stone into my hand. "When I start to move throw this over there." He indicated the direction we had just come from. "Wait a moment, then follow the hedge down to the street and get the hell out of here."

"No."

"Yes. This is mine—my life and my business. You've got a broken arm, you're a liability. Get the hell out of here. I can take care of it."

Deck's hand squeezed my wrist and he slipped off. For a big guy he moved quickly and quietly. I heaved the stone, then I started moving along the hedge. I was quiet but I damned the white pants and the cast. The moon was half full and high enough to throw plenty of light. Parts of me gleamed dully if anyone was watching. I hoped no one was.

Dear Charity,
   What do you think of someone who's a day late and a dollar short?

                                                            Danny

Dear Danny,
   Same thing you do. Not much.
                              Charity

It seemed to take forever, dentist-chair time I call it—when minutes are hours, hours are days, and everything is frozen and abandoned in the tyranny of time, like shrimp in aspic. The temptation to hurry is a fatal one and I resisted it, but it was hard. We were in a waiting-and-watching game, two of us and one of him. He had a gun. So did Deck. So did I. So it was a dangerous game. It would have gone on a lot longer except for the dog.

   It was small; a fluffy, white, fussy-old-lady dog, and it took a dislike to me. A loud one. "Mopsy!" I heard someone calling and whistling. I heard, Mopsy didn't. When I moved it followed, barking all the way. The barks ended suddenly on a high-pitched scream—I hadn't known dogs could scream—and a dull thunk kind of sound. Mopsy went sailing into the bushes like a punted football. I took off too, but in another direction.

"Keep moving and you're dead." There was something about the voice that made a believer out of me. I stopped. My back was to him and I was in the shadows. Slowly I raised my gun hand.

"Drop the gun or I blast you." The same something was in his voice. I dropped the gun.

"Turn around." I did. A short skinny man dressed in dark clothes moved into my line of vision.

"Get over here." I stared stupidly at him. "Do it." He snarled and waved the gun at me. I did it. He came up next to me and grabbed my right arm, holding it tightly. The best thing would have been to twist an arm behind my back but he couldn't. The gun was in his right hand and my left arm was in a cast.

"Don't fuck with me," he snarled, "your life ain't worth shit." His body odor was overpowering, making me gag, making me want to throw up again. He walked me out to a small area of lawn near the koi pond where we stood on the edge of a dappled moonlit patch. Body Odor stood behind me and held me closely.

"You've got five seconds to come out or I off the bitch," he announced in a low, steady voice. My mouth went dry and I started working the gum again. Dentist-chair time resumed.

"Let her go, Harry, it's between you and me." Deck's voice came from the side and behind us. Harry slowly pivoted so we faced Deck. I could just make out his outline in the shadows. Harry laughed or made a noise that, for him, passed as a laugh. "Fat fucking chance. You can leave, I got no beef with you. The broad stays."

I chewed my gum frantically and thought at the same speed. I didn't think he was going to let either of us go and I bet Deck read it that way, too.

"I ain't leaving, Harry."

"Deck—" I croaked.

"Shaddup," Harry snarled and wrenched my arm.

"Let the girl go."

"She don't go."

"Then you got to take me on, too, Harry, and I'm not so easy to take." Deck's voice was soft and menacing. I wanted to believe in the truth of his words.

"I'll do it. Whatever I got to do, I'll do it." I could feel Harry tensing behind me, a cat ready to move. I snapped my gum loud enough to startle anyone who was already nervous—all of us—and then I collapsed, folded up like a card table and went down. I was dead weight and Harry a little guy. He let me go, he had no choice. I heard Deck's gun go off as I folded. Maybe Harry thought I was out of it, that Deck had shot and caught me instead of him. It didn't matter. You don't have time to figure things out in split seconds with guns around. Gut reactions count for more.

Harry started to move. I rolled half a turn and slugged him in the kneecaps with my cast hard enough to mess him up and send shudders of pain up my arm and through my body. He choked back a scream, but barely, and even that must have cost him. Deck shot again and so did Harry. I kept rolling. Then it was silent. I couldn't see Deck and it worried me. Harry was tumbled on the lawn in the moonlight looking strangely peaceful and benign.

"Kat." Deck stepped out of the shadows. "You all right?"

"I'm all right." I struggled to my feet, my arm throbbing, my mind playing "Hard Day's Night." That ended and the "Moonlight Sonata" started. Somewhere, farther away, someone was still calling for Mopsy. "I think," I added, muttering to myself, "I think I'm all right."

Inside my head someone started reciting "*Mary had a little lamb* . . ." It was a six-year-old in a pinafore, chanting sweetly, tapping her foot lightly to keep time. Time. "*Hickory, dickory, dock* . . ." she said. Time moved slowly still. Behind me I heard a noise. I knew what it was without looking but I looked anyway. I hollered to Deck at the same time.

"*Jack be nimble, Jack be quick* . . ." the little girl in the starched pinafore in my mind said.

Harry was on his knees, his gun in his hand. The little girl stopped reciting. "Deck be quick," I said, maybe out loud, maybe in my mind. I couldn't tell anymore. Deck and Harry shot at the same time. Harry sagged to the ground again. Deck fell in the moonlight and didn't seem to be moving. I ran. I tried to, everything still seemed to be in slow motion. Why the hell didn't Mopsy's owner call the police? Deck was half on his knees, half crouching, one hand on the ground, the other pushed into the bloody mess on his chest.

"Deck, lie down. Let me stop the bleeding, then I'll get an ambulance." I was calm now, Chopin's Funeral March played in my head.

"It's too late, Kat." I knew he was right but I couldn't give up.

"I'm going for help."

"Don't leave me, Kat. A friend. Katy, I need a friend."

I sat on the lawn and held Deck in my arms. There was blood everywhere now. My arms were slippery with it. Deck's breathing was heavy and labored. Through it I heard another noise. Harry was up again, the thug who wouldn't die. His gun was in his hand and it wavered and wobbled as he pointed it in my direction. I picked up Deck's .45 and blew him away.

Dead at 88, George Stoddard, in the caring arms of his family. He will be remembered by all with love. No flowers; prayers joyfully received.

I don't know what you say to someone who is dying, whose life is measured in minutes, maybe seconds. I didn't know then, I don't know now. I've never done it before, and I hope to God I never do it again.

"When I met you at the airport—"

"Yes."

"Not an accident. Assignment. Word had gotten out after your calls to Vegas. Supposed to keep an eye on you, take care of the problem." I held him and the blood slipped away, more than I had ever imagined. "Friends. Friendship was stronger."

"Thanks, Deck, thanks for being my friend."

"Katy, what's in a Brave Bull?"

"Tequila and Kaluha." I was crying.

"Don't be tore up, Katy. It was going to be. You die the way you live." He was quiet for what seemed like a long time. "Katy?" I nodded, crying hard now.

"Katy, you there? I can't see anything."

"I'm here, Deck." I held on to him tightly. "Katy, tell Ma—" And he died. I would tell her, but not in Deck's words, they'd have to be mine. I held Deck for a little longer, saying good-bye to a friend. "Vaya con Dios," I whispered into ears that couldn't hear me.

I slid Deck's weight off my lap and stood up. My white pants were covered with blood, my arms and cast, too. I walked over to the fish pond and washed myself off as best I could. Harry lay there but I didn't look at him, just went past like a horse with blinders. In the moonlight one of his hands trailed in the pond. A koi nibbled at it. I noticed that as I walked away.

Dear Charity,

When is it polite to go home? I have a friend whom I visit
out of duty. We have dinner once a month and by the end of
the evening I am so frustrated I am ready to scream. What is
the earliest I can leave?

Frazzled

Dear Frazzled,

Not before dessert. Why don't you go to a movie instead?

Charity

After a while you reach a point where your system can't take any
more: your mind can't assimilate it; your emotions are deadened;
your body is depleted by stress and shock. I'd reached that point
as I walked through the grounds toward the street. I'd run out of
coping mechanisms on every level.

The street was empty and peaceful. Mopsy's person had found

her or given up. I moved into the cold light that street lamps make, put my arm around the lamp post and leaned my cheek and breast against its chill surface. I would walk up to a house, any house, and tell them to call the police. I would as soon as I could. Probably I wouldn't even have to say anything about the police. They would look at me, see the blood on my clothes, and call.

Somewhere in the distance I could hear the scream of sirens. Perhaps the police were already on the way. Harry's gun and Deck's .45 had made noise. It was hard to believe that no one had heard, even with big yards and closed-up houses and air conditioners. Behind me a car door opened.

"Get in," a gruff voice said. I didn't bother to turn around.

"Who are you?" I asked finally, holding on more tightly to the lamp post for the comfort that wasn't there.

"Blackford's insurance policy. Get in."

"They're both dead."

"Yeah. I was late. And he should've handled it okay."

"I'm not dead, why?"

"You were supposed to be. That was orders. Orders is also to bring in anyone still around. That's you."

I shook my head, trying to clear it. "Leave me be. Tell him he's made his point and he won't have any more trouble with me."

"No dice. The boss wants you, he gets you."

"The boss? Who? Blackford?"

"Get in."

He was behind me now and close. I still hadn't turned around. It didn't matter, there was no fight left in me. I let go of the street lamp and slowly pivoted, the lamp post at my back. He had a gun, but he didn't need it. My reserves were long gone.

"Jesus, you look worse than my cousin Lew after a hog slaughtering."

He looked annoyed, not bothered by it. The sirens came closer. I thought about stalling for time, or having it out right there—it didn't seem to matter much. Time crawled again; the music in my head had stopped. Then the sirens, still a long way away, stopped. I let out my breath slowly, not realizing until then I'd been holding it.

"Get in. I'll break your other arm, or your fingers, or whatever it takes, but you'll go." He said unreasonable words in a reasonable tone. I got in.

The car was a late-model blue LeBaron with pale blue upholstery. He winced when I got blood on the seat. A discombobulated voice in the dashboard advised us firmly and kindly to put on our seat belts. He did, I didn't. Concern about my health and safety seemed irrelevant. I settled back and smeared some blood on the door upholstery. It gave me a perverse sense of satisfaction.

The automatic locks thunked into place. The sound reminded me of movies where the prison door slams; you, the prisoner, and everyone in the theater know that it is over, that now it is hopeless. I felt the hopelessness engulf me and I was too tired to fight it, too drained to care or even be afraid. I was lethargic and cold and recognized the symptoms of shock. My arm throbbed painfully.

I leaned back against the seat, smearing more blood, I hoped, and made myself breathe deeply and evenly, then did yoga exercises. I needed the time to pull it together, to bring myself out of shock and get ready for what was coming next. Because I was sure a lot was coming. It wasn't going to be nice and it was going to be soon.

The exercises worked. I got so relaxed I almost fell asleep and was floating in a silver haze with white clouds when I realized the car had stopped. I had time for one more deep breath and then the driver ordered me out. Ostensibly he invited me, but I was past kidding myself.

Someone, a maid presumably, although she could have been a small linebacker, answered the door. She was six feet tall and muscular, and she had a dark, wild, Latin beauty about her. I was shown into an elegant front room. The maid stared at me—not surprisingly, I was a sight—and did not invite me to be seated on the immaculate fawn-colored damask that the living room furniture was upholstered in. I sat anyway. I was still damp with blood and, with any luck, could leave some nice smears. I did my best in that department and then waited calmly enough.

After a bit I strolled over to an imposing set of French doors that opened onto a terrace. I expected them to be locked but the handles yielded readily and the doors opened at a touch. I had started to step out when a stage-left movement caught my eye and a black streak metamorphosed into a Doberman who didn't care for my company on the terrace. 0 for 1. I stepped back into the room and closed the door.

"Ah, Ms. Colorado, Kat, may I say. It is so nice to see you, so nice that you could be my guest for dinner."

I snorted, rather inelegantly.

"I see you have had a busy and eventful day. Perhaps you would care to freshen up first?"

I shook my head, "Let's cut the bullshit, Blackford, and get to the point."

He looked at me sadly. "My dear," he demurred, "how unlike you to be so lacking in the social graces." Blackford crossed the room and rang the bell. "Please call me Don."

I laughed again. It had a hollow ring even to me. "I don't think so. It implies an informality or a friendship that is conspicuously lacking." The maid entered.

"Phoebe, will you show Ms. Colorado to the room that has been prepared for her so that she may freshen up and dress for dinner." Phoebe, who definitely looked more like a linebacker than a songbird, stared at me bleakly.

"This way, Miss."

I shrugged and followed her. I was not the one calling the shots. The sight of myself in the bedroom mirror was a shock and I looked away quickly. I could see why Phoebe had stared. I knew what I looked like but only in pieces: my cast, my pants, my shirt. The total picture was something else. I had gotten most of the blood off my arms but there was a smear on my cheek and my hair was dried and matted with it in several places. It made me feel sick again.

"If you will leave your things out here, Miss, I will see that they are cleaned and pressed. There is a selection of clothing in the closet." She pointed to a large walk-in closet with closed doors. "Please help yourself. Mr. Blackford requests that you join him for cocktails and dinner as soon as you are ready." She said his name in tones generally reserved for royalty or deity. "I will leave you now, Miss, and come back shortly for your soiled things." She padded softly across the carpeted floor and let herself out.

As I loosened the laces of my Nikes, blood flaked off and sifted into the impeccable white pile of the carpet. I toed the shoes off, quickly stepped out of my pants and yanked off the T-shirt, letting things fall where they might. My underwear was stained too, but I wore it into the bathroom.

I locked the door first thing. It gave me a feeling of security and safety, wholly false but momentarily comforting. I stripped my underwear off and put it in the basin with cold water. Then, naked and shivering, I scrubbed and rinsed them until they were spotless and rolled them up in the hand towel.

I turned on the shower as hard and hot as I could stand and stepped in. The smell of blood, hot and metallic, came off my body as the water hit me. It rose in the shower assaulting me. I leaned my arms high against the shower wall and retched in long dry heaves. Finally the smell died and my body quieted.

There were numerous choices of shampoos, soaps, and lotions, and I covered every inch of me with them until I felt cleansed, except for my cast—a mute and ugly reminder. Then I stood in the shower and let the water pound down on my back for a good ten minutes—soaking up negative ions, trying to banish the ugliness and clear my mind. Easier said than done.

Reluctantly I turned off the water and stepped from the shower. I wrapped myself in a large towel and plugged the hair dryer in. First I dried my underwear and put it on, feeling better and more secure immediately. Then I fluff-dried my hair and put on some blush. I needed the color, my own at the moment was a not-very-becoming shade of pale. I was in no hurry certainly. Let

Blackford stew; I planned to meet what lay before me with dignity, style, and grace.

That's what I thought, but that was before I saw the clothes. Someone had gone shopping at the equivalent of Frederick's of Hollywood, Paris, and Hong Kong. I could choose to look like an American, French, or Chinese whore, and not a high-class one at that. I sat on the bed in my J.C. Penney's white cotton underwear and contemplated my options joylessly.

The overall picture did not escape me. Dressed like a whore I would feel, if not like a whore, at least diminished. It's a well-used tactic, probably because it's so effective. I would have preferred putting on my own clothes, bloodstained as they were, but that was no longer an option. Only a rust-colored spot graced the place where they had been.

I decided on Chinese. The cheongsam was tight and form-fitting with slits up the thigh but at least it nominally covered me. I looked around in vain for a wrap and found none. What I did find was a serviceable pair of scissors in a small sewing kit. With them I hacked out a huge triangular shawl from the ornate, white (and very pricey) double bedspread. Using a corner for the short sides of the triangle, I even had fringe. I twirled it around and dropped it across my shoulders. Not bad at all. The effect was Victorian Chinese and it made me look adequately dressed and somewhat elegant. More to the point, it made me feel in control.

I stepped out of the bedroom into the hall where Phoebe was hovering in a holding pattern waiting for me. Her eyes widened in surprise at the sight of my shawl but she said nothing. Maybe she was a maid after all, linebackers are usually more talkative. We retraced our steps, she leading the way with a long, lithe stride and I following. *"Will you walk into my parlor," said the spider to the fly,* played through my mind and dampened my spirits.

The house was sumptuous, tasteful, and sterile, revealing nothing about the personality of its owner, nothing other than that he was rich. I found it oppressive. The silence was loud as our feet sank noiselessly into two-inch-pile carpeting. There were no clocks ticking, no sound of the cooling system, no blender whirring or TV murmuring in the background. Nothing. Just silence and the graceful figure stalking along in front of me.

"In here please, Miss." She opened a door and I entered. The door closed behind me as I faced the stage set before me.

Dear Charity,
 How important is the proper dress for an occasion?
                                        Tupelo Tom

Dear Tom,
 How important is it to you to be courteous and feel comfortable?

                                        Charity

The room was clearly a library. Books, the kind that are only looked at, not read, lined two windowless walls. A large wooden desk, set diagonally across one corner, dominated one end of the room. The other end was taken up by an imposing manteled fireplace with an informal grouping of easy chairs and a love seat. The room was dark and somber with the dreariness of an old-fashioned funeral parlor.

"*Will you walk into my parlor,*" *said the spider to the fly.* I thought it again before I could stop myself. I'm still working on affirmative thinking as an everyday technique.

Blackford laughed when he saw me. I gave him credit for that. "You improvised, I see."

"I don't think much of your taste in women's clothing. It runs to cheap hooker and is definitely not my style."

His eyes flashed but the smile stayed in place.

"Not cheap, actually."

"No? I'm sure it was the look you were after and damn the cost."

"Exactly." His smile changed. "I like my women sensual and sexy."

I shrugged. "I'm not your woman, so shall we get on with it? You didn't bring me here to discuss fashion."

"No, though you look fetching indeed. Except for the bedroom slippers," he added on a note of disapproval. "Why?"

We both looked at the pink satin mules with fluffy tops that were the best of the bedroom shoe lot. They didn't compliment the sleek black-and-green cheongsam I wore by a long shot.

"I didn't care for high heels and your maid took my sneakers. It was this or nothing."

"Ah. Would you like a cocktail before dinner?"

"No."

"No? But you will indulge me." It was not a question so I didn't bother answering. "And you will forgive me, no doubt, if I stick to my usual schedule."

Unasked I crossed the room and sank down in a large elegant easy chair in front of an intense fire. It had been 108 today, but in this room the overall temperature was, I guessed, about 62. The warmth of the fire was welcome, if strange.

"I'm fond of fires, another whim I like to indulge."

I shrugged, past caring about his whims and eccentricities.

He picked up a bottle of champagne from a cooler and lovingly uncorked it. "Ah. Fine wine and fine women. May I pour you a glass?" He proceeded to do so.

I sat there absentmindedly picking my nose. I did not like all his talk about "fine wine and women," or about the way he "liked his women." Picking one's nose is a small, but a crude and disgusting thing. It is repellent to most of us, to our sense of manners and presumably to our romantic and sexual sensibilities. Blackford looked astounded and repulsed. I smiled.

"How very unladylike!"

"I don't pretend to be a lady."

"Just a private investigator," he said scornfully as he handed me my wine. I wiped my hand on the chair arm before I took the wine and watched him wince.

"Exactly."

The control had shifted. I no longer felt remotely like a captive whore and he no longer saw me as one.

"You sent your boys to kill me today?"

"Yes, you were—however delightful—becoming a nuisance. I will not tolerate interference in business matters." He sat down and then leaned forward toward me. "I changed my mind when I learned that Deck and Harry were both dead, presumably at your hands. I was impressed; I wanted to know more about you then."

"Why did you send Harry out after Deck?"

"Several reasons. One, I had my doubts about Deck. He's been on you ever since you flew in, you know."

"I know. What put you on to me, the phone calls?"

He nodded. "You mentioned New Capital Ventures. It came back to me through channels I'd set up. Routinely I put someone on to check it out. That someone was Deck. Too bad—he was a good member of my team. I've never seen him lose it over a woman before, although there is something about you, I admit. Don't," he added hastily as I scratched my nose.

"Not over a woman, over a friend." I fought to keep my feelings under control. I couldn't think about Deck, or mourn him now, and I wanted to live long enough to do both. Blackford stared at me uncomprehendingly.

"We were childhood friends. We fought side by side and bailed each other out, went swimming and fishing in the Sacramento

River and ate hotdogs and watermelon until we got sick. We go back a long way."

"Ah." Blackford nodded. "That explains it. I felt Deck's allegiance had shifted. It wasn't like him, so I watched. I was right as it turned out. He was no longer reliable, he didn't kill you."

"No, and he died for it."

"When a man doesn't follow orders he's expendable."

"And Harry? Was he expendable too?"

He shrugged. "Of course. I'm a businessman. I take my losses, but I like to win. Winning is what counts. Surely you agree?"

"Yes and no. I play to win, but I don't play dirty."

"Deck played fair for the first time in a long time, and he's dead."

"So is Harry, and he played dirty to the end." We paused. It was a Mexican standoff on the philosophical front.

"I have a proposal for you."

"No."

He smiled. "You haven't heard it yet."

"I don't have to. Slime begets slime." I took a sip of wine and held the glass up watching the fire dance through its clear, golden beauty. "The wine is good. Even you can't sour that."

"I knew you were a worthy opponent." As he laughed exultantly and gulped at his wine his eyes glittered in the firelight. Drugs maybe, madness possibly. I did not care for either thought. "You will not consider joining me in business? You are formidable, the intelligence, the spirit—"

"You're wasting your time, Blackford." With an effort he pulled his mind back from the regions where it traveled and resumed the everyday charm and ease. His eyes still glittered.

"Then I must convince you." He said it softly and drew the last *c* out in a sibilant hiss.

"You're wasting your time."

"More champagne?" He topped off my glass and refilled his. "Wasting time? I think not. I am very persuasive. You met Phoebe. Her name was Carmelita once, and she was fiery, voluble, hot-tempered, and passionate. It was I who retrained her; I took my time and did it well. I am very persuasive," he repeated. "The drugs helped," he added as an afterthought.

"And then I changed her name. She was not a Carmelita anymore but a Phoebe, a quiet, dusty brown little songbird, tamed and docile."

There was nothing about him that indicated madness, nothing but his eyes, windows into a soul that was lost in some lunatic wasteland. "A little songbird," he repeated softly.

"Except that she doesn't sing."

"You are wrong about that. At night she begs me, pleads for my attention. I have taught her to want what I give, all the more now for having refused it at first. And then she sings. Long into the night she sings and cries and begs, begs until I tire of her. She cannot have enough now. I am master now."

I was appalled but he didn't notice.

"She was a difficult one to tame. The wild ones always are. The greater the challenge, the sweeter the victory."

He was aroused sexually, hard and swollen in the well-cut lines of his custom-made suit. I felt sick and afraid. I tried to push the fear down, looked away from his crotch and back to his eyes. They glittered and bulged now too, as though the imbalance in his mind had pushed everything out of place.

"You are wild too, not tame. It excites me, that thought, the thought of taming you." He rubbed the base of his hand across his crotch and licked his lips. "Yes, it excites me. Very much, very much indeed."

He turned, poured another glass of wine and stood in front of the fireplace. "It is not the sex, I would not have you think me so crude." He rubbed himself again. "No, it is the power, the joy of humbling another to my bidding that excites me."

I saw again the bent necks, the drooping ears and the glazed eyes of the horses Lefty had broken. The spirit in any living thing can be broken, sometimes to be mended again, sometimes not. Often not. There was a tap at the door and the maid entered.

"Ah, Phoebe, yes, what is it?"

"Dinner is ready, sir, will you have it served now?" She looked at him the whole time she spoke.

"Carmelita." I stood up. Surprised eyes focused on me. "It's Carmelita, isn't it?"

She looked at me for a long moment, then back at Blackford. "No, miss, it's Phoebe." She answered me looking at him.

"Thank you, Phoebe, you may serve." His voice was triumphant.

"Yes, sir." She left the room, gliding out noiselessly.

"You see?"

"You are a despicable human being," I said, and he laughed.

"We are playing for high stakes now, but the odds are even. It is you against me. Only Phoebe is here in the house and she will not interfere. You may not escape, the dogs will see to that. There is a man in the guardhouse outside as well. I will call him, Phoebe has instructions, too, if you force me to it. Otherwise it is you and me, your will against mine."

He smiled and extended an arm, his eyes glittering and wild. "Shall we go in to dinner?"

My full wine glass was in my hand. I flung it against the stone fireplace where it smashed, sending glass and droplets of wine everywhere.

His control slipped but did not break. He laughed again. Then we went in to dinner.

Dear Charity,
  In the office at work some people have given a girl a very cruel nickname. She is a good sport about it and pretends to think it's funny, but I know she is really hurt. What should I do?

  T.R.

Dear T.R.,
  Everyone has a right to be called by the name or nickname they choose. Ask her what she wants to be called and call her that. Perhaps others will follow.

  Charity

I declined his arm but followed him into the dining room. I would not advance my cause by pushing him to call in reinforcements. I had little time and energy and I needed to use what I had well.

For I was under no illusions. He was playing with me tonight, but by tomorrow I would be willing or dead. Perhaps Carmelita had been without friends and family, or they were powerless, easily duped. He had had time there. My friends would be looking for me by tomorrow, if not before. Blackford was playing a dangerous game with me and undoubtedly he knew it. Undoubtedly it added to the spice. I was playing an even more dangerous game with him. I knew it and it did not add to anything. It scared the shit out of me.

The food was plentiful and excellent. I stoked up, needing the carbo boost, but drank nothing but water. Blackford ate little and drank fairly heavily. His eyes glittered more and more as the night went on. The maid waited on us.

He called her Phoebe and I called her Carmelita. I used her name in every breath and twice in every sentence. It got to her. She looked at me and her eyes had a hunted, haunted look about them. It got to him, too. There was anger in the glitter. When he started to dismiss her, I taunted him.

"Why, Blackford, aren't you sure of your training? Maybe not, maybe it's just talk." I lowered my voice so he had to strain to listen. "Maybe you're not so good after all." I laughed. "More water please, Carmelita. Carmelita, that's a beautiful name."

"My training is good. Before she was just a big, stupid, dirty Mexican girl. Now she is something."

"Is that right, Carmelita?" I asked quietly.

She looked mesmerized, clouds passing over her eyes and face. Her eyes met mine briefly and then dropped.

"Is he right, Carmelita?" I asked again. She looked at me. "Were you just a big, stupid, dirty Mexican girl?" I made a gesture with my hands as if to ask, Were you nothing?

"Nothing." Blackford echoed my gesture with the word. "Nothing. Just another dumb Mexican with no chance, no future."

"No." The word came out in a whisper as though someone had hit her in the diaphragm and forced it out. She looked from Blackford to me. Her eyes met mine and held.

"No, I was not dirty or dumb." Her voice was low; I leaned forward to catch the words. "I am big, yes," a little pride crept into her voice, "big and strong. My people and my past—they are good. In my family Carmelita is a proud name." Her eyes were defiant and then, suddenly, scared.

"It is Phoebe now," Blackford said firmly. Carmelita looked back and forth between us. I shook my head.

"Phoebe," he said again. Her eyes dropped in confusion, the clouds straying again across her face. He turned away as though she were scenery, scenery that didn't count.

"We must think of a name for you, too, my dear. Kat will never do. Such a name." He sniffed in aversion. "And anyway, you will be different, so very different," he finished softly. "Kat will not fit you anymore." I almost shivered, barely getting hold of myself.

"Phoebe, will you clear and serve the dessert."

She stood there a long time. He didn't notice. She was still scenery. Finally she moved and brought a platter of fresh fruit, and a gooey chocolate meringue confection and coffee. Blackford dismissed her with a wave of his hand and walked to the sideboard.

"Cognac?" I shook my head and selected a bunch of grapes. I ate them, pulling them off one by one, chewing them slowly. He poured a triple shot of brandy and resumed his seat. The alcohol seemed to be having no effect on him. Ignoring the fruit, he spooned a large amount of the dessert goo onto his plate.

"Soon," he said, "we will begin." I chewed a grape and stared at the ceiling. He wasn't talking about dessert. "Not back to the library," he said, almost to himself, "but to the game room." He smiled as he said game room. I chewed another grape. They were sweet and juicy and surprisingly difficult to swallow. I would make my move soon, I decided, not wait for the game room.

Blackford talked on, about brandy, and vintage, and life. I chewed my grapes meditatively and watched his eyes glitter. I worked on being inscrutable as I made plans, discarded them, remade them.

"Shall we, my dear?" He rose and extended his arm to me.

I started to rise, then sank back into my chair. "Damn, I've lost a slipper." I lifted the tablecloth and leaned sideways to peer under the table. I cried out then with a catch in my breath and slowly straightened. "I can't bend that way. It's because of the accident. Could you please—" My voice trailed off as I saw the frown on his face.

"It doesn't matter."

"Yes, it does." Suddenly it mattered terribly that I not have naked, vulnerable feet. "Please."

He frowned but pulled the chairs out and bent over to look. When his head was level with the table I hit him hard on the neck with the side of my hand. There is a spot there and with the appropriate pressure you can kill or disable a man. He hung motionless for a moment, then fell over. As he went down his left hand clutched spasmodically and caught the table linen. I saw what was going to happen but could not prevent it. In slow motion everything slid off the edge of the table. It made a god-awful mess; it made a god-awful noise.

I turned to face the dining-room door as it was flung open. Carmelita stood there, her arm across her breast, her fingers fluttering in the soft hollow of her throat.

"You must help me, Carmelita," I said softly. "We must work together." She stared at me dumbly, her fingers fluttering still, her eyes wide and motionless. I spoke to her quietly and soothingly, as one would to a frightened child, using her name over and over.

"You must tell no one." I said it three times. "I need you to bring me a knife or a pair of scissors. We must tie him up for a little while. Go and get that now." My voice was soft but it was a command. "Go now." I said it gently. There wasn't much time and I dared not leave Blackford. I dared not count on anything. "Go." She went.

He moved then with lizard-like suddenness. Silently I cursed myself—for thinking that the blow would put him out just because it seemed impossible for anyone to recover that quickly, for not killing him outright, for a long list of things I didn't have time to consider.

His hand fastened around my ankle and pulled. I went down, my knee aiming for a kidney, my hand chopping. He groaned and the grip on my ankle loosened, not much but enough. I rolled off and over and clambered gracelessly to my feet. The cheongsam had split from mid-thigh to waist.

Blackford was on his feet too, eyes glittering. He was a big man and strong. Even with the alcohol and the blow I was no match for him. I backed up to the sideboard and reached behind me. The brandy decanter was first. It sailed across the room and smashed into the wall. He ducked and I threw again, port maybe. He dodged that one, too. I'm fast and with two good arms I would have nailed him, but I had only one.

The last bottle I held onto. Cognac, V.S.O.P. I held it by the neck and balanced it lightly. I had a weapon and was the aggressor. The odds weren't even, but they'd improved. We circled each other warily. The grace and gentlemanly facade was gone now, his lips pulled back in an animal-like snarl. I could have won, I might have—he was rattled, he was weakened and drunk—but then I stepped into the chocolate goo. The odds shifted quickly and not, of course, in my favor.

I slipped sideways and he lunged. I caught myself but not in time. I slammed the bottle down. Hard, but not as hard as it should have been. He took it on the shoulder and grunted, grabbed my arm, twisted me around and held me pinned, my back to him. Slowly the pressure on my wrist forced my fingers to open. The bottle dropped uselessly from my hand onto the carpet. V.S.O.P. He growled and laughed into my ear.

"I love it. I love it when you fight. You're more than I hoped for." One arm was still tight around my body pinning my arms, the other caressed my breasts. "Much more." He laughed again. I couldn't see his eyes but the laughter glittered.

When the door opened slowly, quietly, I saw it first. He was still growling in my ear and touching my breasts. Carmelita advanced across the floor picking her way delicately through the debris. She held a long, slender, carbon steel knife, not up and at arm's length poised to slash but in both hands pointing out from the middle of her body. Her elbows were at her sides bracing her arms. Her eyes were determined. She was heading straight for me.

Blackford finally noticed. "Put it down, Phoebe," he said in command.

"My name is Carmelita and I am not a stupid, dirty Mexican girl. I will not listen to you anymore."

"Phoebe."

"Carmelita," she said proudly. "I am Mexican. I am not stupid or dirty."

"Put it down."

She advanced slowly, eyes on him.

"Carmelita!"

"Ah!" she cried out in vindication, and leapt. He flung me forward and into the path of the knife. I hit it aside with the cast and let the momentum of the swing carry my cast and body back. My arm struck Blackford in the belly hard enough to double him over. I slammed the cast down on the back of his head, pain ripping through my arm and body. Pleasure, too, at seeing him crumple. Then I couldn't see, pain and tears clouded my eyes. I heard Carmelita cry out and rush past me.

"Unh," she grunted, "unh, unh."

I willed the fog of pain to dissolve and wiped the back of my hand across my eyes.

"Unh, unh." She was stabbing him.

"Carmelita!"

"Unh."

I slapped her. In the face, hard. She stood up and looked blankly at me. The knife dropped from her hand. "He called me Phoebe."

I led her to a chair and sat her down. Then I retrieved the V.S.O.P, uncorked it, picked a water glass up from the floor and splashed a double shot in. I handed it over and told her to drink it. I waited while she did and then I walked into the kitchen.

There I opened and shut drawers until I found what I wanted, strapping tape and scissors. There was a cordless phone as well as a wall unit. I stuck the cordless under my arm.

Carmelita was where I'd left her. "Come and help me tie him." My cast arm was almost useless, a testimony to the amount of pain the human body can absorb and still minimally function. We taped his ankles and wrists together. On an afterthought I taped his mouth shut too. I poured a double shot of cognac for me, slugged half of it down and called the police.

I had a hard time, as I knew I would. I didn't have the number Hank had given me to call and they kept interrupting me with stupid questions, with procedure. The pain didn't make me patient.

"Look, listen to me because I'm only going to say it once. I'm a kidnap victim at Don Blackford's house." I gave the address. "There's another woman here, too. Same thing. Blackford is badly wounded. Send an ambulance. There's at least one man on guard on the grounds and he has access to the house. Assume he's armed and dangerous. There are attack dogs, Dobermans. Contact Detective Hank Parker, he knows what it's all about. Don't call me back, it could alert the guard." I hung up.

Carmelita and I sat stiffly in dining-room chairs set side by side. I held her hand and patted her knee and tried not to black out with the pain. We drank cognac. Once she got up and walked over to Blackford.

"My name is Carmelita. I am Mexican. I am not stupid and dirty," she said over and over. She kicked him in the gut, and in the face, and the mouth. I heard teeth breaking. I did nothing to stop her.

"It's Carmelita," she said, sitting down next to me.

I took her hand. "Yes, it's Carmelita."

It took the police forty-five minutes to get to us. It was a long forty-five minutes.

Dear Charity,
  What's the difference between dreams and nightmares?
                                                    Colin

Dear Colin,
  Dreams are hopes and chances and light. Nightmares are
fears and darkness.

                                                    Charity

The rest of that night was a painful blur. The police took me to
the hospital, which is where Hank found me. He shouldered his
way into the X-ray room with a gaggle of nurses hanging onto his
elbow protesting that he couldn't go in there.

  "You'll have to wait outside, sir. The patient is in no condition
to be interviewed," my doctor said calmly. She was the only calm
one there. I had passed the point of calm and was heading toward
comatose.

"It's okay," I said. She raised her eyebrows and looked at me. "He's come as a friend, not as a cop."

"Kat, are you okay?" He flung the last nurse off his elbow and advanced on me, touching my shoulder as though I were spun sugar.

"I'm okay, but Deck—" I stopped talking, was too spent to cry.

"I know." He put his arm around me, ignoring the layer of chocolate goo on my body.

"And Carmelita. There was a woman named Carmelita at Blackford's house. It was a horrible situation and someone has to take care of her. She can't just be turned loose. She needs a social worker or something if her family—"

"It's okay."

"Check on it, Hank. Promise."

"Okay."

"Now. It's important."

"Kat."

"Please."

They loaded me into a wheelchair and told Hank where he could find me later. My arm was all right but the cast wasn't, and they were replacing it. I was thankful. Looking at Deck's bloodstains was no way to live, or to get well.

"Hank, bring me something to wear out of here. All I've got in one piece is underwear."

"Okay, sweetheart." He kissed me and they rolled me off. After that I faded in and out of consciousness while they put the new cast on. The shock, the brandy, and the painkillers made it easy to float.

Hank dropped off shorts, a T-shirt, and some thong sandals; then he disappeared again. The shorts were Day-Glo yellow, one of my least favorite colors, and the T-shirt had Minnie Mouse on it. They still had price tags on them: $5.99, Thrifty Mart. I would have laughed if I could have, but I was too far gone. When they finally finished my cast a nurse helped me comb my hair, clean up a little, and dress. Then she helped me totter out to the waiting room and turned me over to Hank, who kissed me and held me as though I might fall apart any moment.

"It's okay, Hank, I'm fine." He ignored that, which was just as well, and held me tighter. "Let's go to the police station now."

"It can wait until tomorrow."

"I'd rather do it now. Tomorrow I want to forget."

It took a long time, making the statement, answering questions, going over and over things. When they finally let me go I was half dead. Brain dead, heart dead, feeling dead. The other half was asleep.

"Where do you want to go, Kat?"

"Home."

"Where?"

Oh, I'd forgotten how far I was from home.

"To your place? Is it okay?"

"Yes."

I sighed in relief and we headed out, Hank practically carrying me by then. It was morning by the time we got there and Hank undressed me and put me to bed. I slept all day, woke around dinner time, ate what he fed me and then went back to sleep. When Hank was gone Mars stayed by the bed. Every time I woke up I saw him there, which was comforting.

Two days after the ugliness they told me Blackford was dead. He had bled to death but, in all probability, would have died from the multiple head wounds. No charges were to be filed.

It was that night that the nightmares started. I woke up screaming with Hank holding onto me and trying to break me out of the panic. In my dreams there was blood everywhere and I kept slipping and sliding through it, trying to reach Deck, trying to stop the bleeding. And I couldn't. Then the dream changed and Blackford came after me, grinning and calling me Sweetie Pie. I kept hitting him with my cast, the pain went through me in waves, but it made no difference. He just kept grinning and coming and calling me Sweetie Pie. And I kept waking up to the sound of my own screams.

"Tell me, Kat."

"No, I don't want to talk about it."

"Tell me. I know about nightmares and they don't go away until you deal with them."

"No."

"Tell me."

"No."

"Tell me." And it went on that way for a long time until finally I told him. The pain, the sense of helplessness, the fear. I told him more than I'd told the police, more than I'd told anybody. I cried and raged until finally I ran down and slept. When I woke up Hank was still holding me. He smiled and I worked with my mouth until I could smile back. There was a long silence. Hank broke it.

"The nightmares I used to have about Liz?"

I nodded. Then it caught me. "Used to have?"

"They've stopped. Something in me is at peace now. It's over."

"I'm glad, Hank."

"Me too." We smiled at each other. "I'm ready to start over, Kat, to really live again."

"Is it because Blackford's dead?"

"That's part of it."

"And because I helped kill him?"

"No. Because you're you, and you're in my life now."

"I did kill him."

"It's hard to tell, Kat. Either the blow or the stab wounds could have killed him."

"I killed him, I killed Harry."

"Harry was a dead man before you shot him. Deck had seen to that."

"Hank, quit messing with the truth. I killed a man, two men. I've never done that. I've never wanted to. I killed a man with my bare hands."

"Not bare, plaster."

I stared at him blankly.

"The cast was a weapon and you were fighting for your life. Kat, you had no choice, you had to do it. Harry would have killed you. And long before Blackford did, you might have wished you were dead. It's all right, it's a brave and reasonable thing you did. You saved yourself and Carmelita. You chose life, not death."

I tried to believe him because I wanted to and because I thought he was right. I tried, but I kept waking up to the sound of my screams in the night. The next day I got up. They'd told me to stay in bed longer but I couldn't. I couldn't stand the dreams and there was unfinished business still. I did the easy stuff first.

I called Trainor Construction to make sure Ed Trainor was in, then headed on out there. His secretary was haughty and sneered at me, as though she wouldn't have given me the time of day if she'd been wearing three watches. She told me he was busy. I laughed in her face, told her my name and that I was representing the widow of Sam Collins. I said she could let Ed know he had five minutes to get unbusy. I was not in a conciliatory mood. It took him four and a half to walk out into the reception area and invite me back into his office.

"Drink, Ms. Colorado?"

"No. This is business and it won't take long."

"Have we met? I'm at a loss as to the nature of our business."

"We haven't met. I'm a private investigator acting on behalf of Charity Collins, Sam's widow. She wants to know where her two hundred grand is and how her husband died. I can't answer the first question but I can answer the second." His face was slowly freezing over, his eyes were still and cold. I leaned across his desk, my hands resting on the mess of papers there.

"So can you, Trainor, though I don't imagine you're as eager to talk about it as I am. You read the papers, you know what goes on in this town." I stared at him until he nodded.

"I killed Don Blackford. I was with Deck Hamilton when he died. They both made statements that solidly implicated you in Collins's death. Since I always carry a micro-cassette recorder I have those statements on tape—past habit as a reporter." I looked him in the eye as I lied, another past habit as a reporter. "Those tapes are in a safe–deposit box along with a letter of instructions to my lawyer."

I pushed off his desk and stood up straight. He still hadn't said a word. "I imagine you could beat the murder rap with a good lawyer. After all they're only tapes and the principals are dead. Still, you'd be finished in this town. The big boys don't push people off of six-story buildings, they leave that to thugs." I paused, but not for an answer. What was there for him to say?

"Find Sam Collins's money. I want two-hundred-twenty-five-thousand dollars in a certified bank check, that's payback and expenses. I'll pick it up tomorrow morning at ten from your secretary. I don't want to see you again. The tapes stay in the vault as insurance." Then I walked out. The secretary still looked like she wouldn't have given me the time of day. Outside the sun was hot and hard.

And that was the easy one. I had Carmelita and Deck's mother to go.

I found Mrs. Hamilton in a mobile-home park on the outskirts of town, a nice one with cottonwood trees and a park and a senior center. A spry, tanned, elderly man who looked like a brown grasshopper directed me to her place.

"Mrs. Hamilton?"

"Yes."

"I'm Kate Colorado. Katy. Do you remember me from Sacramento? Deck and I were friends."

Her face lightened up and she smiled. "Come in, dear. Yes, of course I do. Sit down. You'll have tea, won't you?" I nodded, not wanting it, not sure I could swallow.

"You've heard?" she asked me, and I nodded again.

"I was with him when he died, Mrs. Hamilton. He asked me to come to you." She put the teapot down and sat at the kitchen table with me, her hands folded and still with all the veins standing out in blue relief. "He wanted me to tell you something but he died before he could tell me what it was. He died to save my life and he didn't have to do that. He was a brave man, a good man, and a good friend."

"Was he? I wonder." Her voice was barely audible. "His job—you know what his job was?" I nodded.

"But he didn't die in his job. He died the way you brought him up. He died a good man. I think that's what he wanted me to tell you."

She got up and made tea and we drank it. I had two cups and it wasn't as hard to swallow as I thought it would be. The silence between us was easy, but sad. When I got up to leave she held my hands and thanked me. She was small and old and frail and it was hard to believe that Deck, who was so large and strong, was dead, and that she was alive. Looking at her and thinking about it I wished I'd had a mother who had loved me and cared how I came out, how I lived and died. Tough luck. I kissed her cheek and walked out into the hard hot sun.

Hank had told me how to find Carmelita. I went because my heart told me I had to but my feet dragged and my mind screamed no. I got lost three times going there and it was an easy place to find.

It was a little, quiet, dull house on a little, quiet, dull street. I stood in the sun on the hot front stoop and rang the bell. Carmelita answered.

"I came to see that you were all right."

"I'm all right."

There was a long pause and we looked at each other.

"I'll go then."

"No." She opened the screen door. "Come in." So I did. I didn't want to, but I did.

The kitchen was cool and quiet and we sat there. It was ice tea this time, and it was still difficult to swallow. In my job it's like that a lot. Often enough it makes me think I've got the wrong job.

"He's dead, did you know?" She nodded. I took a deep breath. "I killed him."

"Or I," she said.

"It doesn't matter. It was self-defense. We had no choice." I thought about it for a while. "Are you sad?"

"No." She shook her head. "I hated him." Clouds gathered in her eyes. "Maybe I cared, too, but I hated him more."

"It was brainwashing, not love or caring. He was good at that. He tried to take you away from yourself and make you his. But it didn't work, you were too strong."

"I don't know . . . without you . . . maybe I'd be Phoebe still."

"No, you were too strong. Will you be all right now?" She nodded.

"I think so. I can stay with my sister and her family as long as I need to."

"Good."

"I have nightmares."

"Me too."

"I wake up screaming."

"Yes. You must talk about them." I gave her the advice I had found so hard to take.

"No. I can't."

"Yes. You must talk about them, to your sister, or a friend, or a priest." She shook her head. "You must. It makes them go away. You are not a bad person, he was." She looked at me. "I know it, I swear it." I got up to go. "The nightmares will stop. It may take a long time but they will, I promise." I tried to give her the hope I longed for. The front door opened and I heard the sound of children's voices. Our hands touched briefly and then I left.

It seemed like hours had gone by but it had only been minutes. The sun was still hard and hot. I walked out into it.

34

I picked up the check at Trainor's office the next morning and then I packed my things. I wanted to leave Las Vegas in the worst possible way. I did not want to pass Go or collect $200 or do anything else. I wanted to leave. My heart wouldn't let me, not without saying good-bye to Joe and Betty, and Hank.

So we had dinner and it wasn't good-bye, not with Joe and Betty, just au revoir. I was glad about that. I invited them to Sacramento and promised them fresh vegetables. They said they'd come and I believed it, a good feeling.

And then Hank. He refused to say good-bye or even au revoir. We made love that night and he knocked my socks off, crossed my eyes, and made my heart sing. We spoke words that don't come easily. And made plans: camping at Mono Lake soon, backpacking in Death Valley in the fall, skiing at Heavenly this winter.

Mono, Death, Heavenly. It scares me. Just like my job and my life scare me sometimes. Have I chosen the shadows instead of the sunlight? I hope not. Mostly I keep trying to bring sunlight into the shadows. I tell myself that; I want to believe it.

Charity met me at the airport and blew out the dust and cobwebs in my mind.

"Why are you wearing yellow shorts and a Minnie Mouse T-shirt?"

"I kept wrecking my white pants and everything else was dirty. I didn't have time to shop."

"Kat, you're such a slob."

It's not true, I thought, not true. I couldn't help it that I got hit by a truck and that Deck bled to death on me.

"I wanted to celebrate, but with you dressed like that we can't eat at Frank Fats or Harlow's. How about down on the river, the Virgin Sturgeon?"

"All right." That would be peaceful, I thought, the water slapping against the pier as boats went by, mosquitoes, large icy margaritas. And no glitz, no glitter.

"Kat, you'll never guess the Dear Charity letter I got this morning."

"What?"

"Someone wanted to know what I thought about a grown-up sleeping with a night-light on. A grown-up! Can you imagine?"

I shook my head and said no, but it was a lie. I could imagine it easily.